The Umbra Collective

Jules D'Isep

ISBN: 978-1-970487-04-6 (eBook)
ISBN: 978-1-970487-05-3 (Paperback)

Published by Bridge Publisher

First Edition

For those who live in the shadows.

Contents

"Loyalty is the only currency that never
loses value in the dark."

—Unknown

Prologue

London, Late October

The limousine melted into the London night, as if neither vehicle nor passenger had ever existed. Inside, Rayne St-John Smythe let the low purr of the engine dissolve into the dark. The Umbra Collective spared no expense for its operatives, but the leather seat beneath her wasn't a luxury. It was a reminder. Everything about her existence was curated, solitary, and cold.

A soft click broke the stillness as a compartment beside her slid open, revealing a chilled bottle of champagne and a crystal flute. She dismissed it immediately; her focus fixed on the dossier in her lap. Facts, weaknesses, routines. The unguarded moments of her mark's life lay bare under dim cabin light.

She shifted, exhaling slowly as her eyes flicked to the city outside. Twelve lives taken, each one an inevitability. And now this: number thirteen. She didn't believe in luck, yet unease settled beneath her composure like grit in a wound. Her fingers brushed the locket at her throat, a piece of the past she couldn't let go, even as the woman in the photo grew more distant with every mission.

The M25 was its usual crawl, and London's sprawl blurred against the window. Any hit in this city would never end in a chase. Traffic-strangled movement, escape reduced to a walk. London wasn't built for flight. It ensnared.

The car turned toward Heathrow. Rayne straightened, checked her compact. Wig perfect, makeup professional but understated. The oversized Velinne Sombra 88 sunglasses snapped into place. Doubt was weakness. Thirteen would be no different.

At Terminal 5, her driver opened the door just as a British Airways staff member approached, polished smile in place.

"Welcome to Heathrow, Ms. Williams," he said smoothly.

Rayne stepped out, tugged at her black Dior suit, and followed inside. At the first-class counter, her alias, Jacqueline "Jackie" Williams of San Francisco, moved seamlessly through security. Discipline, elegance, containment.

She bypassed duty-free and slipped into the first-class lounge, a pocket of polished calm amid the airport's chaos. After a quick 360-degree sweep of the room, the people, and the exits, she settled into a plush leather chair. A waiter appeared, took her order, and returned with her drink; she sipped slowly while scanning the dossier one last time.

She picked up the glass, faintly frosted from the amber liquid within. She sipped slowly, deliberately, her eyes scanning the screen of her device, her mind assessing the details of her mark one last time.

To distract herself, she picked up a fashion magazine from the table beside her, setting it in her lap, and started flipping through its glossy pages with idle curiosity. Ochre was set to be the "it" color palette this autumn, the headline declared. A faint smile tugged at her lips. Did people truly live like this, shaping their identities around seasonal palettes and editorial whims?

She sipped again and skimmed past an article on achieving better orgasms and a travel feature on Greek island getaways, her mind only half-engaged. The moment stretched before her, a fragile calm before the storm she knew was coming.

Rayne spotted him by the buffet. He was a French businessman in his early fifties, well-groomed and exuding the effortless charm that his dossier had only hinted at. The photo she'd studied had been taken during some formal event, polished but lifeless. In person, Paul-Henri Delon was striking, his charisma impossible to miss.

Rayne shifted her wrist subtly beneath the table, imperceptible to the casual eye, and prepared her bracelet for its contact with Delon. The concealed vial primed, releasing a thin coating of toxin along the sharpened edge. Harmless until now, it would remain lethal only for a few short hours, long enough for one touch, one scratch, to finish the job.

Movement shifted the lounge. Heads turned.

The woman was stunning, an athletic brunette who moved like a panther, effortlessly commanding the space. Her outfit was more than just fashionable; it seemed pulled directly from the pages of the Vogue magazine Rayne had flipped through minutes earlier. Every detail was meticulously curated, from the sharp lines of her tailored blazer to the bold splash of ochre that hinted she was already ahead of the season's trends. But it wasn't just the clothes or the physique. It was the confidence that radiated from her, a quiet, unshakable power that elevated her presence to something almost magnetic.

Rayne watched, unable to resist the pull. She had always been "the beauty," the one who turned heads effortlessly, even in the most indifferent of crowds. It was a tool she wielded expertly, a facet of her identity honed by necessity and expectation. But this woman was something else entirely, a force unto herself, unbound by comparison. For a fleeting moment, Rayne felt an unfamiliar pang, somewhere between admiration, jealousy, and unease. The presence of this stranger unsettled her equilibrium, a rare occurrence in her world of shadows.

The brunette strode further into the lounge, her gaze sweeping the room with practiced indifference. It was almost theatrical, the way she seemed to own the space without acknowledgment, the way the quiet murmur of voices softened in her wake. Rayne set her glass down, leaning back in her chair, studying the stranger with a practiced eye. There was always a story behind confidence like that, and Rayne couldn't help but wonder if their paths were about to cross in ways neither of them yet understood.

She tried to ignore the brunette, but the woman's presence lingered at the edge of her awareness like an unwelcome distraction. Focus, Rayne reminded herself. This was her moment.

Rayne put her drink back down, closed the magazine, decided she would worry about better orgasms and Greece later, stood, and made her way to the buffet.

Delon glanced her way, and in that instant, his Gallic charm sparked to life. Another beautiful woman to add to his list, he thought. If not today, he'd plant the seed for their inevitable reunion down the line. He stood up from his table, his smile widening as he approached, and met Rayne just as she reached the buffet.

"Bonjour," he said, his tone warm and inviting.

She returned the smile effortlessly. He extended his hand, and she took it, letting her fingers linger just long enough to hint at familiarity. His smile deepened, rich with intent.

"Paul-Henri Delon," he offered.

"Jacqueline Williams," she replied smoothly, letting the slightest trace of a smile touch her lips. "Jackie to my friends."

"I hope I can call you Jackie," he said, his voice laced with suggestion.

"I would very much like that," she answered, a hint of playfulness in her tone.

As she withdrew her hand, her bracelet caught his wrist, scratching him just enough to elicit a flinch. He pulled back instinctively, bringing his wrist to his mouth to soothe the small sting.

Rayne's apology came swiftly, her voice layered with concern, though her eyes betrayed none of it. "Oh, I am so sorry."

Delon waved it off dismissively, brushing aside her words with a charming smile. "It's nothing," he assured her. "I'll get a plaster from the desk."

She offered to accompany him, a subtle test of her own charm, but he declined with practiced politeness. "I must return to my party," he said, gesturing toward the group waiting for him. "But please take my card," he added, reaching into his jacket pocket. "Call me whenever you are in Paris next. It would be lovely to reconnect."

Rayne nodded and watched him move away, her expression unreadable. With deliberate care, she tucked the card into her purse and turned her attention back to the buffet, selecting a plate of cheeses and retreating to her table.

When she was back at her seat, Rayne's hand dropped casually to her lap. With the slightest motion, she slipped the bracelet loose, tucking it into the lined inside pocket of her jacket.

Now came the hardest part, the waiting. The sharp edge of her bracelet, innocuous to the untrained eye, had been coated with a cutting-edge poison developed by one of the Umbra Collective's bio-pharma subsidiaries. It was a masterpiece of lethality, designed to enter the bloodstream undetected and work its way through the body with ruthless efficiency. Within twenty-four hours, Paul-Henri Delon would be dead. That he had instinctively brought his wrist to his mouth only sealed his fate, ensuring the toxin would spread even more completely.

Airports were perfect for this kind of operation, if you could ensure the meeting. By the time Delon succumbed, he would be in another country, far from London. The local authorities, if they even identified the poison, would waste precious days chasing leads in the wrong jurisdiction. It would take time to trace him back to Heathrow, and by then, Jacqueline Williams would no longer exist. Maddie Peters, with her auburn wig and fresh makeup, would be boarding a flight to Singapore, leaving no trace of the woman who had shared a fleeting moment with Delon at the buffet.

But the next hour was critical. Rayne had to remain calm, composed, and utterly unremarkable. Her heart beat steadily, but the weight of the mission pressed against her chest like a vice. Every glance, every gesture had to blend seamlessly into the fabric of the lounge's quiet luxury.

Her eyes flicked briefly to Delon, his back to her, as he made his way back from the front desk and rejoined his party, oblivious to the clock now ticking against him.

The brunette from earlier still lingered at the edge of Rayne's awareness, a presence she couldn't quite shake. But Rayne pushed the thought aside. Survival demanded focus, and focus was the one thing she couldn't afford to lose.

A moment later, she felt a hand gently touch her shoulder. The instinct to react, to subdue and neutralize the "assailant," flared briefly, but Rayne suppressed it, forcing herself to remain calm. Slowly, she turned her head, her gaze meeting a pair of striking brown eyes that seemed even more captivating up close.

"I'm sorry to disturb you, but is that seat taken? I hate to sit alone. Too much attention from single men."

The voice was soft, soothing, and carried an air of effortless charm. Rayne felt a tingle, goosebumps rising as she took in the woman's beauty, athletic, poised, and radiating confidence. Her eyes flicked toward Delon, only to find his gaze fixed instead on the woman beside her.

"Please, do," Rayne replied, gesturing to the chair beside her, her voice steady despite the distraction.

As the newcomer moved past her and took the seat, a cool breeze followed, carrying with it the faintest hint of jasmine-scented perfume. It lingered in the air, teasing Rayne's senses and pulling her focus away from the magazine she was forcing herself to read.

The woman extended a hand, her movements graceful. "Evie," she said simply, her tone warm but measured.

Rayne hesitated for a fraction of a second before taking the offered hand. "Jacqueline," she replied, then corrected herself with a practiced smile. "Jackie."

Their hands met briefly, and Evie's smile deepened, her presence commanding yet unassuming. Rayne returned to her magazine, flipping through the glossy pages with feigned interest, while Evie pulled out a file marked with the emblem of an investment bank. Silence settled between them, but Rayne found her thoughts drifting. The jasmine scent was tantalizing, and despite her best efforts, her attention kept returning to Evie.

She glanced over the edge of her magazine and noticed several male eyes looking toward them. Damn, she thought, too much attention. She stole another look at Evie, only to be caught in the act. Evie's gaze met hers, and a knowing smile played across her lips. Rayne felt heat rise to her cheeks and quickly returned her focus to the article in front of her, wondering why she felt so off balance.

Their quiet flirtation continued, a dance of stolen glances and fleeting smiles, until the waiter returned with their drinks. He placed them on the table between them, and the women picked up their glasses simultaneously.

Evie raised hers slightly, her eyes locking with Rayne's. "Cheers," she said, her voice low and inviting.

Rayne mirrored the gesture, their glasses clinking softly. As they took their first sip, the tension between them hung in the air, electric and undeniable.

Unable to bear the silence any longer, Rayne broke it. "Where are you off to?" she asked, her voice betraying a hint of curiosity. It was the kind of question frequent travelers used to break the ice, but it felt different now.

Evie's smile widened, her answer smooth and unhurried. "Italy. Rome, then we'll see. And you?"

Rayne was about to answer that she was off to Madrid, but then the front desk called their flights simultaneously, and the women rose from their seats and started moving toward the lounge doors.

Evie glanced at Rayne and asked where her gate was located. A quick check revealed their gates were only three apart. They decided to walk together and continue the conversation.

As they approached Rayne's gate, the pre-boarding announcement echoed through the terminal. Rayne turned to Evie, extending her hand with a polite smile.

"It was lovely to meet a fellow traveler," she said.

Evie took her hand, her grip warm and deliberate, and leaned in for a kiss on the cheek. Their lips caught faintly at the corners, and Evie held the pose just long enough for a flicker of electricity to pass between them. Her brown eyes sparkled with something unspoken, the devil dancing behind her gaze.

"You are lovely," she whispered softly, her voice intimate and laced with mischief.

Breaking away, Evie reached into her purse, producing a sleek card with her first name and a London mobile number. She pressed it into Rayne's hand, her fingers lingering for a moment before she turned and walked away, heading toward her gate with effortless confidence.

Rayne watched her retreating figure, her heart skipping a beat despite her better judgment. Even as she turned away, she caught Evie, out of the corner of her eye, still watching her, smiling. It felt like the room shifted, as if time stretched imperceptibly between them.

Rayne snapped out of her reverie. With her mission still at the forefront of her mind, she slipped away from the gate area and headed toward the ladies' room. She moved quickly, every step deliberate, the calm exterior hiding the whirlwind of calculation underneath.

Once inside, she retreated to a stall and began her transformation. She stripped out of her tailored outfit, trading it for a simple outfit of jeans and a hoodie, unassuming attire for the long-haul flight to Singapore. With the utmost care, she removed the bracelet from her pocket, sealing it inside a plastic pouch before burying it deep inside her disposal bag. Risk management was survival; no trace of the toxin would remain. She tucked her hair beneath a short auburn wig, securing it tightly before pulling up the hood. Her hands moved deftly, packing her old clothes and ID neatly into a small bag. She had been instructed to leave them in a utility access behind the stall, erasing any trace of Jacqueline Williams.

With her makeup refreshed, neutral tones, nothing flashy, Rayne checked herself in the mirror one last time. Her reflection offered no clues to the professional killer underneath. "Maddie Peters" exited the restroom, moving swiftly toward the inter-terminal train. Heathrow's Terminal 5 faded into the background as the train pulled out of the station. By the time she arrived at Terminal 2, she blended seamlessly with the ebb and flow of travelers around her.

The SilverKris Lounge at T2 greeted her with understated elegance, a space designed for comfort and anonymity. Rayne stepped inside, letting the scent of polished wood and freshly brewed coffee settle over her. She glanced around, ensuring no lingering eyes followed her before choosing a corner seat. The long flight ahead promised her time to prepare, to plan, and, most importantly, to disappear.

Unbeknownst to Rayne, a watcher from the Umbra Collective followed her discreetly from the British Airways lounge, keeping a careful distance. While Rayne headed for the ladies' room, the operative was already issuing orders. The cleanup team arrived swiftly, moving with the practiced efficiency of shadows. They recovered Rayne's discarded clothes and ID and meticulously sprayed down the stall with disinfectant, erasing any trace of her presence.

As the cleaning crew left, the watcher remained outside, her attention fixed on her phone. She typed out a report to 100, the Collective's London HQ:

Delon contaminated. Sparrow away clean. Complication: Obsidian engaged with Sparrow.

The message was sent, and within moments, her phone vibrated with a terse reply:

Report to 100 immediately.

Her jaw tightened as she read the order. Obsidian's involvement wasn't in the mission parameters, and deviations, no matter how small, were rarely tolerated. She responded affirmatively, slipping her phone back into her jacket before heading toward HQ.

The weight of her report hung heavily in the air. It wasn't just Rayne's movements being scrutinized now. The watcher knew that every

decision and action would be dissected under the cold, calculating eyes
of the Collective.

There would be hell to pay.

Chapter 1

Vienna, two weeks later

In Vienna's Innere Stadt, within the walls of a centuries-old building, stood an apartment that reflected its owner's storied legacy. This was no ordinary residence but a haven of crafted opulence, a testament to wealth passed down through generations.

The grand entrance, framed by wrought iron and gilded detail, opened into a vestibule of cool marble and a crystal chandelier that spoke of history and elegance. Masterpieces from the Old World lined the walls, each a nod to a family's timeless appreciation for art.

Inside, the apartment unfolded in splendor. Vaulted ceilings and oversized windows revealed a sweeping view of St. Stephen's Cathedral. Biedermeier furniture paired with modern amenities bridged tradition and comfort. In the adjoining study, oak bookshelves housed leather-bound tomes while a polished grand piano stood ready for a waltz.

The master suite was tranquil, its four-poster bed dressed in silk and brocade. Damian stood amid packed cases, indecisive as ever. His valet, Lukas Steinbrecher, observed with quiet patience. Damian rejected one outfit, debated another, then finally chose the dove-gray Loro Piana suit and John Lobb monk-strap shoes Lukas had prepared hours earlier.

Damiano Alphonse Orazio Cesarini, known simply as Damian, descended from the ancient Cesarini family, Venetian aristocrats whose legacy was stitched into the city's history. Their palazzo on the Grand Canal still stood as a monument to their influence. Now, Damian's place within the clandestine Umbra Collective added to that weight. His financial acumen had fortified the family's relevance, bridging history with modern power.

As a boy, Damian had been captivated by tales of his ancestors, doges, cardinals, even a pope, instilling in him pride and duty. Raised in Canada and educated in Europe's finest institutions, he mastered politics, philosophy, and the arts, moving easily through high society. Tall, with blond hair and hazel eyes, Damian's presence commanded attention, his wit respected, though always carrying the weight of responsibility.

Lukas disappeared into the en-suite to retrieve the toiletry bag. When Damian emerged, polished and poised, Lukas suspected he had armed himself. The valet had learned long ago not to ask.

Outside, a black Mercedes idled at the curb. Damian took the travel bag that Lukas handed him, descended the stairs of the apartment and walked to the curb, where he settled into the back seat of the car. Lukas stood at the pavement, watching as the car slipped into Vienna's cobblestoned streets, allowing himself the brief satisfaction of routine carried out flawlessly.

Morning light filtered through the tall windows as Lukas returned upstairs, moving in practiced silence. Service had defined his life long before he entered the Cesarini household. Born in Graz, the son of a police officer, he had grown up steeped in duty. The Austrian Army followed, and later the Special Forces. The Cold War missions along the Iron Curtain had tested him, leaving their marks. A severe injury had cut short his service, but not his resolve.

Fate intervened in the form of Damian Cesarini, then a young man with ambition to match Lukas's discipline. Their partnership grew into trust. For decades now, Lukas had been more than a valet. He was a confidant, steward, and watchman.

Now, in his early sixties, he carried himself with the vigor of someone younger, a tall presence softened only by his quiet warmth. His eyes, sharp and assessing, missed nothing.

Cham, Switzerland, awaited. The villa there was as much Lukas's domain as Vienna. Soon, he would travel to prepare it. For now, he lingered in Damian's absence, the apartment hushed around him, his thoughts resting briefly on the strange course of a life defined by service.

Damian took his phone from his pocket and dialed Lukas.

"Have everything in order for Cham?"

"It will be ready when you arrive," Lukas replied.

The driver navigated Vienna's morning streets. Cafés spilled their scents of coffee and pastry into the cold air, Ringstraße's landmarks gleamed in pale light, and the shortcut through the Naschmarkt revealed vendors setting up their stalls. Soon, they reached Hauptbahnhof. Damian disembarked; coat collar turned against the chill.

With time before departure, he ordered a strong Viennese coffee at a station café. The noise of the concourse faded into the background as he sipped, savoring the velvet bitterness, his mind already in Venice. The clock above turned to 9:50. He got up and made his way to his train.

The Railjet slipped out of Vienna in smooth silence. Damian's first-class cabin gave him solitude as the city fell away. Austria's vineyards and villages blurred into the glass, the Alps and Dolomites rising in rugged majesty. Lakes flashed like mirrors; rivers wound between emerald forests. The train carried him toward Italy, toward home.

Crossing into the Veneto, the air thickened with fog. Damian's anticipation grew with every mile. Venice was close now, the city of his family, his heritage, and his duty.

At 6:04 PM, the train doors opened at Venezia Santa Lucia. The salty air of the lagoon struck him instantly, heavy and familiar. The fog lay thick across the station steps, cloaking the city in mystery. Damian adjusted his coat, tightened his grip on his case, and stepped forward into the night.

Chapter 2

At the station's entrance, Damian paused. The dense November fog hung low, smothering the glow of the streetlamps and cloaking Venice in a shroud of silence. With the canals too dangerous for boats, he would need to navigate on foot. Closing his eyes, he traced the route in his mind, a skill drilled into every Venetian who grew up in the city's labyrinth. He set off toward Palazzo Cesarini.

Crossing the Ponte degli Scalzi, he found it deserted. The usual tourists were gone, leaving the bridge to the mist. Descending into Calle Longa, his footsteps were swallowed by the damp air. Each step gave weight to the thoughts he had been trying to suppress. He had fought for her, argued against colleagues he respected. If the vote had gone the other way, he would have been the one to pull the trigger. That was the burden of their world. No reprieve, no second-guessing.

Along Fondamenta dei Tolentini, the anger in his chest remained heavy. She had made a mistake, a lapse, and it had nearly cost everything.

Campo Santa Margherita was nearly dark, its lamps faint against the fog. The city felt muted, reduced to the sound of water lapping against stone and the creak of gondolas tugging at their moorings.

He pressed on, crossing the Ponte dell'Accademia. At its crest, the fog grew denser, swallowing even the familiar outlines. The Salute, usually commanding the skyline, had vanished. He lingered there a moment, jaw tight. She had no idea what his defense had cost. If she failed again, there would be no second chance.

Descending, he entered Campo Santo Stefano and wound toward San Vidal, each step carrying him closer. Finally, the Gothic façade of Palazzo Cesarini loomed through the mist, resolute against the night.

At the end of a narrow calle, two figures appeared. Women. The fog blurred their features, but their presence at this dead end was wrong. The canals were closed, no boats could land, and yet here they were.

Instinct sharpened. He slowed, his hand brushing the grip of the silenced pistol in his pocket. The taller one, a brunette with a clipped British accent, carried herself with too much confidence to be a lost tourist. Her head moved with controlled precision. The fog distorted the details, but the unease was real.

"Permesso," he said evenly as he passed.

They barely reacted, still bent over a phone screen. Casual. Detached. But he didn't relax.

"May I help you?" he asked, his voice low but direct.

The second woman looked up quickly, apologetic. "We're looking for the Pensione Accademia. The fog makes everything impossible."

Damian studied them, weighing every detail. Tourists? Perhaps. But in Venice, nothing was simple.

"You are close," he replied. "Back down this calle, left at the end of the palazzo, then left again. Cross the Ponte dell'Accademia, turn left onto Fondamenta Bollani, and you will find it ahead."

The brunette held his gaze a beat too long, then nodded curtly. "Thank you."

Her companion added, "We appreciate it."

Damian moved on without looking back. "It is easy to get lost at night in the fog."

The mist thickened as he reached the palazzo gate. His grip tightened on the pistol, the weight a quiet reassurance.

The building rose from the water like a specter. Faded terracotta and weathered marble blurred into shadow. Gothic windows traced with delicate stonework caught faint glimmers of light, while wrought-iron balconies sagged beneath ivy and bougainvillea. At the water gate, his mahogany Riva Aquarama sat idle, its polished wood dulled by the damp. For a moment, nostalgia pricked him. Perhaps Burano, risotto at Da Romano, if there was time.

Inside the courtyard, the fog muted the citrus trees and fountain to vague outlines. Damian paused, inhaling the damp scent of earth and jasmine, childhood memories stirring before he forced them away.

At the iron portone, he keyed the lock. The clang of the gate closing echoed in the silence, and the low buzz of the alarm confirmed his arrival. Two staff approached; surprise quickly replaced by deference.

"Sir, let us take your bag."

"No need, I will take it up," Damian said calmly. "Is Evie here? I have come to collect her. The curtain at La Fenice rises at 8 pm."

"Signorina Evie is in her room. She has been since late afternoon," the senior replied.

Satisfied, Damian climbed the marble staircase, centuries-worn smooth underfoot. The piano nobile stretched ahead, a muted expanse of damask, marble, and shadow. Chandeliers loomed overhead, dulled to faint glows in the mist-filtered night. He moved with purpose through rooms heavy with legacy, their beauty and weight familiar, but tonight irrelevant.

The palazzo, passed down through generations since the fifteenth century, carried the weight of history with every step Damian took. Though he rarely stayed here, the presence of his ancestors lingered in the shadows. Their legacy pressed from every wall, carved into every surface.

Tonight was not for nostalgia. The house was quiet, save for the ticking of a distant clock and the faint rustle of fabric. Damian knew eyes followed him even here. Surveillance was constant, even for the master of the palazzo.

He turned down the visitor's hallway, his steps deliberate, hand brushing the polished oak doors crafted centuries earlier by shipwrights. At the last room, he paused, then knocked firmly.

"Enter," came a lyrical voice.

He stepped inside, murmuring "Permesso" out of habit, though the house was his.

Evie sat at a makeup table, framed in a Murano mirror, applying the final touches for the evening. A black silk dressing gown draped over her, one leg crossed, the fabric slipping to reveal the sharp line of her thigh. She did not look up, but he knew she felt his presence, calculated, unyielding.

Damian cleared his throat, his voice calm and precise. "What you did in London was reckless. Crossing paths with another operative was one thing. Giving her a business card, engaging her directly? Unacceptable. Access to dossiers required significant capital, and the committee is furious. They are calling for sanctions."

She stood, untied the sash, and let the gown fall. Naked but for a thigh holster of knives, she glared at him with defiance sharper than any blade.

"If you are going to do it, do it quickly," she said. "I will even come closer so you do not miss. And a 'Hello, how are you' would have been nice."

She stepped toward him until almost nothing separated them. Vulnerable. Dangerous. Pure Evie.

Damian let his gaze travel from head to toe before meeting her eyes again. The silence thickened, weighted and unbroken.

Her thoughts stuttered. Montreal. A convenience store. A voice telling her she had more potential than this. Memories of scholarships clawed for, of family dinners she never fit into. She blinked them away and turned toward the fractured reflection in the mirror.

"It is not about punishment," Damian said evenly. "It is about discipline."

"And if I fail again?"

His words came low, steady. "Do not think for a moment that I would shoot you in this house. But if the sanction came, despite the years I have invested in you, despite my affection, my resolve would hold. The Collective does not forgive. If ordered, I would pull the trigger myself."

The words cut as clean as steel. Damian had always been more than a mentor, but sentiment could not blunt reality.

He stepped closer, lifted her hand, and pressed his lips gently to the back of it. "Hello, my dear," he murmured. "How are you?"

The question, deceptively simple, carried weight. Concern layered over warning. Tenderness against the cold resolve of their world.

A shiver ran down her spine. She knew this was not just admonishment; it was belief laced with threat. She had made a mistake. She could not make another.

"I understand," she replied quietly. "And I am well."

Damian studied her face, then nodded. "Our world is unforgiving. One misstep can be your last."

Their eyes held, not with intimacy but with the distance of professionals bound by necessity. He released her hand. Evie knew the path forward was clear: prove herself or perish. Not for him, not even for the Collective, but for herself.

"Get dressed," Damian said. "We leave in ten minutes."

He exited.

Evie moved quickly. She chose a black gown, understated and severe. She slipped the knives into hidden seams, second skin, habit unbroken.

In his suite, Damian prepared with equal attention to detail. Black tie, cufflinks engraved with the family crest. His reflection in the mirror revealed nothing.

When they met in the entrance hall, no words were exchanged. A glance, a nod was enough.

A footman held her coat. Damian refused his own.

Outside, the fog clung cold and heavy, swallowing sound.

They walked together; her heels soft against stone. The calli narrowed, shadows pressed closer. Venice moved around them in whispers.

Ahead, the lantern-lit façade of La Fenice materialized through the mist. Grand. Ghostly. A beacon waiting at the edge of shadow.

Chapter 3

La Fenice glowed like a jewel in the mist. Its baroque façade shimmered under lantern light, banners announcing Verdi's Don Carlo swaying gently above the entrance. The fog muffled sound, but inside the theater pulsed with opulence and anticipation.

Damian offered his arm. Evie slipped hers through without hesitation. They moved like figures from another century, their steps measured, precise, an unspoken rhythm between them.

The foyer was alive with Venice's elite. Velvet gowns and tailored tuxedos brushed against gilded balustrades, conversation in Italian, French, and English rising in polite waves. Chandeliers sparkled above, scattering light across marble floors.

Almost immediately, Damian was greeted. Mayor Ricci broke from a circle of investors, his smile always calculated. "Conte Cesarini," Ricci said, extending a hand.

"The pleasure is mine," Damian replied, clasping it. "Allow me to present Miss Isabelle Moreau."

Evie inclined her head with poise. The mayor's practiced eyes assessed her quickly but politely. "I trust you will enjoy the performance," he said. "Verdi's genius never fades."

"Nor does political posturing," Damian murmured as Ricci drifted away.

Evie smirked. "And yet he makes it look effortless."

Damian's attention shifted. "Alessandro Conti," he said, steering her toward a familiar figure. The painter turned, warmth lighting his expression.

"Damian," Conti greeted, clasping his shoulder. "You grace us again."

"I would not miss it," Damian replied. "Issa, this is Conti, a great Venetian painter, responsible for several works in my palazzo."

Evie offered her hand. "Your work is extraordinary."

Conti smiled. "It is always gratifying to meet someone who sees beyond the canvas."

Their conversation turned naturally toward art and survival. Conti spoke of La Fenice's fire in 1996 and its rebirth, a metaphor too obvious to ignore. Damian answered with equal weight: survival, reinvention, power. Evie listened, the crimson curtain catching her eye.

The house lights dimmed. A hush fell, anticipation rippling through the crowd.

"Showtime," Damian said softly.

They were escorted to his private box, a vantage above the crimson-draped stage. Below, the orchestra adjusted sheet music under candlelit sconces.

"The box across, to the left," Damian murmured. His gaze fixed on a man lounging with practiced arrogance. "Silvestro Leonardo."

Evie followed his line of sight. Silvestro was sleek, tailored, careless. His blonde companion in ice-blue looked elsewhere, tapping fingers against the armrest, her disinterest plain.

"The father?" Evie asked.

"Gone. A stroke. The empire crumbles." Damian's voice was steady, almost cold. "The son postures, but the end is close. The Harvest Ball is tomorrow."

The conductor appeared, baton raised. A single sweep, and music bloomed. Strings swelled, woodwinds climbed, brass declared. La Fenice filled with sound, ancient and immediate, a living tide of history.

The soprano stepped forward. Emerald gown flowing, her voice rose into the rafters, each note threading centuries together.

Evie stilled; her breath caught. Opera had never reached her like this. Here, it was not performance, it was survival, longing, and triumph distilled into music. Damian saw her face soften, guarded edges giving way beneath the force of the aria.

The performance surged. Arias of desire, duets steeped in conflict, the chorus swelling like a storm. Damian felt it too, not as spectacle but as truth: the beauty of survival, of reinvention, of power cloaked in song.

The soprano's final note hung suspended, unbroken, aching with finality. Silence followed, vast and heavy, before thunderous applause erupted. La Fenice roared with ovation, centuries echoing in the sound.

Evie exhaled, a faint smile curving her lips. She turned to Damian, and in her eyes burned something he could not quite name.

They lingered as the audience spilled into the night, unwilling to surrender the charged stillness left in the wake of the music. Outside, the fog curled thick and low across the canals, lanterns throwing fractured halos onto water that rippled with unseen currents. The city was hushed, as if Venice itself were still holding the soprano's last note.

Damian guided Evie through narrow streets where shadows pressed close and stone facades glistened with damp. Their steps echoed faintly, softened by fog, until he paused before a discreet entrance along a fondamenta, half-hidden between shuttered doors.

Inside, warmth wrapped around them immediately. Polished wood gleamed under candlelight, low sconces throwing soft pools of amber across marble and brass. The bar was intimate, a place that seemed to belong more to memory than to commerce. The bartender acknowledged Damian with a single nod, as if expecting him, and without a word set down their drinks: a glass of Barolo for Evie, a measure of black rum for Damian.

Evie took her glass and leaned back into the worn leather of her chair, letting the tension of the evening settle. The ruby liquid caught the light, shadows trembling across her fingers as she swirled it slowly. "Verdi understood desperation," she murmured, her voice quiet, almost reflective.

Damian turned his glass between his hands, studying the dark surface before lifting it to his lips. "He dissected people," he said. "Their failures, their ambitions. He laid them bare."

She tilted her head toward him, her eyes steady, unflinching. "Reminds me of someone."

A faint smile touched his mouth, quick as a spark, gone before it could linger. He raised his glass in acknowledgment, the gesture more eloquent than words.

The silence that followed was not empty but layered, carrying the remnants of music, of glances stolen in the opera house, of questions neither had dared to ask aloud. Around them, the bar hummed faintly with the quiet rhythm of a piano spilling from an old gramophone, the notes low and rich, blending with the muted clink of crystal and the faint scent of tobacco smoke.

For a while, they sat like that, two figures apart from the world yet bound to it, sharing a drink in a pocket of time that felt borrowed.

When the glasses were empty, Damian rose, his movements deliberate, and Evie followed. The fog outside had thinned, revealing moonlight silvering the canals, the water gleaming like liquid glass beneath the arches of bridges. Their pace was unhurried, the silence between them companionable.

Inside the palazzo, Damian bypassed the grand salons with their gilded weight, guiding her instead through a quiet corridor lined with sconces and polished stone. The air here was cooler, more intimate, the hush of old walls pressing close around them.

At the corridor's end, Damian pressed open a pair of unmarked double doors. The hinges gave a muted groan, and the space revealed itself in a wash of warm light.

The room was intimate, refined. Floor-to-ceiling shelving cradled cut-crystal decanters filled with amber and gold, their surfaces glowing in the light from concealed sconces. Leather chairs, low and deep, were arranged with quiet symmetry around a small marble table. The air held the faintest blend of smoke, oak, and polished brass, a room that belonged less to the palazzo's public grandeur and more to Damian himself.

Evie stepped across the threshold, pausing just inside. "What is this?" she asked, her voice soft, edged with curiosity.

"The Linen Room," Damian replied, crossing to the shelves. His hand moved with the ease of habit, selecting a bottle without hesitation, the gesture almost ritualistic. He poured a measure of scotch into cut crystal tumbler, the sound of liquid against glass sharp in the stillness.

Evie's eyes flicked around the room, to the shelves, the soft pools of amber light. "Does it mean anything?" she asked, a faint smile tugging at her lips.

"It once held linens," Damian said, setting the glass before her. "Sheets, bolts of silk, damask tablecloths. In the 1830s, when the palazzo was renovated, the linen stores were moved elsewhere. But the servants kept using the old name. It lingered, even after my great-grandfather had the space converted into a private bar."

He paused, letting his eyes travel briefly across the shelves, as though he could still see the ghosts of folded fabric where decanters now stood. "He was a shrewd man. He entertained certain 'neutral' parties here, away from prying eyes in the salons upstairs. Deals were struck over these tables, whispered confidences traded under the cover of grappa and candlelight. The name remained because it was safer. A guest could always say he was visiting the Linen Room, and no one would think to ask more."

He lifted his own glass, the amber liquid catching the glow. "My father used it differently. He was no diplomat. For him, it was a retreat. Nights he didn't want company, he came here alone. This room holds both history and habit. I suppose I use it for both."

Evie traced a finger along the rim of her glass, her smile widening. "So, it isn't just your sense of humor, then. It's inherited."

"Unfortunately, yes," Damian said, his mouth curving almost imperceptibly. He raised his glass, the faintest glint of amusement in his eyes. "Now it holds good decisions. At least, that's the intent."

Her brow arched in amused skepticism. "That's what we're calling them?"

He allowed the hint of a smile. "Depends on the night."

She settled into a low chair, the silk of her gown whispering against the leather as she crossed her legs. Her glass rested with poise against her knee, catching the amber glow of the shelves behind her. For a moment, Damian only watched, the deliberate way she held herself, the strength disguised beneath elegance. Then he lowered himself into the chair opposite, his movements measured, composed.

"And tonight?" she asked.

"The night is still deciding," he said quietly.

Her gaze lingered on him, sharp and unyielding. "And you?"

"I seldom get a vote."

She lifted her glass, sipped slowly, and let the silence expand between them. It was not an absence but a presence, a pause that carried everything they had not yet said. The air between them felt weighted, intimate, as if the walls themselves bore witness.

At last, she tilted her head slightly, her voice deliberates. "Then it's fortunate I'm not asking permission."

His eyes glinted faintly, the barest spark of amusement slipping past the reserve. "When have you ever?"

The quiet that followed was not awkward. Chosen. Heavy with things neither dared name, yet both understood.

At last, Damian rose. "Tomorrow will be longer."

She nodded, sipping the last of her scotch.

"Goodnight, Evie."

"Goodnight, Damian."

The door closed behind him with a soft click.

She finished her drink, rose and poured another night cap and made her way down the hall. In her room, she found the bed turned down, a glass of water set by a hazelnut chocolate. She slipped out of her gown, hung it carefully, and sat by the window with her drink. Venice lay hushed beneath the moon.

Her thoughts circled, restless. Would her end come by Damian's hand? Would she even know when?

She set down the glass, slid into bed, and let the silence press close. The future hung over her like the fog outside.

Chapter 4

Evie lay in bed, staring into the misted window, but all she saw was her reflection, faint and shifting with every breath she took. She closed her eyes. Montreal surfaced first. It always did.

Montreal. Always Montreal.

She let the memories flood back. A quiet suburb, five siblings, shared meals, a warm house, and yet she never truly fit. Orphaned before she could remember her parents, she was the outsider taken in. Loved, yes. But love could not fill the hollow that had settled early and stayed.

For years, she tried to patch the gap. Petty theft, reckless dares, a streak of defiance that only widened the distance she pretended wasn't there.

The convenience store was the turning point. She could still feel the burn of shame as Mr. Moreau caught her with candy tucked under her coat. Instead of calling the police, he knelt and said, "You've got more potential than this, Evie. You can turn it around."

He had not said it with anger, only certainty. That rattled her more than punishment ever could.

She took him at his word. Grades improved. Honours and awards followed. Debate teams, admission to McGill, Oxford on a Rhodes Scholarship. She clawed her way forward, but the unease never left. Even beneath Balliol's vaulted ceilings, even as she outpaced her peers, she felt like an interloper in a world that wasn't hers. That unease followed her to London.

She could still smell the ballroom, the warm crush of perfume and champagne. Chandeliers glittered above a swirl of gowns and tuxedos. Alexander, her boyfriend, stood across the room, his attention fixed elsewhere. An ex. The way he smiled, the lean of his body, said more than words.

Evie slipped out into the courtyard, trading the golden haze for the cool night air.

And found Damian.

He sat alone, relaxed, the ember of his cigar a faint glow in the dark. She hesitated, then walked toward him, bold and foolish. She wasn't thinking about consequences, only about being seen and making Alexander jealous.

"Mind if I sit?" she asked, surprising herself.

He didn't smile, but he rose with measured courtesy. "Damian Cesarini," he said simply, extending the introduction like an anchor. As she lowered herself into the chair, he gestured with the cigar in his hand. "Shall I put this out?"

"Please, don't stop on my account," she replied.

Damian paused, studied her for a moment, then settled back into his chair. The silence between them softened, no longer sharp, and when he finally spoke, it was not with guarded care but with something quieter, more familiar.

Evie let the pause linger, then reached across the table without asking. Her fingers brushed the edge of his cigar case, drawing it toward her. The gesture surprised even herself. She had never been so bold, yet with him, despite knowing him for only minutes, it felt natural.

She flipped the case open, selected one with deliberate care, and cut it cleanly. Damian watched without interruption, the faintest trace of amusement in his eyes as she struck a match and brought the flame to the tip.

The first curl of smoke rose between them, slow and deliberate. She exhaled, meeting his gaze across the table.

For the first time, it was Damian who said nothing.

They began with small talk, but Damian's ear caught the faintest trace of an accent in the way she spoke.

"Montreal," he said suddenly, his gaze steady. "Your accent gives you away. You're not entirely London."

Evie blinked, then gave a small, surprised smile. "Guilty. I grew up there. Suburbs, mostly. You?"

"I did my last years of high school there," he replied, as though it were nothing, though the faintest warmth edged his tone. "I lived downtown. Cold winters, harder lessons."

Her smile deepened, curiosity pulling her forward. "That's… unexpected."

"Montreal leaves a mark," Damian said, leaning back slightly, eyes narrowing with memory. "The city has a way of reminding you who you are, even when you'd rather forget."

Something in his voice steadied her. His calm was a gravity she hadn't realized she needed, and she found herself listening more closely than she intended.

They talked about the city for a while, the corners of memory that overlapped, the cafés on Sherbrooke, the biting wind on Mount Royal, the nightclubs, the stubborn, irrepressible spirit of the place. It felt less like an interview and more like recognition, as if the city itself were a bond between them.

Later, his words lingered long after the night ended. "Sometimes, Evie," he had said, his voice low, almost confiding, "we chase paths that don't bring us happiness. The hard part is knowing when to step into the unknown."

She had not understood then, but she carried his voice with her.

They spent that night together, and in the quiet hours before dawn she had felt, for the first time, something steadier than defiance anchoring her. But when she woke in the Knightsbridge house, Damian was gone. The imprint of him remained only in the order of the room, his absence as deliberate as his presence had been.

It was Lukas who appeared instead, composed as ever, laying out breakfast with quiet efficiency as though nothing were unusual. He asked if she preferred coffee or tea, if she liked eggs lightly scrambled or poached, his tone courteous but unreadable. When she finally asked, he only said that Damian had left on business but would be back. His calm, almost paternal steadiness carried her through the strangeness of the morning.

By the time she stepped back into London's rush and boarded the train north, it was as if the night had been folded neatly away. Oxford awaited, its cloisters and libraries pulling her back into the rhythm of lectures and scholarship. Yet the memory of that evening lingered like the aftertaste of strong wine, subtle but inescapable. The sense of being chosen, even if only for a moment, trailed her through lecture halls and late-night libraries.

Damian never crossed that line again. Never blurred it. Always present, always distant, always contained. But she carried the weight of that night with her, a reminder that something unspoken had shifted, and once shifted it could not be undone.

She told herself the pull she felt wasn't real. She returned to London drawn not only to him, but to the quiet spaces he left behind: a borrowed flat in Knightsbridge, an invitation to dinner, a Soho gallery opening. They spoke from time to time, brief calls and messages that arrived with the same precision as everything else he did, never indulgent, never careless. When she came to London she stayed at Knightsbridge, half for convenience, half in the quiet hope that he might appear again. The place became a tether, a reminder of his presence even in his absence.

It was only later, after the scholarships and accolades, that she learned the truth. Damian had been watching her. Not in the way she once hoped, but in the way, men like him watched potential.

She was not just a brilliant student. She was moldable. Dangerous. Useful.

The recruitment wasn't overt. No promises. No threats. Just a path unfurling step by step, until she realized there was no turning back.

Venice had been the last step.

She sent a brief message two days before departure, light and casual. I will be in Venice this weekend. If you are there, I would love a distraction. It wasn't a question. It didn't ask permission. It let him choose. When he replied, let me know when you land, she knew what that meant. Damian never confirmed unless he intended to follow through.

As dusk settled over the city, Venice greeted her with gold. Light spilled over cobblestones, shimmered in canals, and transformed the city into a living painting. Damian stood waiting near the Riva degli Schiavoni, his cream linen suit glowing softly in the fading sun. A pastel pink Turnbull & Asser shirt offered contrast, his brown slip-ons and tortoiseshell sunglasses finishing the look. Damian absorbed the city's gravitas as if it belonged to him.

Evie approached with casual strides. Her black leggings and golf shirt were starkly practical against the romantic backdrop. A burgundy leather duffle slung over her shoulder caught Damian's eye; it was a gift he had sent during her Balliol days. Without a word, he stepped forward, lifted the bag from her shoulder, the motion seamless, his smile disarming.

"You don't have to," Evie began.

"Indulge me," Damian interrupted smoothly.

She smirked, taking in his polished appearance. "You couldn't just wear jeans and a T-shirt?"

Lowering his sunglasses, Damian gave her a glance of amused calm. "I didn't want to look like a tourist. Though you, on the other hand, seem ready for an aerobics class."

Evie laughed lightly. "At least I don't overshadow the city," she teased, gesturing at his tailored elegance against her simplicity.

Damian smiled and gestured forward. "Shall we?" His tone was easy, but there was insistence beneath it, a hint that this meeting was only the beginning.

She fell in step beside him, curiosity stirring. The contrast between them felt symbolic, almost predictive of what the night would hold.

As they turned into the Campiello della Pescaria, Damian led her to a modest restaurant, Al Covo, its charm understated. Inside, the owners lit up at the sight of him, greeting him warmly. Their gestures put Evie instantly at ease.

"This is Evie," Damian introduced, his tone casual yet meaningful. The couple welcomed her as if she were already familiar, leading them to a secluded corner table reserved for Damian whenever he visited.

Al Covo whispered refinement rather than announced it. No menu was handed to them; Damian simply told the owners to bring what they thought best, as he always did. Evie noticed the ease of it, the way the couple nodded without hesitation, already knowing his tastes. It struck her as oddly intimate that a place could know a man well enough to choose for him, and that he trusted them to do it. She realized then that Damian belonged here in a way she did not, woven quietly into the fabric of the city.

Courses arrived in quiet succession, thoughtful but unpretentious. Evie noticed the balance in it, how nothing overwhelmed, and nothing lingered too long. He asked once, almost idly, if the spice was too much, but the question felt like courtesy rather than concern. After that, silence carried them forward.

A bottle of Friulano sat open, never pressed, left to breathe as the evening did the same. The meal had its rhythm, steady and unhurried, more about the space it created than the food itself.

When the plates were cleared, Evie looked up to find Damian watching her. Not with scrutiny, but with something quieter, as though he measured her presence against a memory only, he carried.

At last, he leaned in, voice pitched low, almost lost to the hum of the room. "Evie, there's something you need to understand about the organization I work for."

They lingered over dessert, sweetness almost an afterthought. Outside, water pressed against stone in a rhythm as steady as breath.

Damian leaned closer; his tone stripped of performance. "What we do isn't just secretive. It's consequential. Discretion is non-negotiable. This life isn't for the faint of heart."

Evie set her spoon aside, eyes on him. The weight of his words settled like a second glass of wine, warm, potent, irreversible.

He didn't rush. Damian never did.

"There is structure behind it," he said. "A Collective. Older than most governments, leaner than any corporation. We operate in the shadows because the work demands it. Intelligence, influence, containment. We intervene where others can't or won't."

She stayed silent.

"I'm not just asking you to know it exists," he continued. "I'm asking you to consider becoming part of it."

Her breath caught, though her face stayed composed. "This is your recruitment pitch?"

He smiled faintly. "No. If it were a pitch, you'd already be inside it. This is your warning."

Evie held his gaze, pulse quickening. "What happens if I say no?"

"You go back to Oxford. Or wherever your instincts take you. And no one follows. You walk away untouched. But you forget. Completely. As if it never happened. Every door closed; every trace erased. You and I do not know each other, and I never existed."

"And if I say yes?"

Damian's expression did not change. "Then you stay. And there is no leaving."

Candlelight flickered across linen, shadows stretching between forgotten glasses.

Evie didn't need more time. Whether it was the allure of danger, the pull of the unknown, or the gravity Damian carried, she said, "Yes."

Just one word. Quiet. Clear. And everything changed.

Chapter 5

As dawn approached Venice, the city stirred with gentle anticipation. In the palazzo, the first light filtered through the lace-trimmed Fortuny curtains of Evie's bedroom. Golden rays crept through the windows, casting a warm glow across ornate furnishings and rich tapestries. The light touched frescoes and gilded mirrors, slowly illuminating the chamber in serene amber hues.

The sun brushed against Evie's face, rousing her from a restless night. Her eyes opened to the Venetian sunrise and the quiet realization that she had survived. Beyond the parted curtains, the Grand Canal awakened, its waters stirred by the first boats of the day. Gondoliers' songs drifted faintly, mingling with the sound of merchants setting their stalls.

She lingered a moment in the stillness before slipping out of bed. The day held promise, and she intended to meet it with clarity. She dressed in workout clothes and descended to the palazzo's modest but well-equipped gym. For the next hour, she moved through her routine: cardio, strength training, yoga. The rhythm of breath and the cadence of her playlist steadied her. Each stretch and rep stripped away the tension of the night before, leaving her sharper, calmer.

Back in her en-suite, marble and glass enfolded her in elegance. She stood beneath the shower, letting the water scour away doubt. Dressed afterward in tailored white linen trousers by Brunello Cucinelli and a soft silk blouse by Dolce & Gabbana, she struck the balance between refined and effortless. Bottega Veneta walking shoes promised comfort. A gold necklace and diamond studs finished the look. The mirror showed her a woman, understated, composed, timeless.

On the loggia, morning light gilded the Grand Canal. Sun fractured across the water; rooftops still muted in shadow. A gondolier's song carried faintly. At the far end of the table, Damian sat with an untouched espresso beside a folded newspaper. His gaze was fixed on the horizon, unreadable. As she approached, he looked up, offering the briefest nod, an invitation without words.

Evie took her seat opposite him. A carafe of coffee waited beside a tray of pastries, fruit, rye toast, and soft eggs with chives. Everything was arranged with care but without ostentation. Like him.

They served themselves in silence. It was not tension but economy, the space between words that belonged only to those who knew how to leave things unsaid. Damian lifted his cup. "You slept," he said. Not a question.

"Eventually," Evie replied, spreading marmalade across toast.

The cigar was already lit. Damian leaned back, smoke from a Romeo y Julieta Churchill curling into the air.

Evie raised her brows. "A healthy breakfast."

A faint smile curved his mouth. "I do not tell you what to wear, Evie. You do not tell me what I choose for breakfast."

She blinked, incredulous. "What? You are always telling me what to wear and where to go."

"Only when it concerns work or assignments," he said evenly. "Beyond that, you are your own person. As long as your choices do not jeopardize the Collective."

Her frustration flared. She began to argue, but Damian rose abruptly, his chair scraping the stone. His voice was sharp, final.

"Do not try me, Evie. I will not argue about cigars. That is the end of it."

His eyes hardened. "You are not my wife, nor my mother. And I did not listen to either while they were alive. Say the word, and I will have you moved to the Bauer within fifteen minutes."

Her fists clenched. "This isn't about the cigars, Damian. I hope you remember it was cigars that brought us together in the first place."

Something flickered in his gaze, though his expression remained guarded. "Our connection changed the moment you put the Collective at risk. You made a choice, and now we both live with the consequences."

"I know," she whispered. "I know better than anyone. But I can fix this. I can make it right. Just give me the chance. Damian, please. Sit down."

After a pause, he sat again, jaw tight. The silence was weighted.

Then, without warning, he reached under his jacket and drew a gun. The movement was deliberate, slow. Evie froze as he ejected a bullet from the chamber, placed it on the table, and slid it toward her. His eyes never left hers.

"Take a good look. That is the bullet that will end you. The one that ties up the loose ends you created in London."

Her hand trembled as she lifted it. Her breath caught when she saw her name etched along the casing. The sight drained the color from her face.

"Wow," she murmured. "You always hear this line in films, but you never think it could be real."

Damian leaned in; voice low. "You are in serious trouble. The Collective does not forgive the kind of risk you created. You endangered yourself and the operation. If Sparrow's cover had been blown, the damage would have been catastrophic."

Her throat tightened. "How bad is it?"

"Fifty-fifty," he said flatly. "Tonight, will tilt the balance. You will either be a hero, or..." He let silence complete the sentence.

Evie nodded, resolve hardening. "What do I need to do?"

"Execute cleanly," Damian answered. "There is no margin tonight. If you deliver, I will have leverage with the board. Enough to silence them. Enough to protect you. If you do not, I will not be able to."

"I understand," she said firmly. "I will not fail."

He rose, slow and deliberate, slipped the bullet back into the gun, and chambered it. The click was stark in the silence.

"Remember," he said quietly. "The choice is yours. Prove yourself tonight or fail and end it all."

He walked to the far end of the loggia, leaving her with her thoughts.

Evie sat, staring at the table where the bullet had rested, its reflection still vivid in her mind. Fear pressed heavily, but slowly it hardened into determination. She would not be undone by mistakes. She would prove herself to Damian, to the Collective, and to herself.

She drew in a steadying breath and let her eyes follow him across the loggia. He stood at the far railing, framed against the morning light, a figure carved from certainty itself. For a moment, she simply watched, the tension between them coiling and uncoiling in the quiet. Whatever line had been drawn, she knew she could not leave it hanging in silence. She needed to reclaim ground, however small, to remind him and herself that she could still stand beside him.

At last, she rose and crossed to him, her steps deliberate. "Damian," she said steadily. "What are your plans for the day?"

He turned from the railing, composed once more. "I plan to walk to the Piazzale Roma, then back to the Rialto. After that, I will collect my boat and head to Burano for lunch at Da Romano."

Unexpectedly, he added, "Would you care to join me?"

A faint smile touched her lips. "Yes, Damian. I would like that very much."

"Then meet me at the front door in fifteen minutes. We have much ground to cover, and the morning is already half gone."

The air in the palazzo still carried the weight of their exchange. Evie steadied herself, drawing a long breath before stepping out to meet him. Whatever had passed upstairs lingered, but Damian was already waiting below, composed and unshaken, as though nothing had cracked the surface.

At the main entrance, he stood with the effortless elegance she had always envied, posture straight, presence commanding. He greeted her with a smile.

"Are the shoes new?" he asked with casual curiosity.

She was caught off guard. "Yes. I bought them when I arrived in the city."

"Bottega?"

She nodded, pleased. "Yes."

"They are lovely," he said genuinely, opening the door to the water gate. He gestured for her to step into the calle.

As they walked toward Campo Santo Stefano, Evie's thoughts drifted. Their earlier conversation lingered, stark against the casual ease of their current interaction. Moments ago, she had been certain Damian was going to end her life; now, he was complimenting her shoes as if they were on a date. The contrast was jarring, and she struggled to reconcile the cold, unyielding man from before with the warm, attentive companion beside her.

The sun warmed the stones beneath their feet as they crossed the Accademia Bridge, the Grand Canal unfolding beneath them in shimmering light. Gondolas drifted below, the palazzos catching the morning sun. Evie took in the view quietly while Damian walked beside her, composed, watchful, always reading the street.

They moved through Dorsoduro, the air alive with coffee, laughter, and the murmur of early business. The Ponte dei Pugni came and went, its history acknowledged only with a glance. Campo Santa Margherita was busy, the square buzzing with voices and clinking glasses. Evie let the city's rhythm steady her.

They turned through Santa Croce, the crowds thinning. At the Calatrava, the steel and glass bridge cut across the canal like a statement, modern against centuries of stone. Damian didn't comment, but his eyes lingered.

Cannaregio came next, quieter, older. They passed synagogues, bakeries, and the modest front of the Jewish Museum. The mood shifted. Not somber, but grounded. History lived here.

By the time they reached the Rialto, the mood broke. Tourists thickened the walkways, and the city's quiet gave way to camera flashes and laughter. Damian watched it all with a faint, unreadable smile. Evie caught the look but didn't ask. Some things, she had learned, belonged to his past.

Under the statue of Goldoni, Venice's celebrated playwright, they paused for a breather. Damian nodded toward a café in the square, and they stepped inside. It was after 11 a.m., a reasonable time for "un ombra," the Venetian custom of a midday glass of wine. The bartender, familiar with Damian, nodded and poured two glasses without question.

They sat and sipped their wine, the throng of passersby flowing around them. The wine was excellent, a simple pleasure in a complex day. As they watched the sea of humanity ebb and flow, Evie couldn't help but wonder how a city so beautiful could feel so heavy with the tension between them. Yet for the moment, the quiet camaraderie between her and Damian offered a sliver of solace.

After twenty minutes, they decided to brave the crowds. Stepping outside, they were immediately swept into a torrent of schoolchildren from Sweden. The lively chaos engulfed them, and Damian, with a glance at the surging mass, gestured for a detour. They chose the back streets, a longer route but a quieter reprieve from the throngs of San Marco.

As they navigated the winding, less-traveled alleys, Evie felt a surprising sense of calm. Venice's timeless beauty, a city of hidden gems and serene canals, contrasted with the turmoil that churned inside her. Her steps fell in rhythm with Damian's steady pace, her breath gradually easing as she drew strength from the city's soothing rhythm.

They returned to the palazzo just before noon. The house buzzed with quiet activity as staff moved with practiced efficiency, anticipating Damian's imminent departure. On the private dock, a sleek mahogany motorboat bobbed gently, polished to a gleam that reflected the vibrant hues of the canal. Damian extended a steadying hand to assist Evie aboard, the gesture as natural as it was reassuring.

Settling into the soft leather seats, Evie allowed herself a moment of comfort. The motor hummed softly as Damian expertly reversed the boat from the dock, merging seamlessly into the bustling traffic of the Grand Canal. The boat glided with ease, passing beneath the Accademia Bridge, where the grandeur of the surrounding palazzos gleamed in the sunlight. Their elegant facades seemed worlds away from the tumult of tourists and the crowded maze of the city.

Turning into the Canale di Cannaregio, they navigated toward the open lagoon. As the boat cut smoothly through the rippling water, the breeze picked up, carrying with it the faint scent of salt and the distant cries of seagulls. Evie felt a fleeting sense of peace, the expanse of water and sky offering a brief respite from her internal storm.

Damian spoke sparingly as they passed various landmarks, his voice soft with nostalgia as he pointed out fragments of his childhood woven into the city's fabric. Evie listened intently, her gaze drifting between Damian and the endless horizon. In this moment of tranquility, the weight of her mission felt momentarily bearable, held at bay by the beauty of their surroundings.

The engine purred softly as the vibrant island of Burano came into view. Its kaleidoscope of houses painted in vivid shades of pink, blue, yellow, and green stood out against the lagoon's serene backdrop. Their reflections shimmered on the water, creating an almost dreamlike scene. Evie couldn't help but feel a sense of awe, her breath catching at the charm and warmth of the island. It was a stark contrast to the cold world she inhabited, a vivid reminder of what was at stake and what she fought to protect.

Damian docked at Burano's marina, the wooden motorboat gleaming under the bright afternoon sun. Evie stepped ashore and secured the boat to a stanchion, her movements smooth and practiced. Damian climbed over the gunwale, extended his arm, a gesture both formal and familiar, and she took it. Together, they set off toward Da Romano.

The restaurant greeted them warmly, its staff recognizing Damian instantly. He had been coming here with his grandparents since childhood, and the customary few minutes of asking about family followed. The host then guided them to a table inside, sheltered from the midday heat.

Menus arrived alongside a liter of white wine and mineral water. As Damian studied the options, Evie's gaze wandered to the art adorning the walls. The lore of Da Romano spoke of meals bought by artists in exchange for their paintings, and the collection now covered the restaurant in Venetian creations.

As they waited for the first course, Evie turned to Damian, her unease plain. Sensing her worry, he placed his hand over hers, offering a reassuring smile.

"Evie, is everything alright?" he asked, his tone steady.

She hesitated before answering, her voice low. "I can't stop thinking about tonight. What happens after we finish the mission?" She spoke of the task ahead, but her underlying fear was London, the unresolved specter haunting her thoughts.

Damian's expression softened as he squeezed her hand. "Tonight is crucial. It is your chance to prove yourself. But the Collective does not forget easily. Your actions will speak louder than any words."

Evie drew a slow breath. "I understand, Damian. I just need to know there is a way back. That I can fix this."

He held her gaze, his voice firm yet kind. "You can. But it will not be easy. Tonight, is your chance to show your worth, not just to the Collective but to yourself."

Determination flickered in her eyes. "I'll make it right."

Damian smiled faintly; approval clear. "I believe in you. Now, let's enjoy our meal. You'll need your strength."

They lingered longer than expected, conversation drifting to safer terrain: art, architecture, the strange serenity of islands like this one. Damian let the subject of the mission fall away, knowing pressure too early could fracture focus. Wired operatives made mistakes, and tonight's success was too important for that. Still, he watched her closely as she spoke, as she moved. London had not left her. If the order came, he would carry it out himself.

With the bill paid and farewells exchanged, they stepped into the sunlight. Burano dazzled; its houses painted in brilliant shades against a cloudless sky.

Evie loosened the boat's lines as Damian started the engine, the hum blending with distant chatter and the lap of water against the dock. The boat cut smoothly through the shimmering lagoon, guiding them back toward Venice. Evie settled into the stern, sunlight warming her skin.

As they drifted away, the vibrant colors of Burano faded, replaced by the subdued charm of Murano. Venice appeared ahead, its skyline a silent beacon calling them home. Passing San Michele, the boat swung around the island before gliding back down the Canale di Cannareggio. Rejoining the Grand Canal's traffic, Damian navigated with ease, steady as a metronome.

When the palazzo dock came into view, Evie felt a wave of mixed emotions: relief and anticipation. The boat pulled into the private dock, and Damian maneuvered it smoothly into position. Evie stepped ashore, securing the lines. The weight of their earlier conversation lingered as they walked toward the water gate.

"I think I'll head to my room for some rest," Evie said, brushing stray hair from her face.

"What time should I wake you?" Damian called after her.

"If I'm not up by seven, come and get me," she replied, her voice fading as the heavy doors closed behind her.

Damian lingered for a moment before heading inside. He returned to the library, selecting a volume at random, and found solace in the garden's shade. The air carried the scent of jasmine, blending with the faint hum of cicadas as he settled into a wrought-iron chair. The book lay open in his lap, but his thoughts were elsewhere.

He reflected on the day's events, the tension with Evie still palpable. Tonight was her opportunity to atone, to demonstrate her loyalty. He trusted her abilities, but the stakes could not be higher. Failure was not an option for either of them.

As twilight dimmed in the garden, Damian closed the book and climbed the staircase to Evie's room. Knocking softly, he waited. No response. Gently, he pushed the door open.

She lay on the bed, still asleep, her breathing steady. Damian approached and lightly touched her arm. She stirred, blinking awake, her eyes widening in alarm until they found his empty hands. Her body relaxed visibly.

"Now that you are awake, I'll let you be," Damian said, his tone low but kind. He stood and made his way to the door. "Would you like me to have the kitchen send up something to eat?"

Evie nodded, brushing a hand through her hair. "Something light," she replied.

Damian inclined his head and pulled the door closed behind him.

She showered quickly, letting the heat mask what adrenaline and doubt refused to show. By the time she stepped out, the shift had happened, movement without hesitation, emotion locked behind detachment.

Crossing into the bedroom, she found a plate of cheese and fruit by the window. Strawberries, grapes, ripe peach slices, and creamy cheeses. Evie donned a soft robe and moved to the table. She took a piece of cheese paired with a peach slice and savored the harmony of flavors.

The late afternoon sun streamed through the window, casting golden hues across the room. But time was short.

She secured the garter around her thigh and moved to the armoire. Her fingers skimmed over luxurious fabrics before settling on an electric blue raw silk gown from Valentino. The hue was striking against her skin. She slid into it, the silk cascading effortlessly.

Her transformation had to be complete. At the mirror, she swept her chestnut waves into a platinum-blonde wig, the polished style catching the light. Ice-blue colored contacts masked the depth of her gaze.

To finish the outfit, she selected a four-strand choker of pearls, a dark metallic gray bracelet, and platinum drop earrings. Smoky eyes and deep wine-red lips completed the look.

She stepped into a pair of Fratelli Rossetti heels, structured and sharp, extending her silhouette.

Turning to the mirror, Evie regarded her reflection. Calm. Composed. Lethal. She looked like a woman who knew exactly what she could take and what she might be offered. One lingering glance, then she turned to the concealed cabinet near the bed.

Her fingers unlocked the hidden mechanism. From the cabinet, she drew two black knives and the glass stiletto, its translucent blade catching the light like a deadly secret. She slipped them into her garter, the gown smooth and unmarked. The weight of the blades was reassuring.

Damian returned a moment later, clad in a shawl-collared Brioni tuxedo. Around his neck, he wore a white silk Gianfranco Ferré scarf. Evie recognized it, a gift she had given him. Probably a winter birthday. It was hard to keep track when there were three official birthdays, if the passports were to be believed, to honor each year.

Her eyes softened at the sight of the scarf. "You wore it," she murmured, brushing her fingers lightly against the silk.

"Yes," Damian replied, steady and understated. "I always do when I am here."

The warmth of his words settled over her. Damian took her hand gently and kissed the air above her fingers. "You would stop time itself, Evie," he said, his tone filled with quiet admiration.

Her cheeks flushed slightly. Despite the tension, her heart betrayed her.

Evie lifted her purse, secured the small .22 caliber pistol inside, and zipped it shut with deliberate care. She could not escape the feeling that this might be her final night in the palazzo.

Her gaze shifted to the Fortuny drapes. She touched the fabric, soft under her fingertips. The view beyond the window, the bustling canal, had brought her comfort in difficult times. The thought of losing it filled her with resolve.

Taking a measured breath, she turned away. This mission was about more than redemption. It was a chance to reclaim the trust she had recklessly jeopardized.

When she joined Damian by the door, his expression was inscrutable. He offered his arm. Evie placed her hand lightly on his sleeve, their steps synchronizing as they left the room, walking into the night that promised reckoning.

Descending the grand staircase, Evie found herself flooded with nostalgia. The scarf, the tuxedo, the way he steadied her, each detail reminded her of simpler times. But tonight, it was not about the past. Tonight was about proving she was still deserving of his belief in her.

Chapter 6

May I have this dance?

At the gate, a sleek gunmetal grey Donzi motorboat idled, its polished surface gleaming under the faint moonlight. The pilot stepped forward, offering Evie his hand with deferential confidence. Two men assisted as she boarded, her raw silk gown catching the light as she adjusted her footing.

They sat in silence on the leather couches as the engines rumbled low, gliding through deserted waterways. Only the gentle lapping of water against the hull and the distant hum of the city broke the quiet. As they joined the late evening traffic of the Grand Canal, the boat's lights shimmered across the water, guiding their way.

Passing the Doge's Palace, Evie reached for Damian's hand. He squeezed hers, fingers interlocking, and they rode like that until the boat slid to the water entrance of the Scuola Grande della Misericordia.

The Scuola caught the amber glow of sunset, rising like a fortress. Once a center of charity and influence, its sixteenth-century ambition, commissioned under Jacopo Sansovino, echoed Roman grandeur. Its legacy had not faded, only shifted. Now, under Umbra's hand, it remained a crucible for unseen power.

Tonight, it hosted the Autumnal Harvest Ball. A study in opulence and irony. There were no fields to harvest within an hour of Venice, but tradition endured. It drew the city's elite, the powerful, and the unwary, all unaware of the older currents moving beneath the pageantry.

The grand ballroom was upstairs. The ground floor, a labyrinth of columns, blind corners, and black light, hosted cocktails. It was a collection point for deals, alliances, and secrets. Four exits led to three canals. Only a mistake could derail a perfect plan.

Damian stepped off first, scanning the perimeter before offering his hand to Evie. She handed him her purse, then accepted his support as she navigated the dock in her heels. Once balanced, she straightened her gown, reclaimed her purse, and took Damian's arm.

The party on the ground floor was already in full swing. A jazz band played sultry melodies in a corner, marble columns and bare brick walls backlit by dramatic black light. Guests draped in finery turned to watch them enter. Evie tensed at the attention, then relaxed. It was part of the game.

Her gown and dangerous allure drew admiring glances. She moved with fluid confidence, her eyes scanning the room. Damian, steady and unobtrusive, guided her through the crowd.

Evie noted everything: hidden niches, exits, clusters of security. Men in ill-fitting tuxedos with rigid postures, wolves trying to pass as sheepdogs. She smiled faintly, sipping the champagne Damian handed her, scanning with cool detachment.

Old friends gathered around Damian, eager with handshakes and kisses. When he introduced Evie as Isabelle Moreau, murmurs followed: colleague, mistress, partner? The closed world of Venetian society buzzed with speculation.

Evie played her role to perfection. She was aloof, charming, unreadable. Every smile and every glance were calculated. Yet beneath it all, a flicker of thought persisted. Les jeux sont faits. The die was already cast. She could only play her hand now and hope she had read the board better than the others.

Then she saw him. Silvestro Leonardi, heir to Leonardo Industries, sauntered up the staircase. She touched Damian's arm, their agreed signal. He excused them both, and together they moved toward the grand stairs.

The marble staircase curled upward in gilded splendor. Evie's steps were measured, her mind running through contingencies. She memorized blind spots and plotted exits. Adrenaline simmered beneath her calm exterior, but a tightness in her chest reminded her that failure would mean more than death. It would mean erasure.

At the top, the grand ballroom unfurled. Chandeliers, frescoes, and gold stretched in every direction. Damian did not pause, and neither did Evie. The beauty was not a distraction. It was data. She swept the room: movement, exits, body language.

Silvestro, surrounded by dignitaries, laughed easily, unaware. Young, entitled, and soon to be dead.

Evie and Damian moved beneath a grand arch as the orchestra struck up a tango. Without a word, Evie slipped into Damian's arms. The music built, so did their dance. Fluid, deliberate, predatory. The crowd parted, drawn in by the hypnotic connection between them.

The blue of Evie's gown flashed with each step, the silk catching the low light as her leg emerged and disappeared in counter rhythm. Their bodies moved in deliberate sync, close but never collapsing, the tension electric and unbroken. Damian's hand on her back was firm, guiding, but his expression remained unreadable. She met his gaze once, briefly, and felt the heat of something unspoken coil beneath her ribs.

The music swelled. Their movements grew sharper, more intricate, heels slicing the floor with elegance, edged in danger. Each pivot and pause drew the crowd deeper into their gravity. The dance held its own breath, as if the room itself had gone still.

The crescendo neared. Evie stepped into him, turned, and held. The final note cut through the air and vanished.

A breathless silence followed. Then applause. Sudden. Hungry.

They remained in the final pose a moment longer, her thigh pressed against his, their eyes locked with something more than performance. Then Damian straightened, pulling her upright with practiced ease, and led her off the floor without a word.

Damian shook hands with the conductor. Evie curtsied, demure but radiant. As the crowd clamored for more, Damian was drawn into conversation, leaving Evie near the bandstand. Alone, but not unnoticed.

Silvestro watched her, glass in hand. He felt a stir of doubt, a rare flicker, but quickly dismissed it. She was too poised, too perfect. His kind of woman.

Smiling at admirers, Evie descended the stairs, weaving through well-wishers, accepting champagne from a passing waiter.

Silvestro approached, taking the old glass from her and replacing it with a fresh one, a grandly theatrical move. He introduced himself simply as Silvestro, his surname superfluous. She smiled, introducing herself as Isabelle Moreau.

"You've lost your dance partner," he said smoothly.

Evie rolled her eyes. "He's here for business. I'm just an adornment until he's done."

Silvestro's smile deepened. Easy prey, he thought. Beautiful, neglected, disillusioned. And yet, there was that look in her eyes, as if she were weighing him. He liked it. It made the pursuit more interesting.

"You intrigue me," Silvestro murmured, swirling his champagne. "There's danger in you. I find it captivating."

"And what makes you think I'm different from the others?" she countered lightly.

He chuckled. "You're not like them. You're sharper. More unpredictable."

He gestured toward the lower floor. "Shall we find somewhere more private?"

Evie inclined her head, cool and composed. As she followed him with deliberate steps, she registered the weight of the moment. Les jeux sont faits. There was no turning back.

Silvestro brushed her wrist, then slipped into the crowd, signaling her to follow.

She lingered, calculating, before descending into the shadows between the marble columns. The black light turned every surface into a study of fractured reflections. It was perfect.

Silvestro reappeared minutes later, carrying two glasses. He offered one to her. Evie accepted, her fingers brushing the glass.

"You move quietly," she observed.

"A necessary skill," he replied. "Enjoying the evening?"

Evie let the silence stretch, then smiled. "It has its moments."

He stepped closer, lowering his voice. "Entertainment comes in many forms."

Evie sipped, composed. "The night isn't over yet."

His grin sharpened. "No, it certainly isn't."

He brushed her chin. "Your eyes are mesmerizing."

She smiled coyly, leaning in just enough. "Thank you, Silvestro."

As his hand lingered, she pressed a concealed plunger in her bracelet, sending a pulse signal and alerting the team. Silvestro, oblivious, took her hand, guiding her deeper between the columns.

Damian, stationed midway down the grand staircase, watched. His team adjusted positions subtly, covering exits. Outside, a gunmetal grey Donzi racing boat activated, slicing through the Rio di Noale.

Silvestro led Evie into a secluded niche. His eyes gleamed, but somewhere deep inside, buried under years of entitlement, he felt a flicker of unease. He ignored it. Tonight was about conquest.

Evie, calm and calculating, allowed herself to be drawn closer. Beneath her cool façade, a single thought hummed steady and sharp. Les jeux sont faits.

Silvestro leaned against a pillar. "Away from prying eyes," he murmured.

"Privacy has its uses," she returned.

"And secrets," he added.

"Perhaps," she said, setting her glass down.

He studied her. "Are you here to enjoy yourself, or to watch something unfold?"

"Why not both?"

Silvestro smiled and stepped closer.

Damian watched from the stairs. Les jeux sont faits, he thought.

Below, Silvestro held Evie's hand, stroking her fingers idly, his questions drifting between flirtation and curiosity. She smiled, inventing her background as she went, reeling him in with practiced ease. His finger traced the outline of her jaw, then drifted lower, following the neckline of her gown. When she did not object, he leaned closer, intent on kissing her, already dreaming of possession.

His hand on her chin, Silvestro didn't notice the subtle movement of her hand to her leg, or chose not to. A flicker of confusion crossed his face as the glass stiletto slid under his armpit, striking just above the heart. His mouth parted in shock, soundless, as he staggered back. He groped for the pillar, confusion clouding his eyes as the blood drained. His knees buckled. Evie shifted slightly, ensuring he wedged neatly between the columns. His body sagged into the shadows, propped just enough not to be immediately seen.

Evie glanced down. A small, dark spot bloomed near the hem of her gown. A shame. She liked this one. Electric blue, sleek and striking. Damian had always seemed a little different around her when she wore it. Perhaps she imagined it. No matter. It would have to be destroyed.

Composed, she turned toward the east exit. One of the guards stationed by the door nodded politely as she passed. She smiled back and stepped down the stairs, removing her shoes. Barefoot now, heels in hand, she matched her pace to the boat approaching the riva.

As she neared the edge, she gathered her gown and, in a seamless movement, took the outstretched hand of the boatman. He steadied her as she stepped lightly onto the Donzi's gunwale and climbed aboard.

The engines roared to life, slicing through the dark waters of Venice. Evie exhaled, her heart hammering not from fear, but from focus. The mission was done. The target has been eliminated. Now came survival.

As the Donzi sped away, city lights fractured across the canal like scattered constellations. Evie replayed the evening, every calculation, every controlled gesture. She had delivered perfection.

Below deck, she opened a gym bag handed to her upon boarding. Inside was a fresh change of clothes, anonymous and unremarkable. She slipped out of her dress, folding it neatly into the bag along with her purse, wig, and contact lenses. Her makeup, carefully wiped away, joined the pile of items bound for incineration. The jewelry she placed into a velvet box marked for Damian, sanitized, not discarded.

She pulled on black leggings and a hoodie, the transformation complete. Without the glamorous veneer, she looked fifteen years younger, her anonymity restored.

Back on deck, she accepted a black wallet from the boatman. Inside were a Singaporean passport, matching IDs, credit cards, and cash in euros and Swiss francs. Her thumb brushed over the passport's cover; a life was waiting in the wings should this one collapse.

Venice receded behind them, its skyline dissolving into the night. Tessera loomed ahead, industrial lights casting warped reflections on the rippling water. A chill skated down Evie's spine. If a bullet found her out here, the Adriatic would swallow her whole.

She steadied herself, scanning the dark horizon. The assignment was done, but the Collective's expectations were never satisfied. The aftershocks would ripple well beyond tonight.

As they neared the docks, the engines softened to a purr. She stepped ashore, the salt air sharp against her skin, the weight of the night settling into her bones.

Meanwhile, Damian lingered at the soirée, sharp-eyed and composed. Champagne in hand, he took a canapé from a passing tray, anchoring himself among the guests. Leaving now would only invite scrutiny. It was vital that he be seen but not involved.

Fifteen minutes later, the inevitable happened. The lights brightened. Doors closed with a thud. A few guests protested, "Don't you know who I am?", but the officers were unmoved. The room buzzed briefly before settling into an uneasy hush.

A commissario, invited through family ties, stepped forward, his face a study in professionalism. "A body has been found on the premises," he announced. "The victim is deceased. The circumstances are suspicious. No one is to leave until questioned."

Damian sipped his champagne, observing with detached amusement. Only Venetians could make murder feel so ceremonious.

A hum rippled through the crowd. "Who could it be?" dominated the discussions. In a nod to the celebrity of the gathering, prosecco was served while everyone waited for the city police to arrive.

Within thirty minutes, officers and crime scene technicians moved through the crowd. Names were taken, statements gathered.

Damian approached the commissario. Their handshake was firm.

"Commissario," Damian said, measured and polite. "It's been a while."

"Conte," the commissario replied, recognition flickering. "A shame it is under these circumstances."

Damian allowed a faint smile. "Indeed. I was upstairs earlier, looking for my companion. She left after a disagreement."

The commissario's pen paused. "Her name, please."

"Isabelle Moreau. Canadian. She is staying with me at the palazzo, unless she has packed her bags, in which case she is at the Bauer."

A smile passed between the two men.

Returning to his notes, the commissario asked if Damian had seen anything suspicious.

Damian shook his head. "No. I was otherwise occupied."

"Will you remain in Venice for the next few days?"

"Of course. Unless something urgently takes me away." Damian handed over his card, the design discreet but unmistakable. "But I am available should you need anything further."

The commissario tucked the card into his jacket. "Appreciated, Signore Conte."

Their handshake was brief. A uniformed sergeant gestured, and Damian moved toward the exit, his pace unhurried.

Outside, the night air was sharp, the city hushed. Damian's footsteps echoed faintly on the stones as a sleek motorboat pulled alongside the dock.

Stepping aboard, he took his place at the stern. The engine rumbled to life, and the Donzi slipped into the maze of canals, leaving the Scuola behind.

The rush of wind cut through him, a bracing counterpoint to the heat of the evening's aftermath. He turned the night over in his mind:

Evie's performance, the kill, the extraction. Flawless, but the Collective demanded more than success. It demanded silence, invisibility.

The pilot handed Damian the velvet box. He opened it and, seeing the jewelry, gave a small nod of understanding. It would be cleansed, sanitized, forgotten.

As the palazzo's familiar silhouette rose from the darkness, Damian straightened his jacket. The boat slowed, gliding into place at the dock. Damian stepped ashore without hesitation, opened the water gate, and entered the palazzo, moving through the grand halls, their quiet splendor steadying him.

Damian entered the Linen Room, the polished wood paneling glinting faintly under the ambient glow. He poured a flute of Krug's Clos du Mesnil champagne, then reached for his cigar, cutting and lighting it with the same determination that marked all his movements. The golden liquid fizzed, bubbles rising to the surface. The aroma, rich and effervescent, filled the air, a welcome distraction from the weight of the night. He took a sip, the champagne's sharp coolness cutting through the heat of his thoughts.

The extraction had gone exactly to plan. Every contingency Evie might need, a new passport, clean ID, cash in two currencies, had been provided. She had earned that much. But success in Umbra did not erase failure. The board might nod, but they would not forget.

Another sip, another measured drag from the cigar. Smoke curled upward, soothing and soft against the stillness. The study offered fragile quiet, a momentary ceasefire between what had been and what must come next. But the bullet still sat in his memory, gleaming with finality, the one etched with her name.

The palazzo had fallen silent, its usual hum of controlled movement replaced by stillness. Damian walked through the dim corridors, footsteps echoing across marble floors that had seen empires rise and fall. In his bedroom, the familiar hush of soft light and crisp linen awaited him. He removed his tuxedo with care, every fold smoothed, every line pressed. Control, at least, could still be exercised over silk and wool.

Sliding beneath the covers, Damian allowed himself a breath, eyes closed, but sleep kept its distance. Every frame replayed: her dance, the blade, the clean escape. The lies told to the commissario, precise and balanced. Nothing was out of place. Not yet.

But it was not perfection that lingered. It was the quiet question: what came next for her, for them?

Evie would be en route to Rome by now, cloaked in her new identity. Neutral ground, clean lines, and temporary anonymity waited there. He had arranged a secure communication line. If she made it to the Waldorf unscathed, she would use it. If not...

He set an alarm. Four hours. Enough to give her time. Not enough to let worry take root.

As the light dimmed, Damian's thoughts drifted to the woman in electric blue, the one who had slipped past death with a whisper of silk and steel. She had proven herself. She had bought herself time.

For now.

But the bullet with her name still gleamed in his mind: patient, inevitable, waiting.

Chapter 7

At Tessera, Evie was greeted by her transport team, the towering twins, their identical suits immaculate, their expressions stoic. Their imposing presence did little to ease the unease gnawing at her. She walked toward the open door of the dark Audi S8, her movements deliberate, her thoughts cautious. Behind her, the Donzi swung around, accelerating into the bay's shadowed waters. Its engines softened to a subdued purr as the running lights clicked on, transforming it into the image of a leisure craft returning to Venice after a day at sea.

The car represented safety, or so she convinced herself. No swift bullet under the black sky. No abrupt burial at sea in the Adriatic shallows. The car meant escape, another day to fight, another chance at survival.

Seated in the plush back seat, Evie felt the door close securely behind her, sealing her in the armored interior. The Audi glided onto the A1, engine humming as it accelerated to typical Italian speeds, leaving Tessera and its shadows behind. Her two escorts sat silently in the front, their eyes fixed on the unfurling autostrada, their presence steadfast but impersonal.

As they approached Padua, Evie reached into the bag beside her and retrieved an iPad, one of Damian's quiet gifts. His impeccable taste in music had been loaded onto it. She selected a best-of Orbital mix, the opening beats creating a rhythm that matched the pulse of the tires. Settling deeper into the seat, she allowed the flow of early morning traffic to merge with the swirling cadence of the music.

False dawn began to break as the car neared Rome, its outskirts glowing faintly in the distance. The men in the front called control, advising of their location with clipped efficiency. Shortly after, a notification was sent to Evie's body double, instructing her to dress and begin a jog along an agreed-upon route. Timing had to be perfect; another vehicle would retrieve the double, ensuring all trails were blurred and the illusion preserved.

Entering the early morning Roman traffic, the Audi maneuvered gracefully along winding streets, climbing toward the Waldorf in the hills. At a blind corner, a few hundred meters from the hotel's grand entrance, the car eased to a halt. Evie slipped out, her movements smooth and swift. Adjusting her posture, she took off at a light jog, her pace measured but purposeful. The crisp air invigorated her, and though perspiration dotted her brow after a few minutes, it was not enough to discomfort her.

Turning into the grand drive, Evie slowed her pace and smiled faintly as one of the hotel's doormen stepped forward, opening one of the heavy oak doors. The gesture was seamless, a mark of practiced hospitality, and Evie carried herself with the confidence of someone who belonged.

Inside the Waldorf, the faint hum of early morning activity greeted her. Evie allowed herself a brief moment of calm, her shoulders easing ever so slightly. The operation was complete. She had done everything necessary to vanish without a trace. Yet she knew better than to succumb to complacency.

Slipping off her hood and removing her sunglasses, she walked purposefully to the concierge's desk. Her tone was measured, effortless, as she inquired about booking a car for her 4 p.m. flight to Zurich. The concierge, eager to impress, offered a car at 1:30, punctuating the arrangement with a knowing smile. "One never knows with Roman traffic to Leonardo da Vinci," he advised. His suggestion of a noon reservation at La Pergola for a light lunch gave her pause. After a moment, she accepted. It would be a fleeting indulgence, a small reclaiming of normalcy before the next leg of her journey.

Her suite was immaculate. Thick velvet curtains muted the sun to a gentle glow, and the air carried the faint note of polished wood and expensive restraint. Her bag rested just inside the door, untouched, as if waiting patiently for her return.

Evie stood still for a moment, letting the silence settle. The space was beautiful, lavishly appointed, all marble and gilt, with deep carpets and hand-painted ceiling panels in delicate shades of sky and gold. The Cavalieri did not traffic in trends. It dealt only in timelessness.

She moved toward the bag and carried it into the bathroom. The marble was cooler to the touch, veined with silver, the light softened by frosted glass and a chandelier that refracted the morning sun into faint rainbows. She began laying out her clothes with methodical ease: ivory trousers, a linen blouse, sunglasses, flats. Neutral. Elegant. Easily forgettable.

She set aside a bathing suit, midnight blue, simple, athletic, and folded it beside the robe the hotel provided.

Her fingers grazed the cool edge of the sink, and she sighed.

It really was exquisite, this suite. Every inch of it is curated for peace. And yet, she had spent no time in it. No slow morning in bed. No long bath in the soaking tub beneath the frescoed ceiling. No coffee on the balcony overlooking the hills of Monte Mario.

She was always passing through. Beautiful places were beginning to feel like illusions, stage sets she occupied for a few hours at a time, never long enough to belong to them.

She slipped into the swimsuit and moved barefoot through the suite; the white robe wrapped snugly around her. Grabbing her slides, she stepped out without hesitation.

The elevator ride down was quiet. The mirrored walls reflected a woman transformed, relaxed, almost serene.

The rooftop pool was mostly empty, bathed in light so golden it looked unreal. The turquoise water sparkled like glass. Rome stretched beyond the terrace in soft ochres and burnished domes, hazy in the heat.

Evie lowered herself into the pool with slow grace, each stroke deliberate, almost meditative. The water was cool against her skin, and she welcomed its quiet resistance. She swam length after length, not for speed or training, but to feel her body move through something calm. Something clean.

Afterward, she claimed a chaise at the water's edge, tucked beneath the shade of a wide umbrella. Her towel hung on the chair behind her, drying slowly in the sun. She slipped on her sunglasses, fitted her headphones, and let music settle her thoughts.

Jazz, low and meandering, wrapped around her as she sipped citrus-infused water and watched the clouds drift lazily above.

Here, for the space of a few hours, time softened. The city faded to a murmur. The mission dulled to memory. Even the Collective, vast and coiled like a serpent in the shadows of her life, felt far away.

And yet, beneath it all, the watchfulness never left her. She could feel it beneath her ribs, that second rhythm, the one that never stopped scanning, weighing, calculating. Even at rest, she remained aware. Not tense, but ready. Always.

At the appointed time, she raised her hand slightly and caught the eye of the passing server. The bill was presented and signed with a single fluid motion, her signature clean and unreadable.

She slipped on her wrap, adjusted her hair, and returned to the private elevator, the one that bypassed the public floors. The hush of its interior welcomed her back like a cocoon. She caught a glimpse of herself in the mirror, unreadable.

The doors opened on the sixth floor, and she stepped into the hallway. The thick carpet absorbed the sound of her steps as she moved with ease toward her suite.

She scanned the corridor with the trained vigilance of someone who had lived too long with danger. The overhead lights cast a warm glow on marble walls, but beneath the polish, something felt off.

It was subtle. The air seemed denser somehow. Still. As if the hallway itself were holding its breath.

Only one other person occupied the corridor: a cleaning lady stationed at the far end; her cart parked perfectly perpendicular to the wall. Her head bent slightly forward, hands resting on the handle. Too still.

Evie's fingers closed more firmly around her keycard as she moved. Every sense flared to life, her awareness narrowing, focus sharpening, time slowing.

The hallway appeared empty, but the silence was not right. It was too complete, too practiced. Like a stage waiting for the curtain to rise.

She approached her suite door. The keycard slid toward the lock, her sixth sense on overdrive.

A flicker of motion. A shoulder tensing. The blur of a hand dipping into the cleaning cart.

Evie dropped instantly.

The first shot hissed past, silenced and deadly, embedding itself in the doorframe inches above her head. Wood splintered and rained onto the carpet. Her bag tumbled as she rolled hard against the door, pulse pounding in her ears.

The lock clicked open. Two more shots cracked through the stillness, their dull impact a thud rather than a report. One buried itself in the door. The other cut so close she felt the air shift at her ribs.

She kicked the door open and threw herself inside, shoulder slamming into the wall. Momentum carried her across the threshold as she kicked the door shut with her heel. The slam reverberated just as a final round punched into the wood outside.

"Amateur," she muttered, fury already burning through the shock. She ducked behind the low sofa, dragging her bag with her.

Her hand moved fast, practiced. The pistol came free, safety thumbed off in one smooth motion. Her phone followed, a single swipe and tap sending the emergency code. Damian and the Collective would know. Five minutes, maybe less.

The room went quiet again. Too quiet.

Evie steadied her breath, forcing the adrenaline into control. The silence pressed heavily, a predator's pause. Then came the faint shift of weight, the careful pressure against the door. Not rushed. Not hesitant. Methodical.

The tip of a silencer slid into view, dark and sleek against the light.

Evie raised her weapon, hands steady.

The woman stepped forward, face emerging, then her arm, then the line of her torso. The uniform read staff, but the grip, the stance, the measured steps spoke of training. Not elite. Efficient enough. Paid to do a job.

Evie did not blink. She waited until the assassin's gaze flicked toward the sofa.

She squeezed the trigger.

One round. Clean. Unerring.

The woman staggered, a guttural sound escaping as her gun skidded across the floor. She crumpled against the wall, clutching her shoulder. Surprise lit her eyes, then rage. She had not expected resistance this sharp, this fast.

Evie rose, pistol still aimed, her expression a frozen mask.

"Who sent you?" she asked coldly.

The woman bared her teeth. "No one."

Evie stepped closer; her tone flat, unyielding. "Try again."

A long pause. Then, finally, through clenched teeth, "I was texted a photo and a location. That's all. No names."

Evie's eyes narrowed. Her mind spun. A burner hit. No traceable link. It had the hallmarks of a Collective op, but without the polish. It was sloppy.

She searched the woman quickly and found a burner phone and a ring of unmarked keys. No wallet. No ID.

Evie dragged the woman to the center of the room, bound her wrists and ankles with zip ties from her bag, then gagged her with a strip of towel. She let her slump awkwardly near the window, blood pooling in a modest, manageable circle beneath her shoulder.

Evie stepped back, breath steady now, thinking, calculating.

Could it have been a rogue operation? Someone inside Umbra moving independently? Or worse, someone outside with inside knowledge? The idea clawed at her.

She sent a second code to Damian, short and clinical:

Engagement confirmed. Extraction requested. Suite secured. Minimal collateral. Suspect restrained. Possible burn trace.

The word burn hung in her mind longer than the others.

She moved quickly and dressed, gathering essentials: encrypted phone, passports, the cash packet in the closet safe, and two changes of clothing. She checked for surveillance devices and swept her hand beneath the mattress out of reflex. Nothing.

A soft knock at the door interrupted her. Three taps: short, long, short.

She exhaled through her nose and moved to the door, weapon raised, checking the peephole. One of the twins stood outside, calm, composed, glancing over his shoulder with habitual paranoia.

Evie opened the door without hesitation.

The first twin stepped in and took her bag without a word. His presence was efficient and reassuring. The second twin lingered behind, already speaking low and fast into a secure phone line, likely to Markus or someone in London. A cleanup team would follow. The Collective's reach never missed a step.

As they exited the suite, Evie cast one last glance over her shoulder. The woman remained slumped, watching her leave with eyes like shards of black glass. There was no fear in them. Just hatred.

Down the hallway, the twin's hand rested briefly at her back, more reassurance than restraint, but commanding nonetheless. It grounded her.

The elevator ride down was a descent through fog. Her body was calm, her expression controlled, but her mind twisted.

Someone had sent a message.

And that meant someone wanted distance. Deniability.

The elevator doors slid closed with a soft hiss, trapping the tension inside.

Evie stared at her reflection in the mirrored walls, calm, unshaken. But her pulse thudded like a war drum.

She would survive this. She always did.

When she found out who crossed her…

They would not.

Chapter 8

Evie stepped into the lobby of the Cavalieri, scanning the space with methodical focus. Her gaze swept across the polished marble floor, the burnished brass fixtures, the high floral arrangements staged for effortless elegance. She catalogued everything: the concierge chatting amiably with a departing guest, a bellhop adjusting a luggage cart, a family lingering near the elevator bank. Innocuous, on the surface.

But she knew better.

The weight of the pistol she had held ten minutes earlier still lingered. Adrenaline pricked her bloodstream; every breath carried an undertone of calculation.

Beside her, the twin kept pace effortlessly. Broad-shouldered, clean-cut, and nondescript in the way only elite operatives could be. His presence was understated but unmistakably dominant, like a blade sheathed in fine wool.

Without a word, he opened the back door of the waiting Audi. Evie slid inside, her movements fluid, setting her bag beside her on the seat. The car's interior was cool and faintly scented with leather and cedar. Bulletproof glass. Reinforced panels. Umbra standards.

The second twin emerged a moment later, his pace matching the first. He climbed into the front passenger seat as the driver pulled away with seamless grace, merging into the river of early afternoon Roman traffic.

Evie retrieved her phone and made the call to the front desk. "I'd like to extend my stay by twenty-four hours," she said to the concierge, her voice perfectly modulated. Calm. A touch weary. "No housekeeping, please. I'm not feeling quite myself."

The concierge, eager to oblige, offered additional services: meals, wellness treatments, and a car. She cut him off gently. "No, thank you. I'd prefer complete privacy." She ended the call and powered the phone down, slipping it into a secure sleeve inside her bag. That hotel room would be scrubbed and repurposed before the sun set. The assassin extracted; no trace left behind.

She leaned back into the seat, legs crossed, eyes distant.

In the front, the driver pressed a discreet button on the steering wheel and delivered a brief burst of heavily accented German into the comms: status report, team update, estimated arrival. A signal that their window had been secured. They had the day. Enough to vanish the scene without a whisper left behind.

The Audi picked up speed, gliding onto the A1, the Autostrada del Sole, with the confident purr of six hundred horses under its hood. The city bled into suburbs, then into the low-slung hills of the countryside. The twin eased the car up to 160 km/h, passing lesser vehicles with smooth, almost arrogant elegance.

Evie watched the landscape flick past: ochre farmhouses, olive groves, gas stations, fading graffiti on crumbling walls. A blur of inconsequence. The rhythm of the road tugged at her thoughts. They did not settle. They spiraled.

Who had sent the woman?

Why now?

Why like that?

It didn't fit. Not with Damian. Not with his signature. If Damian had wanted her gone, she would never have heard the shot. There would have been no gun, no chaos, just silence. Damian's people did not miss.

The journey remained quiet, their passage unnoticed as they moved past Florence, Bologna, and Milan. Nearing the Swiss-Italian border, the Audi pulled into a station to refuel. The driver exited without a word. Evie stepped out to stretch her legs, every movement deliberate. She drew a light scarf around her neck and slid sunglasses into place. A small transformation, enough to change her silhouette in case anyone happened to be looking.

At the border, the guards barely looked up. Swiss efficiency had many faces, and one of them was not wasting time. They were waved through without question, the Audi sliding past into a country where every blade of grass seemed manicured by an unseen hand.

The transition was immediate. Clean roads. Subtle signage. Perfectly timed traffic lights. Even the light itself seemed cooler, more restrained. The driver dropped speed to a regulation 120 km/h as they passed into Ticino, where the Italian language met Swiss law and the streets bore traces of both.

Evie leaned her head against the glass, watching as the vibrant disorder of Italy gave way to the clipped composure of Switzerland. The mountains pressed in on either side, their scale dwarfing everything man-made.

Then came the Gotthard Tunnel, a seventeen-kilometer artery bored through ancient stone. As the Audi entered, its headlights cast long beams down the endless corridor, and the silence grew denser. Evie had always respected this tunnel. It was both a passage and a metaphor: moving between worlds. Between facades.

And she was exceptionally good at facades.

On the far side, alpine discipline returned with full force. The descent into the valley was like slipping into another life: green hills, sharp peaks, and lakes still as glass. Evie tried to let the serenity in. Tried to breathe with it.

But the silence did not comfort her.

Her mind turned again to the attack. The precision was lacking. The tactics are crude. A freelancer, maybe, hired by someone who did not understand what they were meddling with. Still, that did not explain how they had found her. Or why they had tried now.

As they approached Zugersee, the driver spoke softly into his headset. The words were inaudible, but Evie did not need to hear them to sense the shift. His eyes flicked once to the rearview mirror. Her instincts stirred.

Then came the detour.

The Audi veered off the A4 onto the quieter Cham-Ost exit, where tidy roads meandered through picture-perfect villages and well-tended farms. Her fingers curled slightly against her thigh.

This was not part of any plan, but could only mean one thing: the Villa.

The twin driving remained silent; expression unreadable. The other glanced at his phone once, then locked it again without comment.

Evie said nothing. She did not ask. Asking was a weakness. Asking invites lies.

The town passed in shadow, small and lovely: a rail station, a florist, a square lined with bicycles. But as they slipped beneath an underpass and turned sharply into a wooded lane, she felt the dread rise.

Trees closed in like quiet sentinels, tall and ancient, casting long shadows over the narrow gravel drive. Then, through a break in the trees, the mansion appeared. The Villa Villette, built in 1866, stood not merely as a home but as a monument to secrecy. Its stone façade, weathered by time and Swiss winters, exuded a kind of solemn permanence, an estate carved out of both wealth and wariness. Perched on 460 acres overlooking the black mirror of the lake, it had once been the pride of a powerful industrial dynasty. Now, the name had withered into scandal and silence, ownership blurred by shell corporations until even the Swiss registry lost track. Those who remembered the place spoke of it rarely, and always in low voices.

The estate was alive with contradiction. Lush gardens curled around cold stone. Orchards shaded wild memories. Every hedge was trimmed with Swiss diligence, but the air shimmered with a tension that made Evie's skin prickle the moment she stepped from the car. Even the wind carried too much intent.

Stone. Secluded. Silent.

The car rolled to a smooth halt in the roundabout before the front entrance. Gravel crunched under the tires. Then silence.

Just the thrum of the engine winding down.

Evie sat still for a moment, her pulse measured, her expression unreadable. The twin opened her door and extended his hand, not offering, but directing.

She rose, one hand slipping into her coat pocket, fingers brushing the hilt of the knife. A comfort, if not a plan.

She stepped forward, eyes scanning the house, the tree line, the twin's profile. Calculating.

No alarms yet.

But every fiber in her body told her something was coming.

She registered the guards at once, the trained men, Nordic by build and bearing. No insignias, no wasted motion. Not a safehouse. A redoubt.

As she crossed the gravel, her boots sank slightly, the sound unnaturally sharp. One guard watched her. No challenge. Just a nod, recognition without pretense. She returned it.

The great front doors loomed; the dark wood etched with carvings hinting at a buried noble history. She brushed fingers over the surface. Solid. Cold. A door that allowed, never welcomed.

Inside, the air changed. Cooler, dry, faintly scented with beeswax, leather, old paper. The hush was deliberate, broken only by the soft echo of her steps on marble. The main salon unfolded: paneled walls, shuttered windows, a fire snapping in the hearth. Shadows blurred the room's grandeur, making it feel more like a mask than a refuge.

On a side table sat a single dirty martini. Pale gold, perfectly chilled, undisturbed. Beside it, a linen napkin was folded with meticulous symmetry.

She smiled despite herself.

Lukas.

No one else would leave a drink so exact. The twist of lemon curled once, razor-thin. The olive speared dead center. It was not refreshment, it was assurance. A signal that the house ran properly. That someone still had her back.

Evie picked up the glass. The chill grounded her. She took a small sip, the crisp gin, subtle brine, that note of citrus Lukas always drew out just right. He never asked. He remembered.

The fire's warmth lapped at her skin but never reached the marrow. She let her body relax by degrees, not because she was safe, but because she had to look it.

She heard the footsteps before she saw him, measured and deliberate, like the ticking of a watch. No flourish. No hurry.

"You haven't lost your touch, Herr Lukas," she said. "The martini was ethereal."

Lukas stepped from the hallway's shadows, immaculate as ever. Posture ramrod straight, silver at his temples, calm competence written in every line. His eyes missed nothing.

"It is always a pleasure to see you, Fräulein Evie," he said with a small bow. "Your journey was uneventful?"

"Not exactly," she replied, and let it hang, knowing Lukas knew everything.

He inclined his head, no questions. Not here.

"I am relieved you arrived in one piece," he said. "The house has not felt complete without you."

She gave a faint smile. "You flatter me now?"

"Only when it serves a purpose," he said, allowing a trace of humor. "And when it is true."

A pause followed, not awkward, just weighted.

"Is there anything you require while you are here?"

Evie considered. A hundred needs flickered through her mind. She settled on: "No. Your hospitality is flawless."

He accepted it with a nod. At the threshold, he paused, one hand lightly on the frame.

"Your room has been turned down. You will find your things in the closet."

Evie turned back to the fire, the glass warming slightly in her hand.

Another nod. His footsteps receded; the door whispering shut behind him.

Silence settled. No music, no clock. Just the long breath of the house.

She took the stairs slowly, hand grazing the rail. Her body still remembered the pitch of the motorboat, the sprint through the hotel corridor. Here, everything was soft angles and shadow. Nothing demanded anything of her.

The green bedroom waited, unchanged.

It looked untouched. The same wallpaper. The same wide four-poster bed turned down with care. The same armchair by the window, throw blanket folded just so.

She sat on the bed's edge and let her bag slide to the carpet. Fingers lingered on the strap. For a moment, she did not move.

The ensuite bathroom was prepared: towels warmed, robe draped neatly, a bath drawn, steam rising.

Lukas had not asked. He never did. But he always knew.

Evie undressed without ceremony and sank into the water. Heat drew a slow breath from her lungs. No music. No voices. Just the quiet settling of her body.

She did not think of Venice.

She did not think of the twins.

Or the weight of the stiletto in her hand.

She watched the water's surface, letting the day peel away in layers. It would come back. But not yet.

When the water cooled, she toweled off, pulled the robe around her, and crossed to the bed.

The pillow smelled of cedar and starch. It was comfort designed, not felt.

She lay back. Hands curled toward her chest, an unconscious guard against the places still exposed. Her breathing slowed.

She stared at the ceiling until sleep found her.

Chapter 9

Lukas sensed the car before he saw it.

The Audi pulled up the long gravel drive, headlights off, engine low and even. Tires crunched softly in the pre-dawn dark.

5:45. Exactly when expected.

He met Damian at the door.

No words. Just a nod. The kind that required no ceremony. Lukas stepped aside, and Damian crossed the threshold without breaking stride.

The air shifted.

Damian didn't speak. He didn't have to. The weight he carried filled the space: exhaustion buried beneath control; concern bracketed by discipline. He paused, glanced down the hall as if expecting to see her there. When he didn't, he turned to Lukas.

"How is she?" His tone was low, even.

"She arrived. No injuries. No sign of surveillance or tail."

"And?"

Lukas hesitated, not uncertain, only careful.

"She was tired. More than that. Went straight to the green bedroom. She bathed. She slept through the night."

Damian nodded slowly. He removed his gloves with deliberate precision, as though each motion mattered.

"Anything unusual?"

"The house was quiet. No movement since she arrived."

Damian said nothing. He stepped out of his shoes and moved through the house with the familiarity of years.

At the foot of the stairs, he stopped.

Upstairs, a single hallway light glowed dimly, amber, barely enough to cast a shadow. Lukas's touch. Always two steps ahead.

Damian ascended. No creak from the stairs. No break in rhythm.

At the end of the hall, the green bedroom door was closed.

He didn't knock.

He stood for a moment, hand resting lightly at his side, listening. Measuring her presence through the silence.

Nothing.

He exhaled once, quietly, and turned away.

In the sitting room adjacent to his bedroom, Lukas had left a tray with coffee, still hot, and a sealed envelope. Damian ignored the envelope, took the cup, and sat by the window.

Beyond the trees, the lake began to emerge from the darkness, black water catching the first hints of a bruised sky. Somewhere beyond it, trouble waited. But for now, there was this, the quiet before she woke, the stillness before whatever came next.

He waited.

The coffee was strong and grounding. Damian drank slowly, his thoughts circling back to the night in Venice. The ballroom. The blade. The clean precision of her movements. He had expected her to deliver, and she had. But delivery was not forgiveness. Success bought her time, nothing more.

He rested the cup on the arm of the chair, fingers steepled, eyes fixed on the slow brightening of the horizon. He thought of the bullet still resting in his case. Her name is engraved into its brass. A promise deferred, not broken.

Damian drew in a breath, let it out. His discipline was a habit, his patience honed by years of careful calculation. Yet beneath it, a thread of something he rarely allowed himself: doubt. Not in her skill. Not in her will. But at the cost.

She had survived Venice. She had survived Rome. Survival was not the same as belonging. The Collective would not forgive easily, even if he had fought for her. Especially because he had fought for her. They would watch her more closely now, waiting for a crack.

The room was silent except for the faint tick of a clock. Damian leaned back, gaze lifting to the ceiling. The villa carried its own weight, its history pressing down from the rafters. He had brought many through these halls, but only a few had remained. The ones who failed were forgotten. The ones who succeeded carried the scars of survival.

He turned his eyes back to the lake. Dawn had broken fully, streaks of pale gold and muted violet spreading across the surface of the water. A beautiful lie. Stillness on top, turmoil beneath.

His hand closed around the coffee cup again. The porcelain was still warm.

Soon, she would wake. And when she did, there would be no pretense left. The questions would come, and with them the answers she might not want to hear.

Damian set the cup aside and rose, moving to the balcony doors. He opened them slightly, letting in the morning chill. The air was sharp, bracing, filling his lungs with clarity. He let it anchor him.

He would give her time. A few hours, no more. When she came downstairs, he would see in her eyes whether the fire remained, whether she had hardened or fractured.

Until then, he would wait. Watching the lake. Listening to the silence. Preparing for what must come next.

The following morning brought not just clarity but stillness, the kind that comes after a storm. Light filtered through tall windows in soft, golden ribbons. For the first time in days, Evie woke without her body braced for a threat. Her limbs uncoiled, loose and lighter.

She dressed simply. Clothes for readiness, but not war.

Descending the grand staircase, she found the villa alive with quiet purpose. Footsteps echoed on parquet floors. Low voices murmured behind doors. A latch clicked with a steady rhythm.

The scent of coffee and toasted bread laced with herbs pulled her toward the kitchen.

Lukas stood at the center, sleeves rolled, brow faintly furrowed, issuing clipped instructions in Swiss-German. Staff moved with seamless precision: trays whisked away, copper pots stirred, linen folded.

He turned as she entered, expression softening. "Guten Morgen, Fräulein Evie. I trust you slept well?"

"Like the dead," she replied.

"Good. Herr Damian arrived early this morning. He is on a call now but wishes to see you in thirty minutes. To discuss yesterday."

"Of course. I'll be ready. But first… breakfast. I haven't eaten since Venice."

Without pause, Lukas turned to a chef. "Prepare Fräulein Evie's usual. On the terrace."

The terrace was her refuge. Stone-flagged and ivy-draped, it opened to lawns and woods ablaze in autumn fire. The air smelled of wet leaves, woodsmoke, and earth settling into winter.

She stepped outside. Lukas followed with a blanket and a tray. "I do not understand how Canadians insist on sitting outside when the air is freezing."

"It builds character," Evie said, smiling.

"It builds pneumonia," he muttered, though he handed her coffee with care.

She wrapped her hands around the cup. "Thank you, Herr Lukas. You always take care of me."

He inclined his head. "Please enjoy."

Alone, she savored poached eggs, buttered rye toast, and roasted tomatoes with thyme. The garden rustled in the breeze. A gardener raked leaves into neat spirals, a dog trailing close.

Her gaze drifted to the ridge, where fog clung to the hills. It was quiet here, a silence that restored.

From deep within the house, Damian's voice rose, sharp and unmistakable even through stone walls. He was finishing a call.

Evie set her cup aside. Guards changed shifts with silent nods. The great house never truly slept.

Then she felt his hand on her shoulder, grounding and commanding at once. She didn't turn. She didn't need to. Presence was enough.

He stepped forward. As she began to rise, his hand pressed her back into the chair.

"Stay," he said, low. "Please."

A rare word from him.

He reached for her hand, lifting it to his lips. The gesture was not soft, but it was a promise.

His eyes met hers, sharp and probing. Damian didn't look at people; he looked through them.

"Firstly, are you alright? You weren't hit?"

"No," she said steadily. "Just shaken."

He exhaled, a slight easing of tension. "Every indication was that you'd gotten away cleanly. The boat was cleared. Logs falsified. Clothes sanitized. The drive team ran every counter-surveillance layer. Nothing pinged."

His voice was calm, but beneath it the storm rumbled.

"We're following up. But I need to ask, anything unusual?"

She closed her eyes, reconstructing the last forty-eight hours. Boat. Terminal. Hotel. Car. The twins. Disciplined. Routine.

"No anomalies. No tails. No skipped steps. Even if someone saw me in Venice, they couldn't have coordinated Rome that fast. The timeline doesn't fit."

Damian's jaw tightened. "So, it wasn't a reaction."

"No. It was preplanned. Based on information they already had."

He was silent, then said, "Then it was inside knowledge."

His voice dropped, cold. "Someone close enough to have access. They betrayed you."

The word landed heavily. Danger was familiar. Betrayal was different.

"Who do you suspect?" she asked evenly.

"Too early to say. But I need everything. Rome, step by step. Every interaction. Someone threaded this needle. They were close enough to sew."

She nodded. "What about the housekeeper in Rome?"

Damian's expression turned unreadable. His voice lost all warmth.

"She's under review."

Evie froze. Collective code for extraction, debriefing, and termination. No second chances.

"I see," she said softly.

The woman had brought her towels. Had smiled. But in their world, smiles meant nothing. Trust was always burning down to its fuse.

Damian leaned closer. "This is the part they never tell you. The game doesn't end when you win. It resets. More pieces. More knives."

Evie's gaze drifted back to the lake, its surface silver and still.

"I know," she said. "And I'm still here."

For a long, tense moment, neither of them spoke. The silence between Evie and Damian stretched, not awkward but weighted with truths too dangerous to voice. Around them, the villa seemed to hold its breath. The marble floors, the high archways, and the ancient walls all bore witness, but none offered counsel. It was the kind of stillness Evie recognized from years in the field, the kind that settled just before the strike.

The implication was unmistakable now. A hunt had begun.

Someone had moved against them. Against her. And it hadn't been a clumsy outsider; it had come from within. Someone with knowledge. Someone close.

Damian's jaw tightened, the lean angles of his face darkening under the weight of focus. No overt anger, he was too controlled for that, but his fury radiated in subtler ways: the clench of his gloved hand, the perfect stillness of his posture, the sudden drop in temperature around him.

Evie steeled herself, watching him with the quiet familiarity that came from knowing what he didn't say was often more dangerous than what he did. They had survived betrayals before, clawed their way out of collapsing missions, dirty leaks, rogue governments. But this felt different.

More personal.

Damian leaned in, and when he finally spoke, his voice was low, measured, razor-sharp.

"That," he said, each word deliberated, "is what I intend to find out. And when I do, they will pay. No one betrays my people and gets away with it."

The words cut through the stillness like a blade. Evie felt them settle inside her, an oath and a warning both. Damian might be quiet, but his retribution was always surgical. Final.

Then, as if releasing the pressure by force of will alone, his posture eased slightly. His eyes met hers, the edges of that steel tempering into something more human.

"I have some calls to make," he said, standing straighter. "Assets in Berlin, Vienna, and Prague, we haven't heard from. I'll coordinate with the handlers. Verify everyone's clean. If this were a breach, I want the whole chain examined. Twice."

Evie nodded. Her mind was already mapping networks, intercepts, false identities, and former assets. She could help.

But Damian's next words made it clear she wouldn't, not yet.

"In the meantime, take the day," he continued. "You've been through too much. You need to decompress before we ask more of you."

Evie hesitated a beat, then gave in to his logic. "Alright. I'll try to relax."

Damian offered a faint smile, rare and fleeting. "Good. The villa is yours. The library's more than just archives. The gym is updated. The kitchen is stocked. If you need something, ask Lukas."

She returned the smile, tired but grateful. "Thank you. Truly."

But the warmth drained from Damian's expression, replaced by the cold clarity of command.

"One thing," he said. "You're free to explore the villa. Walk the grounds. Use the facilities. Even leave if necessary. But under no circumstances are you to go anywhere without a security detail. Lukas will oversee it. He has the authority to override you, if needed."

Evie lifted an eyebrow. "A little dramatic, don't you think?"

"I don't deal in dramatics," he said. "I deal in contingencies. And right now, you're the center of too many threads."

She didn't argue. She knew he was right.

"Crystal clear," she said. "I won't take risks."

Satisfied, Damian nodded. Already, he was pulling his phone from his pocket, his mind halfway into the next problem. As he walked briskly down the hall, murmuring sharp instructions into the device, Evie watched him go with a familiar mix of admiration and unease.

He carried the weight of too many people. And now, hers again.

She rose slowly, the quiet swallowing the space around her. The day ahead was unstructured yet loaded with implications. She wasn't meant to rest so much as reset. The war wasn't over; it was only in intermission.

She began walking the halls, her footsteps quiet against velvet runners and polished marble. The villa was cool, hushed, watchful, but it no longer felt imposing. It felt like a bastion. A stronghold on the edge of something dangerous.

The details of the house were striking: carved bannisters, frescoes hinting at Roman allegory and Greek tragedy, oil portraits of anonymous patrons, some bearing subtle symbols from the Collective's past. Layers of meaning were built into every corner. It was a house that remembered everything.

She had only made it halfway down the corridor when Lukas intercepted her.

"Fräulein Evie," he said, appearing as though from thin air. His tone was respectful, his presence unobtrusive.

She turned toward him, fatigue easing slightly from her shoulders.

She continued her stroll. The faint aroma of beeswax and old paper trailed behind her. Near the east wing, Lukas waited, as if timed to the second.

"Fräulein Evie," he greeted with a slight inclination of his head. "Might I suggest reviewing the menu for dinner? The kitchen is eager to accommodate. They stand ready."

Evie paused. A long dinner, a glass of wine, and some semblance of normalcy tempted her.

But not yet.

She chuckled softly, a tired smile touching her lips. "Not just yet, Lukas. I appreciate it, but I need to blow off some steam. A workout. Some time at the range. I need to stay sharp."

Lukas nodded with immediate understanding. "Of course. The gym is stocked. The range as well. I'll see that everything is ready."

His tone was warm, but not indulgent. Professional, as always.

"Would you like company?" he asked. "I can accompany you personally or arrange for details."

Evie shook her head. "No, thank you. I'd rather be alone. Solitude helps me focus."

"Very well," Lukas said. "I trust you remember the way to the range. Long and short arms are ready. Ammunition is secured in the gun house. If you need anything, or if anything seems amiss, call me on the house line."

She placed a hand briefly on his forearm, her expression sincere. "Thank you, Lukas. You keep this place running like clockwork."

His lips twitched, barely a smile, but the warmth in his eyes was unmistakable. "It is my pleasure, Fräulein."

Chapter 10

Evie slipped into the open air, drawing a slow breath of crisp alpine morning into her lungs. The sun crested over the tree line, bathing the estate in gold. With the focus of someone trained to compartmentalize, she launched into a brisk 5K run, setting a steady pace across the gravel drive and onto the winding paths that circled the estate's outer edge.

The rhythmic thud of footfalls, the sharp intake of breath, the strain in her legs. Clarity.

No earpiece. No mission directive. No threat. Just her pulse and the soft crackle of gravel.

Behind her, as expected, the twins followed.

Shadow-like, distant but constant, two figures of muscle and discipline kept pace with mechanical ease. Evie didn't look back. She didn't have to. They were hers for now, part of the landscape, like the iron gates or the armory below.

As she rounded a curve near the orchard, the sharp crack of distant gunfire split the air.

She didn't flinch. In Switzerland, such noise was common: weekend militia training, marksmanship tests. For her, it was a cue. Readiness. Vigilance. Control.

After completing her loop, breathing even and skin slick with sweat, she made her way toward the trees. The gun house stood beyond the southern garden wall, a low stone structure, discreet but fortified. Inside, it was spotless. Every weapon is oiled and ordered by type, caliber, and purpose. Lukas's doing, no doubt.

She reached for the Remington Model 700. Cold steel, an extension of will. With practiced ease, she loaded it, checked the scope, and moved to the bench.

Target set. Breathing steady. Elbows down. Squeeze, don't pull.

She fired a hundred rounds, methodically. Adjusting for wind, for angle, for distance. The recoil became rhythm. The moment became meditation.

Then the Glock 19.

A familiar weight. Muscle memory.

Another hundred rounds. Tight groupings. Fast reloads. Double taps. Slow control drills. Her breathing synced with movement. Beyond the crack of the gun, only the whisper of breath between shots.

When she finally stepped back, her arms heavy and shoulders humming, she let the silence return.

This was who she was.

Not just the woman running for her life two nights ago. Not the candidate under scrutiny. Someone forged in iron, in storms, in fire.

She wasn't here to survive. She was here to prove something.

Someone would regret betting against her.

After cleaning and returning the weapons, she paused at the threshold, lungs full of crisp air and the lingering scent of gunpowder. Her body was warm, muscles engaged. The tension from Rome hadn't vanished, but it had somewhere to go now.

She wasn't done yet.

Instead of heading back inside, she turned toward the garage, a modern structure discreet beneath its green roof and climbing ivy. Inside, vehicles arrayed in formation, black Audis, a Land Rover, and a row of gleaming bicycles suspended like artifacts.

Evie selected a matte-black Stöckli road bike. Lightweight carbon frame. She adjusted the seat, clipped her helmet, and rolled it into the sunlight.

The path to Zug Bahnhof wound through some of Switzerland's most picturesque terrain, with rolling meadows, clusters of pine and birch, tidy farms where cows grazed in silence, bells chiming faintly. The sun climbed, light gold and clean, gilding the morning.

Evie pedaled at a steady pace, the rhythm of the road and the cadence of her legs syncing into meditation. The twins trailed discreetly behind in a black SUV, visible only when the road curved or the tree cover broke.

She passed through Cham and Steinhausen, quaint towns with perfect gardens, immaculate shutters, and window boxes spilling over with flowers. People waved. No one stared. Here, she was just another cyclist on a morning ride.

Descending into Zug, the landscape shifted, the pastoral calm giving way to cobbled streets, colorful shopfronts, and bustling cafés. The scent of roasting espresso beans filled the air, mingling with fresh bread and the sharpness of lake wind. She slowed, weaving through the quiet chaos with practiced ease.

The Bahnhof rose ahead, its sleek glass and steel nestled in old-world stone. Commuters moved with purpose. Announcements echoed overhead. For a moment, Evie stood beside her bike, watching the pulse of the outside world.

She made her way into the Altstadt, the old town with its labyrinth of narrow streets and medieval charm. Locking her bike near a café with whitewashed walls and cobalt trim, she took a seat at an outdoor table beneath a striped awning. Her detail stood across the street, "blending in" near a kiosk.

Lunch was a mezze platter with stuffed grape leaves, olives, grilled halloumi, and hummus with warm pita. Nothing fancy, just good food and a tall glass of cold sparkling water.

As she ate, she watched the clouds drift past Mount Pilatus. She remembered that Pontius Pilate's ghost was rumored to haunt the mountain, condemned to wander in exile. A beautiful place, she thought, to disappear.

She glanced at her security team, one of the twins pretending to read a newspaper.

Evie smirked.

For a fleeting moment, she imagined sending mezze platters to the curb, an absurd little rebellion. She stifled a laugh and popped an olive into her mouth.

Absurdity lived just beneath the surface. Even here. But her rebellions, like the episode at Heathrow, could end up costing her everything.

She signaled to her detail. Time to go.

The return ride was even more beautiful. The lake sparkled like cut glass. Swans drifted across the surface, luminous against the blue. The breeze tugged at her sleeves. The rhythm of her tires was steady. Soothing.

Approaching Cham again, she slowed. Lakeside cottages, weathered docks, flower-ringed patios. For a moment, she felt she had touched some version of peace.

At the estate's edge, swans glided, indifferent, part of the impossible serenity.

She dismounted at the villa, legs pleasantly sore, breath even. Her security peeled off to perimeter posts.

Inside, the villa's hush welcomed her back.

But the silence was fractured.

Down the hall, Damian's voice was sharp, barely restrained, cutting through the stillness. A clipped burst of German, a French expletive. Someone on the other end wasn't cooperating, and Damian's patience, always finite, was burning fast.

She heard the scrape of his chair, then his voice again, lower now, edged with annoyance. "And for the record, your building's voice-activated lift is useless. It took me five minutes to convince it I wasn't an intruder and let me out."

She didn't interrupt. Instead, she turned and made her way to the library, drawn toward something she could control. A book. A file. A history.

The hunt would resume soon.

But for now, it was time to read the fine print of the world she was about to step into.

The library was a cathedral of quiet power. Shelves upon shelves of curated history, strategy, philosophy, and consequence. The air was rich with the scent of leather, sun-warmed oak, and time. Every volume had passed through hands with purpose. Many bore the discreet seal of the Collective. Some, she suspected, weren't supposed to exist at all.

Evie's fingers drifted along the spines, noting Greek, Latin, Arabic, French, and German. Treatises on empire. Memoirs of revolutionaries. A first edition De Bello Gallico in cracked burgundy vellum.

One title stopped her: The History of the Jewish Wars by Josephus.

She slid it free with care. War, betrayal, politics disguised as piety. Fitting. Tucking it under her arm, she made her way toward the verandah.

The light had shifted. It was now warm and low, casting gold across the manicured lawn and distant trees. The lake shimmered, reflecting the mountains beyond. No guards in sight, but she felt them. Always nearby.

She settled into a high-backed chair, feet on the ottoman, the book falling open across her lap. For a while, she read, the doomed cities and calculated resistance echoing too close to her own world.

Eventually, the words blurred.

The sun, the air, and the breeze wove together into a calming spell. Her breathing slowed. Her eyes drifted closed.

The villa had settled into late afternoon quiet. Beyond the verandah, the lake reflected the low sun in fractured gold. Inside, clocks ticked with measured steadiness. Outside, Evie's breathing softened, her body finally giving in to stillness.

From a nearby window, Lukas watched in silence.

He noted the way her hands had slackened around the open book, how her head tilted just enough to suggest true rest. Not collapse. Not exhaustion. Rest earned.

He retrieved a cashmere throw, stepping onto the verandah with practiced silence. Draping the blanket over her shoulders, he smoothed it without waking her. His expression was unreadable, but the narrowing of his eyes spoke of vigilance.

"Nothing will happen to her on my watch," he murmured.

Two guards appeared seconds later, summoned by a flick of his hand. Lukas lingered a moment more, then vanished into the house like smoke.

Evie woke nearly two hours later to the faint scrape of a page turning.

Shadows stretched long across the lawn. The book, once on her chest, was now in Damian's hands. He sat beside her, posture relaxed, reading with steady fingers.

"For a big man, you're surprisingly quiet," she said, voice soft with sleep.

"Given enough lumber and time, I probably could build around you," he replied, amused. His eyes flicked toward her. "But it was Josephus who brought me here."

She smiled, brushing hair from her face. The moment was domestic, surreal in its quiet. Two operatives, one of whom had narrowly escaped death, were reading ancient war stories like an old couple at a country estate.

Damian closed the book. "Lukas has prepared something special for dinner. From the smell, I'd bet on duck."

Evie glanced down at her cycling clothes. "I should change."

"You're fine," he said casually.

"Lukas made an effort. So, should I? And you're in a jacket," she pointed out.

He smirked. "Suit yourself. I'll wait downstairs."

When she returned in wide-leg cream trousers and a shimmering emerald blouse, both Damian and Lukas looked up in unguarded admiration.

"Stunning," Damian said.

"Exquisite, Fräulein," Lukas added.

Dinner was simple but elegant, an herbed soup, roast duck, and seasonal vegetables. Conversation flowed, lighter than expected. For the first time in days, laughter rose without caution.

Damian lifted his glass.

Evie touched her glass to his. "To the quiet joys."

Later, Lukas guided them onto the balcony where candles flickered and the scent of jasmine lingered. A bottle of rum and cigars waited.

"Lukas won't let me smoke in the house," Damian chuckled.

"Neither would I," Evie said with a smile.

She chose cognac, and they sat beneath the stars. Damian shared stories, a mission with Al, in Cairo, gone sideways, an operative who faked his own death three times. His voice was low and steady, the cigar punctuating his words with sparks of ember.

The night stretched in comfortable silence until Evie shivered.

"You're cold," Damian said, stubbing out the cigar. "Let's go inside."

They rose together, the night air closing in around them as they crossed the verandah. The sound of the lake followed, soft waves lapping against the stone wall and the faint whisper of wind through the trees. Damian held the door for her, and the sudden hush of the house folded around them.

The corridors were dim, their steps unhurried, the quiet between them companionable rather than strained. She could feel the weight of his presence at her side, measured, unyielding, and yet curiously grounding.

He led her toward the den.

In the den, firelight softened the room. The scent of burning wood mingled with the faint trace of tobacco still clinging to the air. Evie sank into a leather chair, its worn cushions yielding beneath her as if inviting her to stay. Damian settled opposite with a glass of rum in hand, his posture composed but not rigid, the faint glow of the hearth reflecting in the amber liquid.

For a while, they sat in silence, the crackle of the logs filling the space between them. The flames painted shifting patterns across the dark-paneled walls and across their glasses, turning the room into a cocoon of warmth. Evie let her eyes linger on the fire, then on the man across from her, her earlier boldness giving way to something quieter.

She stretched her legs slightly, the heat loosening the last of the chill from outside. Damian regarded her steadily, not pressing, simply present.

Eventually, the stillness worked its way through her body, and she stifled a yawn.

"It's the mountain air, gets them every time." He said, smiling.

"I should go up," she said quietly. "Thank you for tonight. I didn't realize how much I needed this."

Damian nodded, holding her gaze. "Sleep well, Evie."

She offered a faint smile and left. Her footsteps faded upstairs.

He remained, staring into the fire long after she was gone. Only when the embers dulled did he rise.

At the landing, he paused. Her door was slightly ajar, light spilling into the hall.

He listened. No sound.

One step forward, and everything would change.

Instead, Damian turned away. Some lines, once crossed, could not be uncrossed.

He walked to his own room, changed, and lay awake longer than expected, replaying her laughter, her gaze, the scent of jasmine, the way she said thank you like it meant something.

Tomorrow, the hunt would resume. But tonight, there was peace.

Chapter 11

Evie woke to pale sunlight diffused through fine linen curtains, the lake glimmering in the distance. Despite the calm, a subtle ache tugged at her chest, a disappointment she had not expected. She had fallen asleep, hoping Damian would come to her and tap gently at her door.

But he had not.

She pushed the thought aside and sat up, refusing to let it settle. There was too much to be done, and sentiment, however well earned, was a luxury she could not afford. She dressed quickly in workout wear. The routine was comforting. Familiar.

Descending the stairs, she caught the faint sound of china clinking and soft jazz from the kitchen radio.

Inside, Lukas was already at work. Sometimes she wondered if he ever slept, or if the house simply powered him like an extension of itself. His presence always brought a wash of calm.

"Good morning, Fräulein Evie," Lukas said, not turning from the espresso machine. "May I offer you coffee and breakfast?"

"Morning, Lukas," she replied, smiling. "Coffee would be a godsend. Maybe some toast? Fruit if it's not too much trouble."

"It is never too much trouble." He placed a fresh espresso in front of her and slid a bowl of raspberries and figs beside it with elegant efficiency.

She took the cup gratefully, inhaling before the first sip. "Thank you. You really do make this place feel like home."

"I strive for that," Lukas replied. "Even a fortress needs its comforts."

She finished breakfast slowly while Lukas moved quietly around the kitchen. It was a moment of peace, but only a moment.

The following weeks blurred into rhythm: morning workouts, weapons training, long bike rides into the countryside, hours spent with intelligence reports and scenario planning. The villa had become a living machine, every person and every routine dialed toward one purpose: control.

Damian remained elusive. Present, then gone. His hours were erratic, emerging from his office for brief breaks or late dinners, then vanishing again for hours, sometimes days. His work with Umbra had deepened, the network volatile. Evie understood the demands, but still, each absence chipped at her.

Yet the villa thrived around her. Lukas ensured every comfort. She often dined with him when Damian was away. Their conversations, though light, carried depth beneath them. She could tell Lukas watched over her not only out of duty, but loyalty.

One afternoon, returning from a luncheon in Zurich, she stepped into the marble foyer and found Lukas waiting with a tray.

"Welcome back, Fräulein," he said, offering a tall glass with a wedge of lime. "I thought you might appreciate something cool."

She took the drink gratefully. "I do. Thank you."

But it was not the drink that caught her eye. It was the envelope resting on the tray. Heavy stock. Cream-colored. Her name is inscribed in an elegant, looping hand.

"What's this?"

"Herr Damian left it for you. I thought it best to bring it to your attention right away."

She set the glass aside and took the envelope carefully. The calligraphy was unmistakably Damian. She opened it, scanning quickly.

Inside was a note in his steady, slanted script: an upcoming gathering at the villa. Invitation only. Influential guests. The wording was deliberately vague, but Evie could read between the lines. It was not a party.

It was a test.

Or worse, a vote.

She folded the letter and turned to the terrace. Lukas followed without being asked, his presence as grounding as the stone beneath her feet.

The lake shimmered, broken only by a lazy breeze. Evie sipped her drink and let the note rest in her lap, her mind racing ahead of her breath.

"Lukas," she said, voice calm but edged with hope, "do you know if Damian will be back for dinner?"

Lukas's face remained composed, but his answer betrayed faint sympathy. "He left for London this morning. He said he would return in a few days."

"I see." She nodded slowly.

Part of her had expected it. Part of her had hoped this time would be different.

Their relationship was not simple. Damian had saved her once from a man who would have destroyed her, and afterward, they had become entangled in every possible way. He had been her rescuer, her mentor, her partner, and for one brief moment, her lover. Now she lived in his world. Killed at his command. Trusted him implicitly. And feared, equally, that he would never fully be hers.

Despite the private jets, the penthouse, the villa, Evie knew the truth.

She was still an assassin. A calibrated instrument of power. She often wondered, late at night, if things had been different, if the shadows had not come for them both, whether they could have built something quiet. Ordinary.

But those were not questions she could afford to ask.

Not yet.

Not while she still carried a weapon under her jacket.

Not while the Collective continued to measure her loyalty.

Chapter 12

While Evie basked in the comfort of her evening in Cham, Damian maneuvered through the bureaucracy of the Collective in London, each step calculated, each word already weighed. His focus was unflinching, his movements as deliberate as his thoughts. He was playing a different kind of game, one not fought with bullets but with perception, loyalty, and the sharp edge of political power.

Evie's mission to eliminate the Leonardo boy had been a success. The target was neutralized cleanly, with no civilian casualties. But the airport scene had drawn the attention of Umbra's board, and not all of it was supportive.

Old-guard figures like Chambers and Varetti called it reckless. Visible. Emotional. Others whispered the unsaid: that Damian was losing objectivity. That she had become his liability.

Umbra valued many things: efficiency, discretion, and surgical control. Above all, discipline. And Damian knew what the board feared most: unpredictable talent. Operatives who followed instinct before protocol. Wild cards.

He had once been one himself. Now he was expected to manage them.

So, Damian had flown to London not for penance, but for preservation. Of her. Of himself. Of the strategy, they had only begun to unfold.

His ensemble projected everything they needed to believe. The Ozwald Boateng suit, deep blue and sharply tailored. The purple floral tie suggested he was unafraid of detail. The starched white shirt cut clean lines across his chest, and the polished John Lobb shoes gleamed with military regularity.

The family signet ring on his right hand glinted as he adjusted his cufflinks, old silver engraved with a crest few remembered but all respected. Legacy mattered here, but only if it walked with utility.

After one last check in the mirror, a ritual rather than vanity, he shrugged on his Loro Piana overcoat. His umbrella, hand-stitched and weight-balanced, completed the look. In London, the weather was no excuse for being unprepared.

Damian left The Ritz just after dawn, the hotel's opulent hush giving way to the cool rush of city air. The streets were beginning to hum with couriers and those who believed power started at seven.

He walked, not because he had to, but because the rhythm cleared his mind. The route from Piccadilly to St. James's Square took under fifteen minutes, and every step let him calibrate his approach. He missed Lukas, not just the efficiency but the certainty that every detail would be handled. Lukas was back in Switzerland, watching over Evie. One less variable to worry about.

When he arrived at Number 100, a tall Georgian building with no official identity, he paused briefly at the doors. Gathering himself, he stepped inside.

The grand foyer was as he remembered: cool marble floors, an antique chandelier dimmed to half-light, and a receptionist whose posture spoke of military training. He had spent too much time in the field. Now it was time to manage the Collective.

"Welcome to London, sir," James said, stepping forward with perfect timing. James was his London assistant, his business analyst, his internal spy.

Damian nodded, handing off his overcoat and umbrella. "Which room?"

"The Cuvier Room, sir."

Damian's jaw tensed. The Cuvier Room was not for negotiation. It was a tribunal space in all but name, formal, controlled, designed to make its guests feel the weight of every word.

"And who's present?"

James consulted the tablet. "Once you walk in, there will be twenty-one, including Chambers, Varetti, Król… and Magritte."

Damian's breath drew slower. Of course, she was here. Magritte had never hidden her disdain. She found attachments distasteful. Evie's method at Heathrow would have confirmed her worst suspicions: that Damian Cesarini was compromised.

"Very good," he said.

James handed him a slim leather dossier. "Your documents are in order. And you're talking points,"

"I know them," Damian said, taking the file anyway.

He adjusted his cuff, revealing the silver family signet on his right hand and the platinum dragon sigil of Umbra on his left. Legacy and allegiance. He bore both without apology.

A final breath. Composed, sharp.

He walked down the paneled corridor; footsteps measured. Oil portraits of past Umbra leaders lined the hall, men and women of severity, brilliance, and ruthless clarity. Damian knew their names, their victories, and their failures. He carried their legacy now, but only so far as it served his.

At the end, the heavy oak doors loomed. Two security men flanked them. One nodded, opening the door silently.

Damian stepped inside.

The room was circular, lined with dark walnut panels, a domed ceiling fresco giving the illusion of endless sky. A round table dominated the space, its surface bare save for a carafe of water and a few dossiers.

Four members of the board turned toward him. Chambers, blunt-edged and military. Varetti, calculating, slow to speak. Król, young, is the only member younger than Damian. And Magritte, elegant, pale, utterly without warmth.

"Commendatore Cesarini," Chambers said. "Please. Join us."

Damian did not sit immediately. He let the pause hang, then moved to the chair across from Magritte and settled with practiced grace.

Chambers continued. "You know why you're here."

"I do."

"The situation in Venice," Varetti said, "was resolved efficiently. But the Heathrow incident…"

"The actions," Magritte cut in, "were unacceptable."

Damian's expression did not flicker. "They were contained."

"They weren't invisible," Magritte countered. "That is not the kind of exposure this organization tolerates."

"I agree," Damian said smoothly. "And Evie agrees as well."

Król leaned forward. "Does she? From the reports, she acted with clear disregard for protocol. She was in London. Unauthorized. And she was seen."

"She was seen by a watcher and no one else. That's exposure," Damian said coolly. "Internal, but exposure all the same."

He let the admission hang. No excuses.

"But that mistake doesn't erase the bigger picture."

He leaned forward, deliberate. "Evangeline Blackstone is not a wildcard. She is not erratic. That decision wasn't sabotage; it was sentiment. And I have made it clear that sentiment has no place here unless wielded as leverage. She understands that now."

His conviction deepened. "She has the instincts to lead. Discipline can be reinforced. Potential cannot be manufactured. You all knew what I was like when I started. I broke protocol more than once, and most of you were in the room when I did. But I delivered. And I built something lasting."

He paused. "She can too."

Silence.

Magritte folded her arms. "We don't tolerate exposure. Especially from protégés."

"Then don't call her a protégé. Call her what she is: the future."

Even Varetti blinked at that.

Damian pressed forward. "You're not here because she failed. You're here because she didn't fail your way. And that discomforts you."

Magritte's lips thinned. "You protect her because you're invested."

"I protect her," Damian said, "because she is not just an asset. She is a leader. She understands risk beyond the immediate. She has the temperament to manage people, not just missions. That is rare."

His gaze swept the table. "She has the potential to shape this organization from the inside. If we crush that potential now, we weaken Umbra itself. That's not protection. That's investment."

He paused. "Umbra doesn't suffer liabilities. It ends them. Evie isn't a liability. She's the future."

Silence.

Finally, Chairman Denholm spoke. "We'll take your recommendation under advisement. Commendatore Cesarini, you may remain present, but you will not participate in the vote."

Damian nodded. "Understood."

Denholm pressed a button. The center of the table lit softly, twenty-one brass toggles waiting.

"The motion: approve continued advancement with oversight, or impose formal sanction for the breach at Heathrow."

Clicks sounded, soft but final.

"By a majority of thirteen in favor, six opposed, and two abstaining, the board finds in favor of continued advancement under oversight. No formal sanctions will be recorded. This matter is closed."

Damian exhaled, almost imperceptibly. He had won. But he had exposed the divide.

Straightening, he gathered the folder with deliberate care. "Thank you, Chairman. Members."

No further words. He walked out in silence, the click of the door sealing the case and its consequences.

Evie would remain protected.

But the cost had been tallied. The divide was no longer hypothetical; it had been measured in votes and recorded in silence.

Outside, London waited. There were ledgers to settle, allies to call, and influence to rebuild.

The balance had shifted, and he would not allow it to shift further without his hand on the scale.

Chapter 13

James greeted Damian at the door, handing over a dossier bound in Umbra's signature midnight-blue leather. No words were wasted.

They walked in silence to Damian's office, the corridor quiet but charged. Once inside, James began his report without delay.

"Progress on the Leonardo takeover has been steady," he said, tone measured. "The energy group has been spun off and two billion euros cleared. Trucking and logistics sold for another five hundred million. With the liquidation of the satellite subsidiaries, we're projecting a total of approximately three billion in clean profit. Defense, mining, and real estate are integrating seamlessly into the portfolio."

Damian sank into his chair and skimmed the data he already knew would confirm the projections. He preferred precision to presumption. After a moment, he looked up.

"Eight billion in profit, reinforced positions in critical industries, and one less rival on the horizon." A pause. "Not a bad day at all."

James allowed the faintest nod. "The numbers and outcomes align with our forecast."

Damian set the file aside and steepled his fingers. "Prepare dividend cheques for the inner council. Gifts for their spouses. Subtle, tasteful, never ostentatious."

"Yes, sir."

"Coordinate the celebration with Lukas. We will host it at the house in Switzerland. It should be grand. Use the standard list, but leave space for modifications. I will review tomorrow."

"I will liaise with Lukas directly. He will ensure the setting is flawless."

Damian's expression shifted, less austere, more introspective.

"One more thing. Evie."

James stilled.

"She deserves something for Venice. And everything that followed." Damian's voice softened slightly, though steel remained beneath. "Have Lukas draft a list. I want something personal. Not just a gift. Recognition."

"Understood, sir."

Damian's mouth lifted faintly. The Leonardo empire, once noisy and arrogant, was now ash and equity. Evie's name had survived the board. Umbra's reach had deepened. Three billion euros added to the vaults, with more to come. Today was worth celebrating.

"Would you like to join me for dinner at Rules tonight?" Damian asked casually.

James hesitated. "I, yes, sir," he replied after a beat.

Damian raised a brow. "James, you are allowed to say no. This is not a summons."

James looked sheepish. "It is my fiancée's birthday tonight, sir. We have had reservations for some time."

Damian's expression softened. "Then go. No question. Where?"

James named the place. Appropriately upscale.

As James turned to leave, Damian reached for his phone and sent a brief message to another assistant: settle the restaurant bill discreetly, and ensure James never knew.

"Before you go," Damian added, "book me a table at Rules for eight. Window seat, if possible. And reach Alexis before the end of the day."

"Yes, sir."

Damian straightened his collar and adjusted his cuffs. "Enjoy the evening."

James smiled faintly. "You as well, sir."

Damian stepped out of 100 St. James's Square into the late afternoon drizzle. London rain veiled the city in a melancholy sheen. The doorman handed him an umbrella. Damian clipped a Davidoff cigar, lit it with his Cartier lighter, and drew slowly. Smoke curled into the damp air.

The storm in the Cuvier Room was over. The board had sided with him. Evangeline was protected, officially. It had cost influence, but the ledger still favored her.

He nodded once, took the umbrella, and moved into the street.

When Damian stepped into Rules, the air met him like a well-aged whisky: warm, layered, intoxicating. The amber glow lit the dark wood with just enough shadow to keep secrets. He scanned the room and found him.

Alexis was at the bar, seated with deliberate ease. A cigar smoldered between his fingers, smoke circling his face. Aviators concealed their eyes. He wore a formal Adidas tracksuit as if it were from Savile Row.

Damian's face lit with genuine affection.

"Al," he called, "I thought I smelled bad decisions and better cigars."

Alexis grinned. "Damian, my brother. Still slipping into rooms like smoke."

They embraced briefly, strong and wordless.

Over oysters and beer, they toasted.

As they moved into their booth, the conversation shifted. Evie's name surfaced. Damian admitted the fires she had sparked, the capital he had spent to protect her. Alexis's grin faded to steel.

"Tell me what you need."

"For now? Just this. But I will let you know when it is more."

The glasses clinked again; this time, heavier.

Later, they strolled into the night toward The Duck and Rice, laughter softening the weight of old scars. Over tank beer, they shared stories, ribbing, and memories. The hours slipped by unnoticed.

At the door, they embraced once more.

"Until next time, old friend."

"Dinner is on me when I am back," Damian replied.

London rain had dwindled to mist. Damian walked back toward The Ritz, the faint scent of tobacco clinging to his coat. Across the continent, Evie slept safely at the villa.

For tonight, that was enough.

Chapter 14

The suite was still; London muted beyond its tall windows. Damian dressed in a charcoal wool travel suit, crisp shirt, and gloves. By the time he reached the lobby, his security detail had already swept the exits. The city was only beginning to stir, but he was already in motion.

His driver stood waiting beside the black S-Class, luggage already in the trunk. "Sir," the man said with a nod, opening the door. Damian stepped inside, settling into the familiar cocoon of luxury.

The car pulled into the quiet city streets, fog clinging low as the first fingers of light stretched across the skyline. The ride was smooth, unhurried. Damian checked his messages, scanned James's brief, and deleted the rest. No distractions.

They entered the secure General Aviation Terminal at Farnborough, where the Gulfstream waited on the tarmac, its polished frame catching the first gold light of dawn. Within minutes, he cleared exit formalities. The flight crew greeted him with practiced grace. A fresh copy of The Times, a leather folder of intelligence notes, and a pressed linen napkin waited at his seat.

As the jet taxied, Damian took a breath. Zurich was just seventy-five minutes away.

Once airborne, he accepted breakfast more to pass the time than for the food. The Gulfstream skimmed above the clouds, engines a low hum of calm. Below, the world was a patchwork of alpine green and deep blue, snow-dusted peaks piercing through mist. Damian sat comfortably, the serenity of flight a stark contrast to the calculated intensity of the past few days.

He used the quiet to review key documents, board notes, portfolio updates, and intelligence from Berlin. Pen in hand, he marked corrections, his mind sharp despite the hour. Time in the air was never wasted.

A soft chime and the approach of a flight attendant signaled descent. Damian closed his folder, finished his coffee, and slid his papers into his briefcase. The clouds parted as the jet dipped lower, revealing the Swiss landscape: lakes like glass, pastures folded neatly between hills, chalet rooftops catching the first light.

Landing at Zurich's General Aviation Terminal was seamless. His car waited airside, a sleek black Audi A8 idling silently. The driver greeted him with a subtle nod. Luggage was handled, and Damian slid into the back seat. They glided into the heart of Switzerland.

The drive to Cham was uneventful. Damian let the silence settle, the tension of London finally beginning to ease. He allowed himself to exhale.

As Lake Zug came into view, he shifted slightly forward. The waters shimmered in the morning light, mirroring peaks and sky. A sight that never failed to calm him.

Turning onto the private road, Villa Villette emerged through the trees. Lukas was waiting at the steps.

"Welcome home, Herr Damian," he said, voice as crisp as the mountain air.

Damian nodded as he stepped out of the car. "Lukas."

His bags were taken inside and unpacked. The staff moved with the grace of those who anticipated needs before they were spoken. But Lukas lingered.

"There's been a pattern," he said quietly as they walked toward the entrance. "A few unusual inquiries in the past forty-eight hours. Discreet, but not invisible. Enough to be noted."

Damian's stride slowed, expression sharpening. "About Evie?"

"Mostly. Some about the house. Some triangulating around the staff. Unconnected on the surface, but close enough to raise flags."

Damian paused at the threshold. "Keep her close. Eyes on everything. I want every guest vetted again before the party."

"I have already begun," Lukas said, calm but resolute. "Security has been reinforced. No movements go untracked."

Damian gave a curt nod, his face unreadable. "Good. Nothing slips through the cracks. Not this time."

The heavy door closed behind him. The villa's warmth wrapped around him, but his thoughts remained unsettled. Something was stirring beneath the surface.

The rhythmic crack of gunfire echoed across the gravel range, each shot clean and deliberate.

Evie stood firm, shoulders squared, focus absolute as the spent casings fell around her boots. The morning air was brisk, the scent of cordite sharp and grounding. Damian watched from the edge of the range, unseen for a moment, hands in his pockets. The weight of London clung to him, but watching her steadied it.

She was still standing. Still fighting. Still his. Still alive.

When she finally emptied her magazine and holstered her pistol, she turned and saw him.

"Damian!" she called, her face breaking into a grin as she jogged toward him. The hard edge she carried at the line softened into something brighter, warmer.

He met her halfway, catching her in a tight embrace that said everything neither had time to write down. She smelled of gun oil and lavender soap. Familiar. Dangerous. Home.

"You're back," she said into his shoulder.

"I'm back," Damian replied, pulling away to study her face. "And you've been busy."

Evie shrugged, brushing a stray hair behind her ear. "Had to keep sharp. Lukas said the range was open, and, well, you know me."

Damian smiled faintly. "Yes. I do."

But the smile faded. He took her hand, guiding her to a bench near the gear table. She followed, sensing the shift in his energy.

"There's something we need to talk about," he said, voice low, measured.

"London? The committee?"

He exhaled. "Yes. I met with them. We discussed the Heathrow incident."

She stiffened. "And?"

"They've chosen to excuse your actions. Formally. The vote passed: thirteen in favor, six opposed, two abstaining."

She looked away, guilt flashing. "I shouldn't have gone to London. I thought I could get away with it. That I was being careful."

Damian placed a hand gently on her arm. "You were seen. That was the problem. Not the tail. Not the outcome. The exposure. That is what they care about. The operative who spotted you was doing their job."

"I know," she whispered. "I was careless."

"You made a mistake," he said plainly. "And it nearly cost you. But Venice turned the tide. They saw what I see. What I have always seen."

Her eyes met his again, cautious. "Which is?"

"That you don't just belong here, Evangeline. You have the potential to lead. To command."

The use of her full name startled her. It was rare. Intimate.

"They gave me a condition," he went on. "No more errors. No more wildcat. From this point forward, you must be exceptional. You know what 'or else' means in this business."

Evie sat in silence, the weight of it settling.

Damian smiled, and for the first time since arriving, some of the tension in his shoulders eased. He touched her chin gently, then stood.

"Come on. Lukas has coffee waiting. And you've earned a break."

She rose, falling into step beside him. "Thank you, Damian. For going to London. For defending me. For… not giving up."

"I didn't defend you out of obligation," he said quietly. "I did it because I believe in what you are, and what you could become."

Evie didn't reply. She didn't have to. The look in her eyes said enough.

"I understand," she said softly. And meant it.

As they walked back toward the villa, Damian glanced sideways at her.

"Evie, there's something else I want to discuss with you."

She looked at him, curious.

"As you know, the party this weekend is a significant event," Damian said, his tone shifting to something more formal. "I've decided I'd like you to be my companion for the evening."

Evie glanced up at him. "Companion?" Her brow arched, dry amusement sharpening the word. "Is that the polite term for arm candy in your world?"

"In our world, Evie, it means something quite different. You wouldn't merely be attending. You'd be my partner for the evening."

That pulled her upright. "Partner?"

"In name, and in presence," he said. "You've earned the right to be seen. I want the Collective to see you not just as my operative, but as someone I trust enough to stand beside me. In full view. No shadows. No layers. You'd be at my side the entire evening."

Evie tilted her head. "Is this a test?"

"It's a signal," he said. "To them. And to you."

She didn't respond immediately. The space between them seemed to tighten. She knew better than to take him at face value. Visibility was not always a shield; sometimes it was the sharpest edge. Still, she nodded slowly.

"The evening marks the official acquisition of Leonardo Industries by the Collective," he continued. "It's not public, of course. But those who matter will understand the symbolism. Even the invitations carry the message. Look closely and you'll see the dragon swallowing the 'L.'"

Evie's lips parted in a silent oh. She had seen the thick ivory cards on Lukas's tray earlier, embossed with a coiled dragon in deep red foil, its teeth grazing a serifed capital L. Clever. Ruthless.

"It's a message," Damian said. "That the old guard has been absorbed. That Umbra expands not just in influence, but in reach. Many of the Inner Council will be present. Some allies. Some undecideds."

"And you want me there to play the gracious hostess," she said, tone measured. "Why?"

He met her eyes. "Because they need to believe you are more than execution. They need to believe you are legacy."

A long silence stretched between them. The villa loomed ahead, hushed and solemn against the mountain air.

Finally, Evie smoothed her sweater with a slow exhale. "Then we'd better make sure I look the part. I assume there's a dress code?"

Damian gave a faint smile. "It's formal. Timeless elegance is always safe."

She tilted her head. "And I get to choose?"

His expression warmed. "Of course. You've never needed help commanding a room."

Evie nodded, already calculating the right blend of strength and sophistication. "All right," she said. "Let's give them something they'll remember."

Damian watched her a moment longer, then offered a quiet nod. "Let them see what I see."

The morning broke clear and sharp over Switzerland, sunlight gilding the burnished hues of autumn. The mountains stood crisp against a flawless sky, and the air carried the cool bite of change. Evie drew the curtains wide, already dressed for her run, a quiet thrill of anticipation rising in her chest. Today was the day.

She laced her shoes and descended the grand staircase, finding Lukas overseeing the final touches for the evening's reception.

"Good morning, Lukas," she said, her voice light. "Everything looks fantastic. Have you seen Damian?"

Lukas nodded. "Good morning, Fräulein. Thank you. The team has been diligent. Herr Damian had to run into Zug briefly. He will return shortly."

Evie slipped outside. The trails circling the estate were lined with gold and crimson leaves, crunching beneath her feet as she ran. The cool breeze, the distant glint of Lake Zug, everything worked to clear her mind, centering her. The rhythm of footfalls and breath gave her thoughts a sharper edge.

By the time she finished, her pulse steady, she felt ready.

At the shooting range, she began with her pistol. Each shot was measured, each breath deliberate. Lukas's voice echoed in her mind, Adjust your grip, control your breath, and the tighter groupings confirmed the improvements.

Satisfied, she moved to the long rifle. A hundred disciplined shots, the rhythm as familiar and grounding as prayer. Her focus narrowed: rifle, target, breath. The world shrank to the scope and the center.

When she lowered her rifle after the final shot, Evie paused, surveying the tight, consistent groupings. Progress. Proof.

She packed up carefully, conscious of the stillness around her. Lukas had slipped away silently.

As she returned toward the villa, the estate was well into its final transformation. Staff moved briskly under Lukas's sharp eye. Tables were being arranged on the east terrace, and floral displays in deep jewel tones carried past. A string quartet rehearsed in one of the drawing rooms, the music drifting into the air in elegant swells.

The grand house was shifting from sanctuary to stage.

At the landing, Lukas awaited with a clipboard in hand. He looked up and nodded once. "You were consistent today."

Evie smiled, brushing a loose strand of hair from her face. "I was focused."

His gaze flicked toward the range. "You will be fine tonight. Eyes forward. Shoulders back."

"You make it sound like a military parade," she teased.

"For some of the guests," Lukas said, his tone dry, "it will feel that way. Some like to strut. Others prefer to watch who is watching."

She glanced toward the distant hills. "Any word from Damian?"

"He returned while you were finishing your session. He is in the study reviewing the security file, no doubt." Lukas paused. "He asked me to let you know he would like to see you before preparations begin."

Evie nodded. Already, the morning's ease was giving way to something sharper. Formal. Performative.

"I'll shower and change."

Lukas's rare smile was approving. "He will appreciate that."

Back in her suite, Evie stood for a moment before the tall mirror. Flushed from exertion, hair tousled, she looked strong. There had been a time when she would have doubted that reflection. Not now. The steadiness in her gaze was earned.

She stepped into the shower, letting the hot water loosen her muscles. Her thoughts drifted to Damian and his careful reserve, the flickers of warmth he allowed, the memory of his voice the night before: You should.

By the time she wrapped herself in a robe and twisted her hair into a towel, her focus had sharpened to the evening ahead. Not just the party, but the politics and power plays, the signals and silences that would pass between her and Damian, in full view of the Collective.

After her shower, Evie chose an outfit both elegant and practical for the busy day ahead.

Downstairs, the villa was already humming. Staff moved with brisk efficiency, and Lukas was everywhere at once, invisible yet omnipresent.

As the day unfolded, Evie moved from task to task with calm focus. She checked the floral arrangements, coordinated with caterers, and reviewed the security sweep with Lukas. She inspected the terrace, adjusted the seating chart, and rechecked the guest list. Every detail accounted for. Every risk is minimized.

The hours flew by.

Returning to the main hall, she joined Damian and Lukas near the hearth.

"Everything looks excellent," she said, satisfaction quiet in her voice.

"Just a heads-up about the guests," Damian said, voice low but measured. "There will be two waves. The first group arrives after lunch: overnight guests, board members, foreign dignitaries, and people who require attention. The rest arrive at seven for the main event."

Lukas consulted his watch. "We have time for a breather before the guests arrive."

"Good," Damian said, glancing toward the marquis. "Let's walk."

They moved through the villa, a quiet tour as the house transformed around them. Every space bore the touch of intention: vases with seasonal blooms, candles trimmed and placed, the scent of bergamot and fresh linen in the air. Chandeliers sparkled in the morning light, scattering rainbows across the parquet floors. In the music room, a quartet rehearsed Mozart, just audible, restraint layered over elegance.

"It has come together," Evie said, taking it in. "Feels like something bigger than the sum of its parts."

"It should," Damian replied. "That is what power is. Illusion, reinforced by detail."

Down the garden steps and toward the marquis, the great tent rose like a cathedral of silk and steel, its ivory canvas glowing in the sun.

Inside, the air shifted, cool and perfumed with flowers, polish, and the faint tang of rich food.

The interior was immaculate. Long tables draped in white linens stretched the length of the tent, each place setting perfectly aligned: cut crystal, burnished gold flatware. Autumn-toned arrangements in deep burgundy, rust, and gold cascaded from the centerpieces, punctuated by pale roses and sprigs of eucalyptus. Light filtered through the canvas in soft, dappled waves, lending the space a dreamlike cast.

At one end, a bandstand had been erected, elevated and professional. Musicians checked mic levels and tuned instruments, a trombone player laughing as he ran a few bright, brassy bars.

Further along, bartenders in pressed black waistcoats aligned delicate glassware with military order. The subtle clink of crystal and the low hum of coordinated movement filled the air. From behind a curtain, the scent of roasted garlic and slow-cooked meat drifted out.

Evie paused in the center, eyes sweeping the scene. "It's perfect."

Damian followed her gaze. "The perfection comes from how people move through it. What they feel."

Their eyes met.

As if on cue, the band launched into a bright, swinging rendition of Take the 'A' Train. The tempo was brisk, playful, the kind of easy confidence only a proper jazz band could conjure.

Damian turned to her, a glint in his eye. "May I have this dance?"

Evie blinked, caught off guard. "Here?" she asked, smiling already.

He extended his hand. No explanation. Just the offer.

"I'd love to," she said, and placed her hand in his.

Within seconds, they were in motion. Damian swept her into a clean, confident hold, his steps light but deliberate. Evie followed effortlessly, her years of ballet, discipline, and instinct flowing between them. They moved across the floor, weaving between tables and chairs, spinning and turning with the band's rising energy.

The music filled the marquis, warm and insistent, and for Damian and Evie, the rest of the world narrowed to the polished floor beneath their feet. Their movements were instinctive, a quiet conversation in the language of turns and steps. He guided with the lightest pressure of his hand; she answered with the subtle shift of her weight. The rhythm between them was easy, unforced.

Evie laughed, unguarded and bright, the sound carrying through the open space. Damian's smile was smaller but no less intent, his gaze holding hers as though measuring how far she would let him go.

The staff had paused to watch, their work momentarily forgotten. Beyond them, the silk drapes stirred in the afternoon air, the marquis still waiting for the night to begin. For now, it belonged entirely to them. They were not operatives, not hosts, not bound by the machinery of the world outside. They were simply two people moving together, her blouse catching the light like liquid fire as he drew her close.

The final chords swelled, trembled, and faded. Damian slowed them to stillness, his hand lingering at her back, his eyes fixed on hers until the last note dissolved into quiet.

Applause broke the spell, warm and genuine. Staff clapped, the band grinned, and somewhere at the edge of the room a single whistle rang out.

Damian bowed with a flourish, still holding her hand. "You have a dangerous talent for rhythm, Evangeline."

Evie curtsied with a wink. "You're not so bad yourself, Cesarini."

They turned to the band, offering a nod. The musicians saluted back.

As the applause faded and work resumed, Damian and Evie exchanged a glance, one that said more than words could. The connection had been real. Unstaged. A glimmer of something bright in a world built on control.

In the quiet that followed, surrounded by flowers and linen and golden light, they felt, if only for a moment, the possibility of something more.

Evie looked around the marquis again. This time, she saw it not just as beautiful, but ready.

As they walked back to the house, Lukas emerged from the door onto the balcony and signaled that the first car was at the gate.

Damian glanced at his watch, then back at her. "It begins."

Evie smoothed the fall of her blouse, straightened her posture, and lifted her chin.

"Let them come."

Chapter 15

As the afternoon light faded, the villa shifted into a softer hum. Conversation drifted through the halls, mingling with the occasional clink of crystal. The earlier bustle had given way to a graceful rhythm. The first wave of guests, those staying overnight, were settled with aperitifs, admiring the gardens in the slant of the setting sun.

By five o'clock, the tempo changed. Chatter ebbed into a gentler murmur as guests excused themselves to prepare. Footsteps climbed the grand staircase, heels and leather soles tapping across polished stone. Upstairs, staff moved with silent precision, turning down beds, placing fresh towels, adjusting lamps to a warm glow.

Outside, the first notes of the band carried through the evening air. Bartenders polished crystal until it gleamed, chefs bent over simmering sauces with the concentration of surgeons.

Dressing hour began. Silk whispered, perfume bottles clicked, and gowns of jewel tones, metallics, and timeless black shimmered as women stepped from their suites. Men emerged in tuxedos, Savile Row, and Milan tailoring, settling across shoulders, cufflinks, and cologne in place. The villa had become a stage.

By 6:45, the moment arrived.

Damian stood at the top of the staircase in a midnight-blue Armani tuxedo, calm command radiating from every line. Beside him, Evie appeared in plum silk by Oscar de la Renta, moving like a liquid shadow. Her hair swept into an updo, diamonds glinting discreetly, and she exuded contained power.

Their eyes met, unspoken recognition passing between them. They linked arms and began their descent.

At the base of the stairs, Lukas waited in a black tie, precise and composed.

"Everything in place?" Damian asked.

"Yes, sir," Lukas replied. "Security live. Dinner service at nine. All accounted for."

Damian gave a final glance at the glowing marquis outside. "Excellent. Keep quiet. Eyes on the board members. And someone on Castonguay. He wanders."

"Understood," Lukas said before disappearing.

The first black car turned onto the gravel drive, headlights sweeping arcs across the dusk. Evie caught sight of it through the tall windows. She leaned closer to Damian; her voice soft.

"Thank you," she whispered.

Before he could answer, she pressed her lips to his cheek, lingering a fraction too long.

"Remind me not to let you out of my sight," Damian murmured.

She arched a brow. "Then stand close."

The hush that fell was almost reverent, the stillness before a symphony's downbeat.

Soon, limousines curved up the drive-in procession. Silk, satin, and polished shoes crossed the red carpet under lantern light. Inside the marquis, jazz swelled, champagne flowed, and Evie played her role flawlessly: poised, gracious, and sharp-eyed.

Then came the voice, loud, off-key, and unmistakable.

♫ "It's a long way to Tipperary," ♫

Damian sighed. "Perfect timing."

Alexis, Big Al strolled up the drive, tuxedo worn like a challenge, bow tie slung around his neck, pint of beer already in hand.

He swept Evie into a one-armed hug, kissed her cheek. "Don't settle for him, darling. There's still time for archdukes and ex-race car drivers."

Evie laughed. "And miss this chaos? Never."

Lukas appeared with a fresh pint, matching temperature, matching beer. Al blinked at him, solemn. "How did he know?"

Damian only gave him a look.

Al raised his glass. "Cheers, mate."

"Sir," Lukas replied evenly.

Damian motioned toward the marquis. "Your Jane is at table three."

Al squared his shoulders. "Let's see if I can ruin that."

"Save me a dance," he called to Evie.

"Don't spill on me this time."

"No promises."

He vanished into the glow of the marquis, the band swelling behind him.

Evie shook her head. "He's impossible."

Damian's lips curved faintly. "He's inevitable."

He lifted her hand, brushed it with his lips. Their eyes held a silent oath. Not just tonight. Always.

Together, they followed him into the light.

Chapter 16

The marquis dazzled. Crystal chandeliers scattered light into a thousand fragments, candleflames doubled in their facets. Autumnal centerpieces, burnished leaves, sprays of berries, flowers deep in crimson and gold glowed like fire against white linen. The air hummed with conversation, the measured cadence of the powerful at ease.

Damian and Evie moved through it not as guests but as currents in the room, shaping flow and direction. Every handshake was deliberate, every greeting a performance layered with intent. A nod here closed a question. A smile there reopened a negotiation. They were hosts, diplomats, arbiters, and something more, an axis around which the evening spun.

When they reached the head table, Evie understood the weight of what was unfolding. Not dignitaries, not financiers, not patrons. Here sat the full assembly of the Collective's Inner Council, all twenty voting members arrayed in a single line. Faces she had studied only in dossiers, the grainy surveillance images, annotations of influence and weakness, now turned toward her across polished silver and crystal.

Ernst Müller of Zurich, broad and frost-haired, adjusted a heavy gold cufflink as his pale eyes measured her with banker's coldness. Sophia Keller of Vienna leaned back, a single diamond drop at her ear flashing when she tilted her head, her expression unreadable but her silence deliberate. Across from them, Conte di Rossi of Milan tapped a finger against his wine glass, the faint scar at his temple a reminder of a car bomb three decades ago. Evie caught each detail in an instant, her mind matching them against the dossiers she had memorized.

For a flicker of a moment, surprise threatened her composure. She masked it at once, spine straight, expression poised. Damian's glance caught hers and told her he had seen it and approved of how quickly she controlled it.

Dinner unfolded in polished stages, each course a choreography. Champagne first, served with a precision that silenced the room. A bisque of lobster, rich and delicate, chased by the pour of Puligny-Montrachet that glinted like liquid gold. Plates arrived and vanished as if on invisible strings. The hum of a string quartet rose and fell like breath.

Conversation surrounded them, layers of politics, markets, and shadowed history. The fall of Leonardo was a favored topic. His holdings, his arrogance, his end. Yet within it, Evie caught the undercurrents: questions of what came next, of who had gained, of what would be done with the empire carved from his bones.

She moved within it seamlessly, her own voice measured, her smile exact. She spoke with the elegance of a diplomat and the calm of an operative who knew she was being weighed. Each council member who addressed her did so with intent, some with curiosity, some with calculation, and a few with suspicion. She answered each in turn, every response measured to give just enough and never more.

Then the signal came.

A velvet box set before each woman. An embossed envelope was placed before each man. The movement was quiet, subtle, yet unmistakable. The air shifted, a collective pause.

Damian rose. He lifted his glass with the ease of a man who had commanded rooms greater than this and men far more dangerous. His voice carried without strain. "Operazione Leonardo has concluded. The acquisition is complete. And the linchpin in that effort," he turned, his gesture precise, his eyes on her, "was Miss Evangeline Blackstone."

A silence followed, breathless and taut. Then, crystal rose, lifted as one. "To Evie."

The sound rang sharp.

She froze for a fraction of a second, then exhaled, her body remembering to move. Every council member was standing, their eyes fixed upon her. Glasses clinked in unison, a chorus of conviction and scrutiny. Admiration glimmered in some faces, calculation in others, suspicion in a few. Yet all eyes marked her.

And in that chorus, she caught the fractures.

Sophia Keller raised her glass but did not drink, her lips forming a smile too polished, her eyes already elsewhere. Ernst Müller sipped, then leaned toward his neighbor with a whisper hidden by the rim of crystal. Conte di Rossi drank deeply, but his gaze remained fixed on Damian rather than her, as though measuring the man rather than the woman he had elevated. Farther down the table, a Russian delegate she did not yet know well kept his glass at chest height, raising it only a fraction before setting it back down untouched.

Small tells. Barely there. But to an operative trained in shadows, they spoke volumes. Not all toasts meant loyalty. Not all gifts meant gratitude.

The women opened their velvet boxes to find bespoke bracelets, white or yellow gold, each set with stones chosen to match their tastes, their lives. The Collective did nothing without purpose. These were not gifts; they were symbols. Bonds forged in candlelight; obligation disguised as elegance.

The men unfolded their envelopes to find drafts for fifty million euros. Not bribes. Not payment. Tribute, rendered in public ritual. Respect and loyalty quantified, binding obligations without a word spoken.

Evie leaned toward Damian, her voice low and steady, though her pulse raced. "What exactly is going on?"

His answer was steel wrapped in velvet. "Leonardo is no more. For less than a year's earnings, we now control shipping, aerospace, biotech, and defense assets across Europe. This is not a conquest. It is ascendance."

She looked at him with new clarity, her eyes catching his in the candlelight. Not just her mentor. Not just her protector. This was a strategist shaping empires, moving entire industries like pieces on a board.

"And I was part of it," she whispered.

"No," he said, his gaze unwavering. "You were the hinge."

The word landed like a brand, searing and unshakable. She felt the weight of it settle into her bones.

Later, when the applause softened and the music rose again, Evie excused herself from the table under the pretense of air. She found Damian already waiting in the shadowed edge of the marquis, half-lit by the glow of a sconce.

"You saw it," he said quietly, as if reading her.

"The fractures," she replied.

He inclined his head once. "They always show in moments of unity. That is why we stage them."

For a heartbeat, neither spoke. The music swelled, the council laughed, the glitter of empire carried on.

Evie's voice was little more than breath. "And me?"

Damian's gaze held hers, steady and unyielding. "You are the one they cannot ignore."

It was not comfort. It was a fact. And it left her both fortified and unsettled.

The marquis glittered on, but for Evie, the night had already changed.

Chapter 17

The marquis was alive with light and music, the air heavy with laughter and the rich scent of wine. Crystal chimed, heels tapped against polished floors, and the Collective's elite moved with effortless elegance, their conversations layered with meaning.

Evie was radiant, her plum silk gown catching the glow as she turned on the dance floor, partners circling, voices rising around her. She smiled, she laughed, she listened with care, but even in the heart of the crowd, her eyes searched.

And then she found him.

Across the tent, Damian stood near the bar, his bow tie loosened, posture deceptively relaxed, yet every angle of his presence still commanded the room. Their gazes caught and held. The noise of the marquis dimmed, the swell of the band receding into the background as the current between them grew taut and unmistakable.

She excused herself with a gracious smile, slipping through the dancers until she reached him.

"I thought I'd lost you," she said, her voice low, warm.

Damian's mouth curved faintly. "Had to step out for a moment. Business, of the quieter kind. But it is finished now." He offered his arm. "Walk with me."

Her hand slid into the crook of his arm without hesitation. The contact was simple, but the spark was undeniable. They moved together through the marquis, past tables glowing with candlelight, past council members leaning close in their own hushed conspiracies. Some eyes followed, curious, but none dared intrude.

They stepped out into the night air, the music dimming behind them. Lanterns lined the path toward the lake, flickering gold across gravel and grass. The breeze carried the perfume of roses and the faint strains of jazz from the marquis, softened now by distance. Stars stretched sharply above them, and the moon cast silver across the dark water.

Neither spoke. They did not need to. The rhythm of their footsteps was its own language.

At the boathouse door, Damian paused. His hand rested briefly against the wood before he opened it for her.

Inside, the space was warm and close, scented with cedar and aged leather. Two deep chairs faced each other across a low table. A silver bucket held a sweating bottle of Krug, and beside it, a martini gleamed as if placed only moments before.

Evie's brow arched with a knowing smile. "Lukas."

"Of course," Damian said, his faint smile carrying layers of history. He shrugged out of his jacket and set it aside with measured ease.

He uncorked the champagne, the pop soft but ceremonial, and poured two flutes. The bubbles caught the firelight as he handed one to her.

For a moment, the gesture seemed ordinary. But his gaze lingered, his posture still. He reached into his inner pocket and withdrew something small and heavy.

A coin. Platinum, intricate, gleaming cold in the firelight.

The world seemed to narrow to the space between his hand and hers.

"This," Damian said, his voice low, "is your token of membership."

Evie accepted it carefully, the cool metal pressing into her palm with a weight out of proportion to its size. A dragon coiled around a ring was engraved. Beautiful. And finally, her reward.

Her breath caught.

"You are no longer an employee," Damian continued. "You are Umbra."

He let the words settle, watching her closely. "With that comes equity. A stake. But also, responsibility. We do not revoke membership. There is no stepping back. You must understand what this means. Not just the honor, but the weight."

Evie traced the edge of the coin with her thumb, her voice quiet. "So, this is it."

"Yes," Damian said. "A lifetime. Your actions reflect on all of us now. I went to London in part to defend you after Heathrow. But I have been working toward this for a while. Leonardo simply accelerated the decision. Venice tipped the scales."

She exhaled, a smile pulling at her lips. "And I suppose you celebrated with Al."

Damian's chuckle was low. "The Duck's beer tanks may never recover."

The warmth eased the tension, but only for a moment. Evie's gaze sharpened again. "What did it take to make this happen? To get me approved?"

"Favors. Debts. Reminders," Damian said simply. "I invoked alliances, argued for potential over perfection. I reminded them what happens when we invest in strength instead of punishing flaws." His tone hardened. "But do not mistake it. You were nearly terminated after London."

Evie did not flinch. "I know."

Her voice held no denial, only memory. She could still see the glint of brass in the Venetian sun; her name etched into the bullet. A fact, not a threat.

"And yet," she said softly, "you didn't pull the trigger."

"I didn't want to," Damian replied evenly. "But I would have, had it been ordered."

Silence stretched between them, taut but alive. The firelight painted his face in shadow and gold. The weight of choice hung in the air.

Then Damian leaned forward. "If you accept, there will be an investiture in London. Formal. Irrevocable. But you must say it, Evie. Out loud. And mean it. You have twenty-four hours."

The room held its breath.

Evie looked at the coin, then at him. Her heart slowed even as her decision sharpened.

"Accipio," she said.

Damian's answer was immediate. "Salve ad Collectivum. Welcome to the Collective."

He turned and shouted at nothing in particular: "Lukas, she accepts!"

He lifted his glass. She raised hers. The crystal rang in the warm air.

Her lips curved faintly. "And this is my reward?"

"No," Damian said, quiet steel in his voice. "That is your sentence."

She laughed softly, shaking her head. "That little declaration: 'Lukas, she accepts!' was that just for show?"

"Possibly," Damian deadpanned.

"Was he actually listening?"

"Almost certainly."

Her laughter spilled into the boathouse, warm and unguarded. "If I find a bug in this coin,"

"Don't bother," Damian said, straight-faced. "You'll never find it."

For the first time all night, her laughter rang out freely. His followed, quieter but real.

Outside, the lake shimmered like black glass beneath the moon. Inside, firelight and candlelight painted their faces, and between them lay the coin: cool, bright, heavy with oath.

For that moment, there was no Collective, no tribunal, no politics. Only them, and the unspoken weight of what came next.

Evie turned the token in her hand, the platinum gleam catching the light. Her thoughts slipped back to the envelope Lukas had given her days earlier, the invitation embossed with the dragon devouring the "L." Damian had left it before flying to London.

She blinked; the realization was quiet but undeniable. "You knew," she murmured, her voice more awe than accusation. "You left the invitation before you went to London because you already knew you would win."

Damian did not answer at once. He held her gaze, letting the silence draw taut. Then, with the faintest curve of his mouth, he smiled.

137

Chapter 18

They lingered in the warmth of the boathouse, the candlelight flickering between them, their laughter still echoing faintly from the moment before. Beyond the windows, the lake stretched out black and still, a pane of obsidian kissed by moonlight. Somewhere distant, the last notes of music from the marquis floated across the water, softened by distance into a private symphony.

Evie sipped from her flute, savoring the crisp effervescence, while Damian set his glass down with a quiet finality. He reached into the inside pocket of his dinner jacket, the motion slow and deliberate.

"I have something else for you," he said quietly, his expression unreadable, but soft around the edges in a way only she would notice.

He withdrew two small black boxes, setting them gently on the low table between them. They made no sound when they touched down, but the air in the room shifted all the same, subtle and expectant.

He placed slightly ahead of the other.

"This one," he said, tapping the first, "is for weekdays."

Then the second "And this one, for weekends."

Evie raised a brow, a playful smile curling at the corners of her mouth. "You're full of surprises tonight."

Damian gave a small shrug, the kind that somehow still managed to look determined. "Only the important ones."

She reached for the first box, her movements slow, reverent, like a child unwrapping something too good to be real. Inside, nestled in a bed of soft leather, was a set of keys. The silver emblem caught the light, sleek and unmistakable.

She looked up, eyes wide. "A Maybach?"

He smiled, something fond in it. "I couldn't have you showing up in Paris in that sad little excuse of a car you've been driving."

Evie laughed, warm and delighted. "That 'sad little excuse' got me out of Prague at least twice."

"Barely," Damian countered, his tone dry but not unkind.

Still grinning, she set the first box down and reached for the second. Her fingers hovered briefly over the lid. "And this one? I'm afraid to open it."

"You should be."

She flicked open the lid and froze.

Nestled inside, cool and gleaming like a coiled secret, was the key to a Bugatti Tourbillon.

Her breath caught. Her lips parted, but no sound came out at first. Then, quietly, "No."

Damian leaned back, arms crossed loosely, enjoying every flicker of disbelief crossing her face.

"You cannot be serious," she whispered.

He just looked at her.

"A Tourbillon?" Her voice rose a notch. "Are you out of your mind?"

Still, he said nothing.

Then she launched across the space between them, keys clutched in one hand, throwing her arms around his neck. "Oh my god, oh my god, oh my god!" she squealed, pressing a kiss to his cheek, his jaw, anything she could reach. "Thank you, Damian. Thank you. This is insane!"

He laughed, caught off guard by the sheer force of her joy. The sound was rare and warm, smoothing the last edges of tension from his frame. "It's just a car," he murmured.

"It is not just a car," she gasped. "It's a rocket ship wrapped in sex."

"Well," Damian said, amused, "you'll need some practice before launching."

Evie pulled back, her hands still trembling slightly. "How am I supposed to drive this thing? Like, actually drive it?"

"I've scheduled you for the Bugatti driving experience in France. Anneau du Rhin track. Two days of guided training. Private coaching."

Her mouth opened, closed, opened again. "That's near Colmar, right?"

"About two hours."

Evie blinked, then laughed, a genuine, helpless sound. "You think of everything."

He rose, straightening his jacket with a deft tug. "You'll be registered under your operational alias, of course. But I suggest you still wear a helmet."

She looked at the keys again, their weight solid in her hand. Then, "And how exactly am I getting this beauty to France?"

Damian turned toward the door with a smirk. "Ask Lukas to drive you."

She blinked. "Lukas?"

"He has two."

Evie snorted, then burst into laughter. "Stop."

"I'm not entirely joking."

"I hate how I can't tell when you are."

Damian opened the door, letting the cool night air spill in again, fresh and clean. The scent of pine and lake water threaded through the warmth of the boathouse. The music from the marquis filtered softly across the water, distant and sweet.

She stood, gifts in hand, and stepped beside him. He offered his arm again, and she took it without hesitation.

"You spoil me," she murmured, settling against him.

"No," he replied, his voice lower now, near her ear. "I just recognize an investment when I see one."

She glanced at him sideways, heart skipping again, but this time with something deeper. Not adrenaline. Not even romance. Something like permanence.

Together, they stepped out into the moonlight, the gravel crunching softly underfoot, the champagne and secrets still sparkling behind them. The path ahead gleamed silver and uncertain, but they walked it without hesitation.

As they reached the marquis's entrance, Damian paused beneath the lanterns, his hand resting lightly at the small of Evie's back. The warm glow cast their shadows long and golden on the gravel, flickering as the lamps swayed gently in the alpine breeze.

The murmur of celebration floated out to meet them: laughter, music, the clinking of glass on glass, a private orchestra of privilege and power.

"Before you get swept up again," Damian said, his voice low, meant only for her, "thank the head table. Every one of them. You'll understand why in time."

Evie gave a single nod. No protest. No question. Just that quiet, anchoring awareness again, of how the ground was shifting under her feet, how her place in this world was no longer incidental. It was becoming fixed. Visible. Permanent.

Inside, the marquis pulsed with energy. The band played a brassy, infectious number that laced through the warm air like champagne bubbles. Couples spun across the dance floor, gowns flashing like spilled wine, tuxedos gleaming beneath the chandeliers. The mood was looser now, intoxicated by elegance, by triumph, and just enough Sauternes to make the edges blur.

Before she could rejoin the current, Lukas appeared, silent as ever, materializing from the shifting crowd with practiced subtlety.

"Fräulein," he said with a slight bow, voice pitched low. "Would you like to see them?"

Evie turned her head slightly, curious.

"The cars," Lukas clarified, not unkindly.

Behind her, Damian's voice followed, threaded with quiet amusement. "Wired."

Evie smiled at that. "Of course."

He offered a faint nod in return. "Go. See them before everyone starts asking for a ride."

She touched his hand briefly, nothing showy, just a small gesture of connection, deliberate in its understatement. Then she turned and followed Lukas out into the cool night.

The path curved along the estate's perimeter. Lanterns swung from wrought iron posts, casting warm pools of gold across the gravel. Overhead, the sky stretched wide and empty, a starless sweep so clear it almost rang with silence. The distant mountains loomed, ancient and indifferent, as if weighing the night's ambitions against the permanence of stone.

Neither of them spoke. Lukas kept pace beside her with his usual grace. The quiet wasn't uncomfortable; it was deliberate. A discipline. A mutual understanding that some moments were best left unmarred by words.

They reached the garage, a discreet, bunker-like structure carved into the slope, hidden in plain sight. Lukas pressed his access card to the panel, and the heavy steel door slid back without a sound, revealing a cavern lit from above by discreet recessed LEDs.

Light bloomed slowly inside, unfurling over polished concrete and gleaming curves.

The Bugatti Tourbillon took form first, its silhouette low and sharp, the bodywork catching the light like liquid obsidian. Flecks of midnight blue shimmered in the paint, seen only when the light hit just right, like a secret only the car would reveal to those who earned it.

It didn't just look fast.

It looked inevitable.

Evie approached; her steps unhurried. She didn't speak. Her fingers hovered near the hood, just grazing the emblem. The surface was warm, responsive. Built not just for speed, but for the kind of command that made speed feel incidental.

Next to it, standing in quiet contrast, the Maybach gleamed, a pale silver-grey, whispering of elegance. It didn't need to shout. It didn't chase attention. It was built for the long game.

Inside, through tinted glass, the interior gleamed: ivory leather, brushed chrome, details that spoke in fluent understatement.

Evie stepped between the two, absorbing them not just as objects, but as statements, power distilled into two philosophies. One for control. One for escape. Both weapons in the right hands.

She ran a hand once more along the Bugatti's flank, the metal impossibly smooth beneath her touch, then stepped back. From a distance, the two vehicles looked almost staged. Not presented. Not paraded.

A future.

Behind her, Lukas remained at a polite remove, silent, vigilant, offering neither commentary nor explanation. She appreciated that more than she could say.

Evie turned toward the garage doors, the engraved token still heavy in her pocket. Her hand closed around the silver key, warm now, the imprint of her palm faint but certain.

Inside the marquis, the party carried on, unconcerned by what lay beyond its silken boundaries. Music and laughter rolled across the lawn, a tide of brass and candlelight.

She stood a moment longer, her breath visible in the cold air. Inside her, something was settling, clicking into place like clockwork.

It was recognition.

She exhaled once, steady. Then she turned back toward the marquis, the keys warm against the skin of her palm.

No ceremony. No words. Just the knowledge that nothing would be the same again.

Chapter 19

In the marquis, elegant couples spun in practiced arcs, their movements fluid and hypnotic beneath the soft wash of golden light. The dance floor shimmered like a living painting, gowns catching candlelight, polished shoes whispering across lacquered wood, laughter rising in waves. It was a portrait of celebration, and at the center of it stood Damian, the quiet architect of the evening's perfection.

He moved through the crowd with ease, each interaction polished without feeling rehearsed. He stopped to shake hands, exchange pleasantries, and raise a glass. He laughed, not loudly, but warmly, and his attentive presence gave weight to every conversation. No one ever felt like a guest at his event; for the span of their exchange, they felt like the only person in the room.

At the bar, he paused with a small cluster of familiar faces, industrialists, gallery patrons, and a European MP who had danced with surprising grace earlier in the evening. A toast was raised. Laughter bubbled up like champagne, bright and effortless. The bartender refilled their glasses before they even needed to ask.

Nearby, the younger crowd had claimed a corner of the floor. Their dancing was more exuberant than refined, but no less joyful for it. Damian watched them for a moment, arms folded, a subtle smile brushing his lips. Youth had its own kind of charm; one he didn't envy but liked remembering.

He turned then, instinctively, and there she was.

Evie had returned.

She stepped into the marquis like someone born to this world, elegant in her plum silk gown, the coin still tucked against her skin, her eyes bright and unguarded. The ambient light caught the edges of her features, painting her in warmth and promise.

She didn't seek the center. She made her way toward the head table, where the architects of her fate sat still engaged in low, pointed conversation.

There was a pause as she approached.

Then, without announcement, she extended her hand to the first council member. A tall man with silver hair and an old-world bearing took it, bowed slightly, and pressed a kiss to her knuckles. One cheek, then the other. His expression was measured, but not cold. Beneath the formality was something rare: pride.

She moved to the next. A woman in a silk jacket, elegant and reserved. Their eyes met, and with a subtle incline of her head, the woman accepted Evie's hand, repeating the gesture, cheeks, hand, eye contact held just long enough to say: You are seen.

Evie moved with quiet grace, each thank-you more than protocol. This was a ritual with teeth. Each kiss on the cheek is a signature on a pact that could not be undone.

An older gentleman, his fingers calloused despite the polish of his tuxedo, held her hand a second longer than expected. "We've been watching you a long time," he said, his voice low, weighted. "Don't stop now."

Next was a younger woman, sharp-eyed, military in bearing. She didn't smile, but her grip was firm and respectful. "We don't welcome tokens," she said quietly. "We welcome value. You've shown yours."

Evie nodded once. "Thank you."

By the time she reached the final seat, her chest felt tight with something bigger than pride. The warmth of their acceptance hadn't overwhelmed her, but it had settled deep, like fire behind her ribs.

These were no longer gatekeepers.

They were peers.

From a short distance, Damian watched, drink untouched in his hand. He hadn't guided her there. He didn't need to. She had arrived on her own.

Later, Damian stood at the entrance of the marquis, his demeanor gracious and unhurried as he bid farewell to each departing guest. He shook hands, kissed cheeks, and exchanged a few last words, his genuine appreciation evident in every interaction. The guests, many whisked away in chauffeured limousines, left glowing with praise, a quiet, rolling testimony to the night's success.

One by one, the cars disappeared into the darkness, their headlights cutting long paths through the trees before vanishing down the drive. Laughter, music, the clinking of glass, one by one, they faded into stillness. Only the faint rustle of wind through high hedges remained.

Damian lingered a moment longer, watching the final taillights blink out of sight. A quiet sense of accomplishment settled over him, like the slow exhale after a held breath.

Inside, the villa shifted to a softer rhythm. The overnight guests, fewer now and familiar, made their way to the main house for a last drink and a midnight buffet. The formal elegance of the evening gave way to easy laughter, tired shoes, and champagne replaced by cognac and scotch. Staff moved discreetly, replenishing small plates, keeping glasses full.

Evie, still humming with a private energy, slipped away down a side path, drawn like a magnet to the garage. She padded silently under the stars, the faint music from the villa brushing her heels.

There, beneath soft recessed lighting, the Bugatti Tourbillon and the Maybach S-Class waited. Silent. Gleaming.

Evie walked between them, fingertips brushing cool meter, her smile curving up unbidden.

She had arrived.

Back inside, Damian leaned against the low cabinet in the library, surrounded by a handful of close friends, Alexis among them, sprawling comfortably in an armchair, shoes off, drink in hand. The room was warm, wood-paneled, thick with the scent of old books and finer things: leather, candlewax, good cognac.

Damian glanced toward the door and shook his head with a chuckle. "She's like a toddler on Christmas morning," he said, fond amusement lacing his voice. "Back to the garage for the third time."

The room broke into laughter.

"Is she polishing the tires herself now?" Alexis asked, grinning. "I should've brought her a microfiber cloth."

"Give her five minutes," Damian replied, raising his glass. "She'll name them both."

True to form, Evie returned a few minutes later, eyes brighter than they'd been all evening. She stepped into the library like she belonged there, which, of course, she now did.

Damian was already handing her a drink, without needing to ask what she wanted.

She slipped into the circle of chairs beside him, tucking her legs beneath her, the hem of her dress pooling elegantly around her bare feet.

Meanwhile, Lukas moved quietly through the now-empty marquis outside, seeing off the band and caterers, double-checking that nothing had been left behind. The full strike would happen at dawn. For now, the night still held its shape.

As midnight crept on, the library grew quieter. One by one, guests said their goodnights, trickling upstairs with softened voices and careful footsteps. Staff moved with ghostlike precision, clearing glasses, straightening cushions, ensuring that nothing would be out of place by morning.

Evie lingered, her fingers wrapped around the champagne flute, the engraved coin still tucked against her collarbone, a quiet weight she could feel even through the silk.

She crossed to Damian, glass still cool in her hand. She opened her mouth to speak, but the words caught. There was too much.

"I have no words," she said, barely above a whisper.

Alexis, lounging nearby with his pint, lifted a hand. "Then let me talk for you."

That pulled a laugh from her. She bent and kissed Al squarely on the cheek, impulsive, affectionate, glowing. Then she turned to Damian. Their eyes met.

She didn't say a word. She just mouthed it: thank you.

Then, barefoot and unhurried, she turned and began up the stairs, the hem of her plum dress whispering behind her like a trailing secret.

Damian called after her, "What did you name them?"

Evie stopped halfway up the staircase.

She didn't turn around.

In a voice clear and certain, she answered, "The Bugatti is Seraphina. The Maybach is Odin."

The room broke into laughter and applause, unexpected, warm, spontaneous.

Al chuckled, eyes following her until she disappeared around the landing. "Of course, she did."

Somewhere above, Evie smiled, the engraved coin cool against her skin, the laughter below her like a promise.

The night was over.

She had crossed the velvet threshold.

The laughter had faded, the last car had pulled away, and even the marquis now stood dark and silent beyond the trees. Inside, the house glowed in soft pools of light, echoing with only the faintest footsteps and the rustle of fabric as evening clothes were exchanged for comfort.

The villa had gone still.

In the library, the fire burned low, casting amber shadows across the parquet floor. Damian and Lukas sat in companionable silence, a final brandy between them. The heavy velvet curtains cocooned the room in a hush of old leather, woodsmoke, and cognac.

Big Al sprawled in a deep armchair, his tuxedo jacket draped carelessly over the rest, collar undone, bowtie missing. He nursed a neat cognac, a faint curl of cigar smoke still drifting above him.

Lukas poured the last of the Delamain into three glasses, the quiet efficiency of ritual among old hands. Their glasses touched with a muted chime. Silence returned, not empty but weighted with memory, consequence, and the rare sense that something had gone exactly right.

After a moment, Damian exhaled. "She named the cars."

Alexis chuckled, "Best part of the night."

"She didn't even hesitate," Damian murmured.

"She had already decided," Lukas added.

Alexis swirled his drink. "Seraphina and Odin." He snorted, "Once you name the machines, it's over."

Damian's smile was faint but real.

"She's not like us," Alexis added.

"No," Damian agreed, "She isn't broken like we are."

Alexis drained his glass. "She isn't, but she will carry weight now. You saw it when she took the coin. It changes people. But she has earned her place."

"She has," Damain agreed, "and now it is our place to protect it."

A log shifted in the hearth, sparks rising. Outside, the wind moved softly through the trees.

Eventually, Alexis stood, stretching, "If I sit here any longer, I will start quoting Yeats."

He slung his jacket over his shoulder and gave Damian a nod, "You did good, my brother. Be proud"

Damian smiled and nodded in return.

As he made for the stairs, Alexis looked at Lukas and walked over to shake his hand. "Good night, Lukas, and thank you for everything."

Lukas, who was visibly surprised for a moment before regaining his composure, nodded. "It has been my honour. Gute Nacht, Herr Alexis."

When Alexis disappeared into the hall, Damian and Lukas lingered a moment longer, the fire and silence enough. Then Damian stood, smoothing his cuffs, finishing the last sip of brandy. "See you in the morning, old friend."

"Gute Nacht, mein Herr."

The library quieted again.

Upstairs, Evie hung her gown carefully in the armoire, bare feet sinking into the thick carpet. The night still lingered in her bones, sharp and brilliant. Steam curled around her face as she stood beneath the shower, thoughts drifting, flashes of the marquis, the dance, the coin, Damian's hand in hers. The steel of the Bugatti was under her fingertips. The weight of acceptance, final and irreversible.

When she emerged, skin flushed and clean, she wrapped herself in a robe and paused in front of the mirror. She didn't fully recognize the woman staring back, but for the first time, she didn't need to.

Downstairs still hummed faintly. A door closing. She wasn't ready for sleep.

In the kitchen, one of the night staff straightened when she entered the room.

"Shall I fetch Herr Cesarini?" He asked attentively.

She shook her head. "No, just a glass of champagne, if there is any left."

He disappeared into the back and returned with a chilled flute on a salver.

Taking the glass, she thanked him.

"Would you like me to turn up the lights? Or can I prepare something to eat?" He was eager to please.

Smiling, she declined and returned to the stairs on her way to her room.

At the top of the stairs, she paused and glanced back, offering a silent nod of thanks and acknowledgement of his efforts.

Back in her room, Evie set down the glass, slipped off the robe, and slid beneath the sheets. The coin turned slowly in her fingers, its engraving reflecting the moonlight.

She smiled, took a sip of champagne, pressed the coin in her palm, and thought, "It is real."

Chapter 20

By morning, the villa had become a hive of purposeful motion once more. Trucks rumbled up the gravel drive, work crews in waterproof jackets swarmed the lawn, and the once-majestic marquis was being dismantled, its canvas sagging like a circus tent after the final show.

Rain tapped a steady rhythm against the tall windows, unrelenting, grey, and soft. From her bedroom, Evie watched the drizzle streak down the glass and sighed. The fantasy she had imagined, driving the Bugatti with the top down, the Alps roaring by in a blur, sunlight flashing off chrome, would have to wait.

She dressed for a rainy morning. No makeup, no pretense. Even in casual clothes, the engraved coin tucked inside her pocket weighed on her like a second spine, a quiet reminder.

Downstairs, she found Damian on the covered verandah, already deep into a morning call. He was seated comfortably, laptop open, feet propped on a low ottoman. His coffee steamed beside him, half-forgotten. Shirt sleeves rolled to the forearms, collar open, eyes sharp with focus. The trademark cigar added a hint of coffee aroma. Even on a Sunday, even in the rain, Damian worked.

Evie leaned against the frame of the glass doors, watching for a moment. A smile tugged at her lips, equal parts affection and amusement. There was something reassuring about the way he moved through the day: calm, relentless, composed.

Lukas arrived at her elbow with impeccable timing, offering her a fresh coffee.

"Thank you, Lukas. Just what I needed." She said, accepting the cup with a grateful smile.

Damian ended his call, closed the laptop with a satisfying click, and turned toward her. Rain misted the edge of the overhang, blurring the garden into watercolor.

"Everything is under control. Lukas has the workmen in hand," he said. Then, with a glance back toward the hallway: "Al? You and Jane up for a bit of risotto in Milan?"

A moment later, Jane appeared, casually dressed but radiant in that effortlessly composed way she always managed. She was already shaking her head, a scarf draped loosely around her shoulders. "We've got the grandkids coming for tea," she said with a grin. "I promised them roast and two kinds of dessert. You'll have to manage Milan without us."

Al followed behind her, mug in hand, expression somewhere between mischief and fond resignation.

"And Damian," Jane added, arching a brow as she pulled on her coat, "if the two of you spend any more time together, people will start to talk."

Damian offered her a smile that was all quiet mischief. "Let them." Evie laughed into her coffee.

Jane kissed her on the cheek, then Damian. "Enjoy the rain. Or the risotto. Whichever wins."

With that, she disappeared down the corridor toward the guest wing. Al lingered a beat longer.

"You two behave," he said, squinting at Damian. "And try not to buy anything you cannot lift."

He winked, then vanished as well, the scent of Cuban cigars trailing behind him like a signature.

Damian turned back to Evie, the smile still lingering at the corner of his mouth. "Well then, I guess it is just the two of us."

Evie blinked. "Milan?"

"Rain calls for risotto," he said simply. "And I need a clear view of the week ahead."

She agreed, and he nodded toward her outfit. "No need to change. I'll match you."

His eyes flicked down, briefly, to her thigh. The shape of the garter beneath the leggings was unmistakable. But no knives today. He did not comment, only noted it, cataloguing the absence like a battlefield adjustment. Perhaps she had left them upstairs. Or perhaps she was adapting.

They parted briefly to gather what they needed, and when they met again in the garage, it was not the Bugatti that waited, but the sleek black M5. The Tourbillon could wait for drier skies. For now, discretion and comfort ruled.

Rain hissed gently against the windshield as they pulled away, the tires slicing through the wet like memory through silence. Inside, the car was warm, familiar. Evie tucked her feet up beneath her and opened a tablet, scrolling slowly, reading without haste. Occasionally, she looked up to take in the misty slopes of the Gotthard Pass, the low clouds wrapped around the Swiss peaks like whispered secrets.

By the time they reached Ticino, the rain had begun to ease. Pale light broke through the clouds in soft shafts, and when they crossed the border into Italy, the sky opened fully. The Alps fell away, and the road unfurled like a ribbon toward Milan.

Damian drove the way he did everything else, without waste. Evie watched him out of the corner of her eye now and then, catching details she had not before: the way he tilted his head slightly in the tight corners, the almost imperceptible glance to the mirrors every few minutes, the quiet tension in his jaw when they passed other high-performance cars.

By the time they reached the sleek façade of La Rinascente, the sun was in full command of the sky.

Damian handed off the keys with a silent nod to the valet. They entered the glass atrium and rose in the elevator, the Duomo's white spires coming into view as the floors slipped past. The rooftop restaurant, Maio, was alive with understated glamour: crisp linen, mirrored sunglasses, laughter in three languages, and the soft strains of a jazz trio playing somewhere just out of sight.

Evie paused at the terrace railing, taking in the sight of the cathedral, its marble facade burning in the sun like a monument to endurance. "You've never been here?" Damian asked, more observation than question.

She shook her head. "It's surreal."

They were seated in a quiet corner, sheltered just enough to speak freely. The host seemed to know Damian by name, or reputation, or both. Evie ordered the saffron risotto. Damian selected the tagliolini with truffle. They shared a bottle of chilled Friulian white, minerally and crisp, elegant without pretension.

Their conversation came in waves, soft and unhurried. They spoke of the investiture, of names that must be included and those who must be handled delicately. Of logistics and optics. Of appearances. Then, after a pause, of nothing at all.

As they lingered over espresso, Damian leaned back, the sun cutting a soft line across his cheek.

"I'm glad we did this," he said. "I needed the quiet. And you…" He paused, tilting his head slightly. "You belong in this city more than you think."

Evie gave him a look, half amused, half grateful. "Is that your way of saying I look better in black than you do?"

Damian smiled, slow and knowing. "I'm saying Milan has never looked at me the way it just looked at you."

She rolled her eyes, but warmth softened her expression.

She glanced down at her empty plate, then at the horizon beyond the Duomo's spires. The sun was angling lower now, bathing the rooftops in that late-afternoon gold found only in cities built of marble and history.

The breeze stirred softly at the edge of the terrace. The tablecloth lifted just slightly, then settled again. For a long moment, they said nothing.

Damian sipped the last of his espresso, his gaze not on the view, but on her, studying the line of her profile, the way the sunlight touched her cheekbones, the thoughtful way she twirled the spoon in her empty cup without noticing.

As the dessert course arrived, a dark chocolate marquise with a gleaming mirror glaze, Damian leaned in, his expression sharpening. "Now," he said lowly, "let us discuss the investiture."

Evie set her fork down, attentive. His voice had taken on that precise, measured quality she associated with serious preparation, clinical but never unkind.

"It will take place in London," Damian continued. His tone was even, but there was a gravity beneath it. "I'll be sponsoring you, and you know the committee already. Last night's dinner was not just a celebration."

Evie nodded slowly, bracing herself as he laid out the terrain. "The ceremony is formal. You will be addressed directly. Some questions will be pointed out. Do not let that rattle you. Stay polite, stay brief. Concise answers earn respect. Clever ones provoke suspicion. Say too much, and they will start wondering what you are trying to hide."

She felt her spine lengthen, the subtle shift of posture born from training, from old instincts.

Damian studied her, then continued, voice cooling a degree. "If Heathrow is raised, and it likely will be, acknowledge the mistake briefly. Apologize without embellishment. Pivot immediately. Make it clear it will not happen again. What they want is proof that you have learned. Proof you can exercise restraint."

Evie nodded again, more slowly this time, already rehearsing tones, phrasings, the rhythms of controlled humility. "There will be a section in Latin," Damian went on. "Ancient rite, largely symbolic but binding. You will be asked if you accept the oath. You will respond with 'Accipio.' And you must mean it."

Evie's fingers tightened slightly around the stem of her glass. It was becoming real now, not a ceremony but a consequence.

Damian's expression softened just slightly; the edges less severe. "You will do fine. Stay polite. Measured. And very, very alert."

"This will change you." He said quietly.

Evie looked up. "The investiture?"

He nodded. "Not just the title. The weight of it. The way people look at you. What they expect. What they assume."

She let that sit for a moment. "Will I stop being myself?"

"No," he said. "But you will start learning who that 'self' really is. And what you are willing to do to protect it."

"Was it like that for you?" She asked.

His eyes held hers. "It still is."

A waiter appeared to clear their plates. Damian gave a polite nod, and they waited until he retreated before speaking again.

Evie drew a breath, then reached for her glass of water. "I am not afraid," she said. "Just... aware."

"That is the correct state of mind." Damian leaned back, his fingers idly tapping the rim of his cup. "Awareness is what keeps you breathing in our world."

"And knives." She added lightly.

His gaze flicked to her thigh. "I noticed their absence."

Her mouth curved into a slow smile. "Who says they are not somewhere else?"

He arched a brow, amused. "Spoken like a true ghost."

They stayed a while longer, watching the city exhale around them, its rooftops glowing, its avenues humming with life, the moment suspended like a frame from a film.

There would be more days like this, she thought. But none quite like the first.

He called for the bill, but his gaze shifted just briefly over her shoulder. His body language did not change, but she caught it, the subtle alertness sharpening the air.

Without raising his voice, he leaned in. "Get up slowly. We are leaving."

Evie froze for half a second, then obeyed. The change in his voice was instinct, not dramatics. And she trusted it.

As he stood, Damian's hand moved casually into his jacket. She caught the faint click, the release of a safety.

"You brought a gun to lunch in Milan?" she murmured, incredulous. Damian's mouth curved in a ghost of a smile. "The valet works for Umbra. He gave it to me in exchange for the keys."

Evie suppressed a laugh. Barely. "You people!" she whispered under her breath.

"Remember," he said, handing her a small, unassuming boutique bag, "you are now also 'you people'."

"There is a little something extra in there," he added lightly. "A box of La Molina chocolates. And tucked beneath it, a pistol and two loaded clips."

Evie arched a brow. "Guns and ganache. How very Umbra."

They left the terrace without haste, Damian settling the bill, leaving an unremarkable but generous tip. Evie walked ahead, casual but alert, her pulse steady.

Damian followed after a final glance at the man who had been watching them. No visible weapon. No movement. Just a man, staring the way men did when they did not realize their interest was showing. It was not a threat. Not yet.

Evie turned to him, the boutique bag swinging easily from one hand. "It is Milan," she said with a grin. "We cannot not shop," Damian smirked. "Of course. You almost died at the Duomo, so naturally, we buy shoes."

They wandered Via della Spiga, the heart of Milanese luxury, where the air smelled of leather and expensive perfume. Evie moved through the boutiques with ease, her fingers tracing cashmere, silk, and velvet with the same precision she used when checking a weapon. She was quick. Decisive. She did not second-guess.

A deep forest-green dress caught her attention, a high neck, sculpted shoulders, a cut that spoke of authority without shouting. Damian watched her turn it over once, appraising it the way a jeweler might a flawless stone. She emerged from the fitting room ten minutes later, the dress already molded to her, commanding without being loud.

Damian offered a small nod. Approval, understated.

Then came the shoes.

Evie tried on pair after pair, until she slipped her feet into black stilettos with a fine gold inlay. They made her two inches taller, her posture straighter, her presence more absolute. She smiled down at them, flexing one foot slightly.

"I feel like I could run an empire in these."

Damian did not disagree.

They capped the afternoon with gelato, pistachio for her, black sesame and lemon for him. Then, with an impulsive grin, Evie tugged him toward the Duomo's rooftop.

High above the city, they stood beneath the white spires, wind tugging at her hair. Milan stretched below them, sun-drenched and buzzing. Damian let her walk ahead, arms folded against the railing, her silhouette sharp against the skyline.

She belonged here.

And for just one long breath, he allowed himself the thought: maybe they both did.

The bells of the Duomo struck four, solemn and heavy. Damian's gaze flicked to the unexpected sound, then to his watch.

"It is time," he said softly.

They wound back down through the quiet piazza, the afternoon light painting the stones in gold. But as they approached the car, Evie felt the shift in Damian's mood. His jaw was tight. His eyes, distant.

"You are being quiet." She said.

He hesitated, one hand already on the car door. "It is nothing." She nodded, sensing there was more, but she did not press. Not here. Not yet.

The autostrada north unwound before them in smooth, silver-grey ribbons. The sky deepened into soft rose and blue as Italy slipped behind them.

The ride home was quiet, punctuated by occasional murmured jokes about Milanese drivers, reflections on shoe selection strategies, or the best way to smuggle chocolate past Lukas.

By the time they crossed the Swiss border and rolled back into Cham, the villa was cloaked in lavender haze, dusk falling like a benediction.

Evie looked out over the grounds and blinked. The marquis was gone. Every table, every lantern, every trace of last night's celebration had vanished. The lawn looked untouched, as if it had never happened.

"Lukas," Damian said simply, reading her thoughts. "Surgical as ever."

Evie smiled faintly, struck by the seamlessness of it all, the way the storm of the night before had been cleaned, erased, rewritten into silence.

Lukas met them at the steps, composed and unflappable. Staff appeared to take their coats and bags, moving like water around stone.

"The kitchen has prepared something light," Lukas said, voice low.

"In anticipation of your Milanese indulgences."

"A safe assumption," Damian replied dryly. "Soup and salad sound perfect."

Evie changed into something soft, cashmere and cotton, comfort woven into form, and rejoined Damian in the dining room. The table was set with bone China, delicate consommé steaming gently, fresh greens waiting beside it.

Dinner was quiet. Grounding.

Damian broke the silence first.

"I am going to Venice tomorrow."

Evie's spoon paused. "Can I come?"

His eyes met hers, serious. "Evie, you inhumed someone there last month."

Her gaze did not waver. "There were no witnesses."

Damian shot back. "There were five hundred people who saw you there."

"I made it away cleanly," she said simply.

"You shot up one of my favorite hotels in Rome."

"Please. You decamped to the Hassler years ago."

The silence between them was not tense, just full.

"I could stay in Cham," she conceded, "Or Knightsbridge."

Damian nodded slowly. "I will leave it to you."

Evie stood a few minutes later, brushing her hand lightly over his shoulder as she passed. "Goodnight."

He watched her retreat, the whisper of her bare feet soft on the old wood floors.

"I am just thinking of your safety," he murmured, almost too low for even himself to hear.

But as the house quieted, as the fire sank to embers, the thought of Venice lingered. Silent. Unresolved.

Chapter 21

Without Damian, the villa felt too symmetrical, too still. The quiet was its own pressure, a reminder of absence. Maybe she should have flown to London.

Evie kept to her routine with military precision: early mornings, punishing workouts, range time. Sensing the restlessness beneath her calm, Lukas doubled down on hand-to-hand.

She was improving, but he had a way of showing her, discreetly and devastatingly, that she was still far from his level. One moment, she thought she had him off balance, the next, she was on the mat, breath gone, pride bruised.

He never gloated. He never needed to.

The frustration burned, and she learned to use it. She got sharper, quicker. She stopped aiming to win and started aiming not to lose.

Still, despite the drive and the discipline, she brooded. Not openly; she was careful not to let it show. But the absence of Damian hollowed the days. They felt thinner. She told herself it was silly. He was not her boyfriend, not her husband. He was her anchor, the one who made the strange world of Umbra feel, if not familiar, at least navigable.

When he returned Thursday morning, three days late, relief flooded her before she could smother it, tangled with a thread of irritation that he hadn't been in touch since he left.

Damian walked in with his jacket slung over one shoulder, travel-worn but composed. A faint scruff shadowed his jaw, and there was a lightness about him, subtle but there.

He smiled when he saw her, that half smirk she knew too well. "You sulking, wife?" he asked lightly.

Evie arched a brow, arms folded. "I did not realize I was your wife."

"You are not," he replied, "which is precisely why I did not have to call."

She tried not to laugh and failed. "Touché."

"The car will be here at 1 PM to take us to the airport," he reminded her.

By mid-morning, they were packing for London. This time, there were events, dinners, briefings, and the investiture itself. No room for her usual minimalist approach. Lukas had already laid out suit bags and trunks. She needed daywear, eveningwear, and other options.

A black SUV idled at the front steps. The driver climbed out as Lukas emerged from the house a one precisely. Bags were loaded; Damian and Evie settled into the rear seats, Lukas up front, already syncing with the convoy that would shadow them to Zurich's General Aviation Terminal.

The drive was quiet. Damian worked through messages and calls, switching between French, English, and Veneziano with the same fluidity he brought to everything. Lukas navigated in silence. Evie, cocooned in the back seat, rested her head lightly against the glass and watched the alpine landscape roll by in muted greys and greens.

The Gulfstream awaited them, engines a low hum of readiness. Boarding was seamless, and they buckled in for the seventy-five-minute flight to London.

Evie sipped an espresso and let the cabin's quiet luxury sink into her bones. She could get used to it.

London City Airport greeted them under low, heavy skies. An Umbra team stood ready at the private terminal, efficient, silent, invisible.

Their bags were transferred into a waiting Range Rover, and the convoy slid west into the city.

As they passed the Tower, then the Embankment, London unfolded beyond the glass, familiar and alive. She had not realized how much she missed it.

When they pulled up at the Ritz, she glanced at Damian. "Why here, and not Knightsbridge?"

Lukas, scrolling through his phone, looked up sharply. Damian caught the look, gave him a slight nod, then turned back to Evie.

"The London house is unused now," he said. "I spend more time in Vienna, Singapore, and the palazzo. It is unstaffed. And while Lukas could whip a temp team into shape by teatime," he shot a sidelong glance at Lukas, "it hardly seemed worth the trouble for a four-day weekend."

Evie studied him. "And if it were just me?"

Damian's smile was faint. "I would have opened it in a heartbeat."

The car slid beneath the gold-lettered awning. Doormen appeared as if conjured, doors opening in a choreography so smooth it barely read as motion.

"Honestly," he said, voice dropping, reflective, "I have been thinking about selling it."

Evie blinked. It was not what she had expected.

"I cannot seem to get organized about it," he said with a light shrug. "And for once, I do not know if I care to try. It is starting to feel like ballast."

Damian, disorganized. Damian, letting go of an asset. It did not fit. Then again, even the most composed people needed to let something slip.

Check-in was effortless. Staff moved around them like chess pieces, precise and unobtrusive. Their suites were adjacent: Evie's on the sixth floor, a corner room with pale blue walls and wide windows over Green Park; Damian's next door.

The coming days settled on her shoulders like an invisible weight, the ritual, the scrutiny, the moment of transformation. She took it without hesitation.

She tried to read in her suite and could not focus. She stood when James's text arrived: lunch was here.

She read it twice. James was not expected until later in the week. An early arrival meant something had shifted.

The corridor outside was hushed, the carpet muffling her steps. She moved past closed doors, gold sconces casting a warm, diffused glow. Damian's double doors were closed.

She paused. Voices carried, low and steady: Damian's measured tone, James's clipped precision. No laughter. Business.

She knocked twice. The voices stopped, and a moment later the door opened.

"Come in," Damian said.

James glanced up from the call he was on and gave a brief nod before returning to the file. Damian closed the door, and the work resumed.

Inside, the room had transformed. It was no longer a hotel suite. It was an operations center.

Lunch arrived not on a trolley, but by discreet courier from a Mayfair sushi restaurant that Damian trusted. No flimsy cartons, no plastic forks. Lacquered bento trays, porcelain dishes, and a bottle of Junmai Dai Ginjo he had clearly anticipated.

James ended his call and smiled. "Ah, Evie. Always lovely to see you."

"Thanks, James." She took in the files, the screens, the quiet hum of real work. "If there is something I can do, I would like to. I feel a bit sidelined."

"You are not sidelined," James said gently. "You are being prepped. But I understand." He gestured to the couch. "Sit. We will rope you in soon enough."

She sank into the cushions, riding that familiar mix of exhaustion and adrenaline that followed long, uncertain days.

Damian looked up, a glint of dry mischief in his eyes. "James," he said, deadpan, "find someone for Evie to kill. She is bored."

"Random or sanctioned, sir?"

"Let her choose."

Evie smirked. "Do I get to vet the dossier first?"

"I will have a shortlist in fifteen minutes," James said, tapping his chin.

They cleared space on the table and began to eat. Between bites, Evie watched Damian. Knightsbridge. He had said it like parting with a watch or moving a painting. To her, it was not just another asset.

It was where it had started. Her first real brush with his world. The first place she had felt, not safe, but anchored. The hush of the study. Her laughter against the stone after long dinners. His coat around her shoulders on walks through Kensington's sleeping streets.

She did not want him to sell it. Fiercely, silently, she hoped he would not.

Damian refilled her glass without comment. She wondered if he knew.

A booming voice burst through the room.

"You should not have that foreign muck. You should be getting proper fish and chips."

Evie turned to see Alexis filling the doorway, face red with mock indignation.

Damian looked up, and an honest grin broke across his face.

"Al, how did you know we were here?" Evie asked as he strode in, every step loud and certain.

"You cannot get within fifty miles of His Majesty's airspace without me knowing," Al declared, dragging Damian into a hug that lifted him off the floor. "It is his cologne. I would know it anywhere."

Evie laughed, helpless at the sight of Damian dangling, mildly exasperated and tolerant.

"Do they have security in this two-bit hotel?" Damian deadpanned when Al set him down. "I want a discount. You cannot let any lunatic wander in off the street."

"Rich, coming from you," Al shot back.

The moment melted into easy laughter born of old wars and older friendships. Even as Damian smiled, Evie caught it, the faint strain at his mouth, the shadow behind his eyes.

The suite snapped back to headquarters. Lunch cleared to one side, files and laptops retook the table. Damian and James barely looked up.

Later, Al rose from a chair near the window when Evie came in. "We are heading out for a bit," he said. Damian gave a brief nod, already tracking the numbers James pointed out.

Outside, the afternoon had the pale gold of early autumn. They walked down Piccadilly, past reflective shopfronts and rumbling buses. The smell of roasted chestnuts drifted from a cart.

They turned toward St. James's and followed the path to The Mall. Trees framed the avenue, Buckingham Palace distant and steady.

"I do not want him to sell Knightsbridge," Evie said quietly, eyes forward. "I do not know how to bring it up."

Al slowed. "Wait until after the investiture," he said. "Then talk to him. I will be there, no matter what."

Her shoulders eased. "Thank you."

They walked on, arm in arm, through the slow-turning streets. By the time they looped back toward Piccadilly, lamps flickered on, and the sky deepened toward twilight.

"Nearly seven," Al said, checking his watch.

They slipped through the revolving doors into the marbled hush of the Ritz. The lift attendant nodded them into the brass car. The ascent was smooth and silent.

On six, they walked to Damian's suite. Al opened the door without knocking. Low conversation and the soft shuffle of paper carried across the room. Damian and James were still at work.

"There has been a change," Damian said once the greetings faded. "We are dining in tonight. Lukas will not be joining. He requested the evening off for a personal matter."

Evie nodded. Without another word, the four of them made their way to the Ritz dining room.

The meal was elegant and unhurried. Fine wine flowed. Courses arrived with polished grace. Al was in rare form, charming, outrageous, and entirely inappropriate. Evie laughed more than she meant to, the week's tautness loosening.

Damian was engaged, but not himself. Halfway through the second course, his phone buzzed. He glanced at the screen, excused himself, and disappeared.

When he returned, his smile was subdued. He picked up his fork and rejoined the conversation, but Evie felt the shift.

As dessert arrived, thin layers of hazelnut dacquoise under silk smooth ganache, Damian leaned in, voice low. "We need to go to Rome tomorrow."

Evie turned, startled. "Rome? Damian, the investiture is Saturday."

"I know," he said calmly. "We will be back on time. But we have to go."

There was no give in his tone. Whatever it was, it was not optional.

She nodded, uneasy but trusting.

"I vote we finish this wine and hit the Duck," Al announced, oblivious to the change.

"Out," Damian said smoothly. "Early flight. I need lucid, not laminated."

"Since when has that ever stopped you?" Al scoffed.

"Since tomorrow matters more than tonight."

"I will pass, too," Evie replied, "I am dead on my feet."

Everyone looked at James questioningly.

James sighed with mock resignation. "Looks like I am the sacrificial lamb."

"Try not to die," Damian said without looking up.

"It is not dying that is hard," Al grinned, clapping James's back. "It is surviving me."

As Al and James drifted toward the lobby, Evie leaned closer to Damian. "You might need to call recruitment. James has a one in four chance of surviving a night at the Duck with Al."

Damian's chuckle was soft.

Back upstairs, as he unlocked his suite, she paused. "Can you tell me anything about Rome?"

He shook his head. "You will see. Bring workwear and a casual change of clothes."

Something in his voice made it clear there were no more questions.

He disappeared into his suite. The door clicked shut.

Evie stood in the quiet hallway a moment longer, the taste of wine and uncertainty on her tongue.

Rome, she thought.

Outside the tall windows, London glittered in whites and silvers, lights from the Ritz forecourt casting pale reflections across the glass.

Knightsbridge lies a few miles west. Quiet. Waiting. If she asked him not to sell it, he would listen. Could she buy it from him? The cost would stretch her. Furniture could come later. Would he sell? And if he did, would he sell to her?

Chapter 22

Evie's alarm blared, splitting the calm with mechanical insistence. She silenced it with a groggy swipe and lay back against the tangle of pillows. The bed was too large for one, and the empty space beside her whispered with memory. She imagined Damian there, still and composed, one arm flung over the pillow, his breathing even in the morning hush.

There had been a time she would have shut those thoughts out. Now they came uninvited, a quiet, steady presence.

But sentiment had no place today.

She swung her legs over the side of the bed, feet brushing the cool carpet, and set her mind to the day ahead.

Damian's instructions the night before had been crisp: black tactical pants, a turtleneck, tactical boots. Neutral, forgettable. Not what she would normally wear for breakfast at the Ritz, but she had learned to heed his judgment without argument.

She dressed quickly, efficiently. She packed a small backpack: jeans, trainers, a clean tee, and a fleece pullover. Nothing glamorous, just enough to move in. To vanish if needed.

Downstairs, Damian was already seated with coffee and a tablet. He did not look up when she joined him, but she knew he had registered her the moment she crossed the threshold.

She ordered an espresso. He laid out the logistics, his voice low and deliberate: Rome. Tight timeline. No margin for improvisation.

When the coffee was finished, they moved through the gilded lobby with practiced ease. Outside, a black Audi S8 idled at the curb, a chase car tucked behind. Discreet. Umbra's signature.

Evie slid into the back seat, muscles taut with readiness.

As they drove, she turned to him. "With this security detail around you, how did you get to Venice alone?"

He glanced at her, then leaned in slightly, voice pitched low. "No one can follow me in Venice. I am safer there than anywhere."

She believed him. She had tried once, an exercise in futility. He had vanished into stone and shadow before she reached the first turn.

London City Airport came into view, private hangars gleaming in the pale light. The Gulfstream waited on the tarmac, engines idle, less a machine than a second home, lately.

Boarding was seamless. Takeoff was smooth, the fields of England slipping past like an old memory. Breakfast followed: croissant for her, smoked salmon for him. They ate in silence, the kind that said more than conversation could.

Landing at Fiumicino was a whisper. No crowds, no ceremony, only Umbra agents waiting at a distance, sunglasses and tailored black suits, mirrored composure.

Evie watched them approach. "Do they all shop from the same catalog?"

Damian allowed himself the faintest smile. "Custom tailoring. Standard issue."

A waiting Mercedes carried them away, past the postcard beauty into Rome's grittier edges: warehouses, chain-link fences, cracked concrete.

The car stopped. Security fanned out. Damian led the way inside.

The warehouse was a vacuum, with no windows and no distractions. Under a ring of hard lights stood a woman, arms restrained above her head, cables biting into her wrists. A ring of surveillance equipment framed her like a brutalist portrait.

Evie stopped.

The woman looked like her. Taller, maybe. Sharper at the jaw. But the eyes, the mouth. Uncanny.

"This is Veronica," Damian said, clinical. "She was your double at the Waldorf during the Leonardo operation."

Recognition flickered: morning runs, drinks at the bar, a sunlit nod by the pool. A decoy. A shadow.

"But?" Evie asked, voice flat.

"She sold you out," Damian said, gaze sharp. "Freelanced your schedule to a rival faction."

Veronica's head snapped up, defiant. "No. I helped you. I would never."

Damian pressed a button on a small remote. A screen is lit.

Veronica's voice filled the room, cool, transactional. "I told them when she left. I set the whole thing up. If they blew it, that is on them. I practically put the gun in her mouth."

On screen, Veronica accepted a slim briefcase, cash inside.

When the video ended, Veronica broke. The fight went out of her, knees giving way as she slid down the wall.

"Please, you do not understand!" Her voice cracked, words tumbling. "I have a daughter! She is seven. She needs me. I only did it for her."

"It was the money! I did not think they would actually... I thought it was a scare! School fees…rent…we were behind. You know how it is! You must know!"

"She is smart. Top of her class. Loves animals. If I am gone..." Her breath hitched. "If I am gone, they will put her in the system. Please. I am all she has."

The words fractured into sobs. She threw every card left on the table: fear, guilt, motherhood, the fragile humanity that might pierce an operative's armor.

Evie's gaze did not waver.

The blade was in her hand before the thought fully formed.

She approached without haste, steel catching the hard light.

"This is no business for a single mother," Evie said quietly.

The motion was clean. One efficient draw. Blood rose and spilled, betrayal leaching out like ink in water.

Evie watched until the body stilled. She rinsed the knife, dried it, and rejoined Damian at the door.

No one spoke.

As they exited, a cleanup crew passed them. He had known she would do it here and now.

The car door shut with the finality of a sealed vault.

Damian sat beside her in silence. At last, he spoke. "I hope you did not buy the mother routine."

Evie stared ahead. "No one with a child takes a job like that. She was playing the angle."

He nodded once. "Little did she know."

They did not speak again until Trastevere.

The restaurant was small, hidden on a shaded lane. Inside, the air was thick with garlic and tomato, the warmth of real food and lives lived well. A window table appeared without request.

They sat. Ordered. Ate.

Midway through the meal, Damian set down his fork. "Al wanted to handle it," he said.

Evie looked up.

"I told him no. You had to see it through."

She nodded.

After, they walked with gelato from a vendor whose silver tins gleamed in the noon light. Hazelnut and pistachio for her, lemon for him. They moved through Rome like two ghosts.

"You know," Evie said after a while, "when I fill out the customs form, what do I write?"

Damian quirked a brow. "You tell me."

"I came to Rome to execute someone and then have pasta. Lovely stay. Would recommend. Five stars."

A faint smile touched his mouth. "They do not ask why we are here."

They turned off the lane and crossed the square to Santa Maria in Trastevere. The basilica's door was cool under her palm. Inside, gold tesserae shimmered in the half light. Tourists murmured. A choirboy's whisper skimmed the apse and was gone.

Evie stood for a moment at the back, letting her eyes adjust. She did not pray. She lit a candle anyway and watched the flame take. Heat. Light. Proof.

"For who?" Damian asked, voice low.

"For what I will not put on a form," she said.

He nodded and moved a step aside, hands in his pockets, the habit of a man who waited often. She felt the weight in her chest change shape, not lighter, just arranged.

On the side aisle, a woman guided a little girl past the mosaics. The child pointed up and whispered questions. Evie watched them go. No story attached. Only a picture she would keep.

Damian's gaze shifted past her shoulder. "Second column, left," he said quietly. "Blue jacket, white trainers."

Evie glanced once. Early thirties. Tourist wristband. No tell in the stance. The man's attention slid to his phone, then to the ceiling, then back to his companion. "Not ours," she said.

"Agreed."

They walked out into the square. The fountain chattered. She rinsed her sticky fingers in the cold spill and wiped them on a napkin. Damian bought water and a newspaper from the tabacchi. No one hurried.

Along the Lungotevere, the plane trees held a flattened light. Traffic hissed. She fell into step beside him and matched his pace. Neither spoke. The river moved on, the city doing what cities do when no one is watching.

At the corner, a small van idled with its hazards on. A man stepped down, held the door, and looked past them without looking at them. Damian slid the folded newspaper under his arm and kept walking. Evie did the same. No exchange. Nothing to see.

At the end of the block, he glanced at her. "Ready to go home?"

"Yes," she said. And meant it.

Back at the airport, the plane waited.

As they boarded, rain began needling the windows. Evie settled beside him. He leaned back and, within minutes, slept.

She watched him, features relaxed, tension drained. He looked younger like this. Softer. The sight unsettled her more than she expected.

She turned away to the rain streaking the glass.

Behind her eyes, Veronica's face lingered. Not in life. In death.

Damian had not brought her for vengeance.

Her line in the sand.

The sky over London sagged under familiar rain, flat and pewter gray. Droplets clung to the windows as the jet taxied across the private apron, each streak warping the skyline into a smudged memory.

Evie watched in silence as the city emerged by degrees. London did not wait for her. It never waited for anyone.

When the stairs lowered, she descended first, boots striking wet metal with muted finality. Lukas stood at the base, impeccable in a black coat, posture straight and unreadable. Beside him, Al loomed like weather about to turn, tailored coat flaring in the wind, one hand curled around what looked suspiciously like a beer.

Order and chaos together made her smile.

Al's grin cracked wide. "There is my girl," he said, ruffling her hair with the fondness of someone who did not ask permission. Lukas gave a single nod, brisk and respectful, his eyes softening a fraction.

Damian followed, descending with his usual economy of motion, already murmuring to Lukas. Without preamble, he turned to Evie. "Go with Al. I will be at One Hundred."

No explanation. No need.

She fell into step beside Al, who was already striding for the car as if London might be repaved in his wake.

Behind them, James emerged, haggard and immaculate. His suit was flawless. His eyes were not.

"You survived," Evie said with a sideways smile.

"Barely," James muttered, a ghost of a grin. "Think I danced with a duchess. Might have insulted a prince."

"That is how you know it was a proper night," Al barked.

Evie chuckled. For the first time since Rome, the knot in her spine eased.

Under it, the weight remained. Veronica's memory. The cold finality. That silence lived in her now, a permanent resident.

She was in.

There was no going back.

Al drove the way he walked, steady and sure. London slid past in wet sheets.

"Tomorrow is not theater," he said, eyes on the road. "It is accounting. Answer what is asked and nothing else. If they push, give them less."

"And if they smile?"

"Assume the teeth are real."

She almost smiled. "Latin?"

"You will hear the question. You will say 'accipio.' Out loud. Once."

She nodded and watched the rain belt the bridge rails, a thin silver curtain between now and what came next.

At One Hundred, the tempo shifted.

The induction team was entrenched, huddled over ceremonial scripts and encrypted schematics, tension humming like static before a storm. At the center, on a polished black table, sat a velvet-lined box. Open. Waiting.

Damian stood beside it, turning a ring slowly between his fingers. Heavy gold, plain but for a Latin inscription inside the band. No embellishment. No vanity.

Only permanence.

Evie arrived for a short walk-through. A staffer read from a cream folder, voice low and careful.

"You will be addressed by name. You will stand. You will be asked if you accept the oath."

"I answer 'accipio,'" she said, letting the word settle. The ring was measured against her knuckle, the weight exact without flourish. A pen hovered, then paused. Not yet

"Again," the staffer said.

"Accipio."

They closed the folder. The room's hum resumed.

James hovered at Damian's elbow, silent and attentive.

"I want the Knightsbridge house signed over to Evie," Damian said, voice low and final.

James blinked once. "That is significant."

"It is appropriate," Damian said. He did not look up. He did not need to. "She is not a guest anymore."

James gave a short nod. Understood. Not a gift. A signal. She was not ascending. She was being installed.

Later that evening, James appeared again at the doorway, tie loosened, a glint in his eye. "Sir, just after eight. Al is asking about dinner out."

"No," Damian said without looking up. "In camera. Evie needs to live to see tomorrow."

James bowed, dry as good gin. "I will redirect him to more manageable pursuits."

Dinner was summoned, fast and discreet, quietly extravagant. The team worked into the night, cross-checking every line of the ceremony, rehearsing contingencies, polishing the transition from operative to member with the rigor of a drill.

Outside, London sank into darkness. Inside, One Hundred held its blue glow.

Evie left early with Lukas, the corridor at the Ritz quiet as snowfall. In her suite, she laid out tomorrow's dress, pressed the seams with her palm, and read the ceremony once, slowly. The coin sat on the bedside table, catching a sliver of city light.

She said the word once to the empty room.

"Accipio."

Then she switched off the lamp and let London breathe around her.

By midnight, Damian closed his laptop, the weight of the day settling like a familiar coat. "That is it."

James gathered his notes. They left together, stepping into the cold, glassy hush of the London night.

At home, James stood in his doorway and toed off his shoes, exhaustion finally seeping into his bones. He should have gone straight to bed, but a thought held him.

Evie.

In less than a year, she had moved from shadow to significance. Her name already threaded the Collective's highest corridors, edged with legend.

And him.

He smiled wryly. He played his part quietly and well. A supporting character in someone else's myth.

On the sofa, eyes drifting shut, the thought curled tighter.

Maybe someday.

A ring. A house in Knightsbridge. A nod from the man at the top.

But not yet.

Not yet.

Chapter 23

Damian woke to a rare indulgence: a quiet London morning and sunlight filtering through heavy curtains. He blinked once, disoriented, then settled deeper into the weight of the duvet. It was nearly ten, uncharacteristic, but the rest had done him good. For once, he allowed himself the simple luxury of stillness.

His hand found the phone on the nightstand. Notifications blinked, quiet but insistent. Most could wait. Today could wait. One message did not: a flagged document from James, listing companies marked for liquidation. Clean work, ruthless in its efficiency. He remembered the first such list he had ever signed, years ago in a smaller office with cheaper glass, the pen too light in his hand, a mentor's voice like gravel saying, Decide cleanly or do not decide at all. He typed a short reply, "Proceed. Begin paperwork," and set the device down; the outside world held at bay a moment longer.

The shower was hot and bracing. Water sluiced away the remnants of sleep, replacing them with clarity. He dressed in casual trousers, a collared shirt, and a lightweight jacket. His thoughts drifted to Evie. She would be sequestered today, as tradition demanded. No contact. No distractions. The ceremony is at eight.

Still, an odd energy tugged at him. He could not sit still.

He stepped out of the Ritz and into the city's living heartbeat. Morning London: smudged light, sharp air, the scent of wet stone and coffee. He walked without direction, letting the city set his pace. Delivery trucks clattered. Street vendors lifted shutters. He remembered a different morning, years back, when he had walked this same stretch with a ring newly pressed into his palm and the strange feeling that his name had been soldered to something larger than himself. The weight had felt cold then. Today it felt exact.

A small bookshop caught his eye between a wine bar and a tailor. He wandered in, fingers skimming spines until one title arrested him, an early printing of a twentieth-century work on political strategy, its jacket worn but intact. He had quoted it from memory in rooms where men mistook calm for consent. The copy he had once owned was filled with marginalia in a younger hand. He bought this one without comment and went back into the day.

A day of reading in the park called. Children shrieked at one end, chasing bubbles in the damp grass. An old man scattered breadcrumbs for indifferent pigeons. Damian found a bench beneath a half-bare tree and opened the book with the reverence reserved for ancient texts and old friends. He read a line he had once underlined twice. He thought of Evie standing in his study at Knightsbridge, the first winter she had been there, her laughter catching in the wainscoting after a long dinner, her hands buried in the sleeves of his coat on the walk back. He had told himself then that she was useful. The truth had arrived later.

For the first time in days, the static hum in his mind stilled.

He read. He watched. He listened. Hours passed unnoticed. He let them.

By late afternoon, the light softened, thin and gold. He closed the book, thumb resting on the worn cover. For a few stolen hours, he had been a man, not a strategist, not a custodian of other people's storms.

The return to the Ritz was unhurried.

Back in his suite, ritual resumed its reign. The ceremony allowed no slack. A second shower, colder. White tie is unforgiving, the Savile

Row tailor had told him the first time, guiding his hands at the mirror until the knot lay true. Shirt starched to severity. Bow tie exact. Platinum cufflinks gleaming. The black coat, cut for power and tailored within a breath of its life, settled over him like armor. He looked, for a quiet second, at the empty chair by the window and thought of the chair in the anteroom where he had once waited alone, twenty minutes that had felt like a year.

A knock at the door.

Lukas stood there, impeccable, expression carved in stone. "Time to go, Herr Damian," he said, checking his watch with understated gravity.

Damian nodded once. Together, they descended.

Al was already in the lobby, holding court at the bar, resplendent in evening tails. He lifted a glass in salute as they passed, a soldier's blessing in crystal. There had been nights when that same hand had steadied him on a stairwell after the kind of phone call that shortens lives.

James waited off to the side, the only one not in full regalia. Sharp black suit, crisp white shirt, elegant but reserved. Damian met his eye and offered a brief nod. James returned it with the crispness of a blade raised in salute. He remembered the first week James had worked for him, the careful way he had asked a hard question at the right time. It had told Damian everything he needed to know.

It was time.

Chapter 24

Evie woke before dawn, long before the alarm could intrude. Pale, uncertain light filtered through the tall windows, softening the sharp corners of the suite. She lay still, listening to the muted hum of London below, delivery vans groaning, a siren carried thin across the rooftops, the restless heartbeat of a city that never fully slept.

Eight p.m. The ceremony. Until then, seclusion. No calls. No interruptions. Lukas had delivered the decree the night before with a formality that brooked no argument. He had stood at her door like a sentry, his posture absolute, his voice devoid of indulgence. You will rest. You will prepare. You will speak to no one but the appointed staff. He had not lingered, had not explained. He had simply turned and left, leaving the weight of the order behind him like a seal pressed in wax.

She sat up slowly, muscles tight from a restless night. Rome still haunted the edges of her mind: Veronica's betrayal, the act, the blood. The weight had not lessened. It was not meant to. That was the point.

Barefoot, she drew back the curtain. London sprawled beneath her, gray, endless, indifferent. Morning mist hung low, veiling rooftops, softening spires into smudges of shadow. A double-decker bus lumbered along Piccadilly, oblivious to what the evening would bring. The city was alive with its own small dramas, traffic, commerce, quarrels, and reconciliations, while she waited above it, apart from it. Tomorrow it would feel different. Tomorrow, she would not just walk its streets. She would own her place within them.

The suite had been provisioned with ascetic care: simple meals on covered trays, a selection of teas, meditation prompts written in Lukas's hand, and a leather-bound notebook she had not touched. A note rested on the desk in his careful script: Use the time. Prepare your mind.

She tried. Silence became her companion. She showered long, steam wrapping her like armor. She drank her coffee in measured sips, the bitterness grounding her. She opened the notebook, stared at its blank page, then wrote a single word: Why. She stared at it for a long while before closing the cover.

Her mind circled. Venice. The bullet with her name on it, pressed into her palm by Damian's hand. The night she nearly ceased to exist. Damian himself, with his impossible calm, his relentless will. The way he had fought to bring her here, to this point. She thought of the weight he carried, and of what she owed him, and of what she owed herself.

By early afternoon, a discreet knock. When she opened the door, no attendant waited; only a garment bag, sleek and black, hung from the handle. Beside it, a velvet case bearing the Umbra sigil, heavy with unspoken meaning. The corridor beyond was empty, silent. No footsteps receded down the hall. The delivery was ritual, not errand.

Inside the bag lay the dress Lukas had chosen. Floor-length black, long sleeves, a silhouette clean and spare. Tailored for power without vanity. No embellishment. No distraction. The fabric carried weight when she lifted it, as though woven with the gravity of the night itself.

The velvet case held a single item: a ring, silver, its surface etched with the faint suggestion of the Collective's sigil. Not to be worn yet. Not until the moment. But its presence was undeniable, like a verdict waiting on the table.

The hours crawled. She tried the tea, found it thin, and left the cup half-finished. She paced the suite, memorizing its angles, its windows, the muted artwork on the walls. She tried to meditate, to slow her breathing, but her thoughts pressed in, insistent. She lay on the bed, eyes closed, drifting into a half-dream of marble corridors and masked faces, of music echoing from somewhere she could not reach. She woke with her heart pounding, the room unchanged, the silence intact.

At six, another knock. Lukas again.

This time, he spoke through the door as if reciting a line from an old rite. "Half an hour."

There was no impatience in it, no softness either. Only precision, the cadence of a man who had delivered such words before. The reminder was not for her alone. It was for the order itself, a measured step in a ritual larger than both of them.

Evie stood for a long moment after he left, letting the words settle like dust on polished wood.

She dressed with methodical care. She lifted the gown and stepped into it slowly, as though each movement locked her further into place. No jewelry. Hair pinned up, severe but elegant. Makeup minimal, almost stark, her features sharpened to clarity. When she finished, she caught her reflection and stilled.

She did not see the girl who had slipped through Heathrow with steel strapped to her thighs. She did not see the woman who had stalked Istanbul's streets or knelt in the Venetian palazzo under Damian's gaze. She saw something forged. A blade honed by fire and purpose, stripped of ornament, sharpened to its edge.

At seven, the final knock.

Lukas.

This time, he entered. He closed the door quietly behind him, stood tall, and studied her. His eyes moved with soldier's thoroughness, but when they met hers, they carried something else, an appraisal not of her attire but of her readiness.

"You look prepared," he said, voice even. But beneath it, she caught the flicker, approval, pride, something tightly leashed.

For a moment, she thought he might say more. That he might offer comfort, or warning, or memory of all she had endured to reach this point. But Lukas was Lukas. He held his silence with the weight of stone.

Evie met his gaze and exhaled, steady. "Yes," she said.

He gave the smallest nod, one soldier to another, one custodian to the charge he had shepherded through fire. "Shall we?"

She stepped into the corridor; the heels of her shoes were silent on the carpet. The air outside the suite was cooler, touched with the faint scent of polish and stone. Each step carried her further from solitude, closer to ceremony. Lukas walked half a pace behind, sentinel and witness, guiding her toward an altar only she could ascend.

And as the corridor stretched ahead, Evie understood. This was not merely an evening of ritual or recognition. It was the closing of a life, and the beginning of one that would no longer belong entirely to her.

Chapter 25

The motorcade moved quietly through the early evening streets of London, flanked by blacked-out chase vehicles that drew no attention but meant everything. Inside the lead car, Evie sat in silence beside Lukas, the smooth hum of the engine beneath them doing little to calm her nerves. Her hands rested in her lap, fingers curled inward, nails biting lightly into her palms.

The building was unmarked, its brutalist exterior giving no hint of what lay within. But Evie knew. The Umbra Collective's London conclave: a private gallery above ground, a sanctuary of shadows below.

Lukas escorted her inside, where every detail had been arranged with solemn care. Soft lighting glinted off marble floors. A long corridor opened before them, guarded at each end. As they walked, Evie caught brief reflections in the dark glass: her own composed figure, Lukas a step behind, and nothing else.

At the final set of doors, he stopped her. "You go on alone from here," he said quietly.

Evie nodded, pulse loud in her ears.

The doors opened.

She stepped into a room unlike anything she had imagined. It was cavernous and silent, lit only by pendant lights that cast warm pools across the black stone floor. A ring of chairs, twenty, spaced evenly, encircled a central dais. Each seat was occupied by a member of the

Committee, all in black. Faces lay in shadow, presence unmistakable. The final chair, the twenty-first, sat empty. Damian's.

At the center stood a marble plinth. Upon it, a black velvet pillow bearing a single ring, heavy gold, inset with an obsidian cabochon carved with the Umbra seal.

Damian waited at the far end, dressed in a full white tie, his platinum ring glinting under the lights. He did not smile. He did not speak. He held her gaze, steady and unwavering, and gave the faintest nod.

Evie stepped forward.

Each footfall echoed. Measured. Intentional.

She halted before the plinth.

From the shadows, a voice emerged. Female, French accented. "Evangeline Blackstone. You stand before the Committee. You have been nominated, tried, and provisionally accepted. Before you receive the insignia of membership, you will respond to three questions."

Evie drew a breath and inclined her head. "Yes."

Another voice, male, clipped British.

"Abnegasne priora foedera? Et nunc tibi vincula Umbrae imponis, pro eius commodis, eius iuribus futurisque?"

"Ita, abnego. Et imponor."

A third voice. American. Warmer. "Intellegisne societatem hanc perpetuam esse? Exitus non conceditur, solum exigitur?"

"Intellego."

Silence held.

Then the Frenchwoman again.

"Promittisne fidem, silentium, et servitium in aeternum? Et si oportet, cum vita ipsa?"

Evie's voice was clear. "Accipio."

A ripple passed through the circle.

A fourth voice, old, Italian, faintly amused, intoned, "Admittere novam lucem."

The others responded in unison, "Et tenebris vivere."

Damian stepped forward. He took the ring from the pillow and held it in his palm. His voice was level and grave.

"With this ring, you are bound to the Umbra Collective. With this vow, you enter our trust."

He took her hand.

The ring slid onto her finger.

It was heavier than she expected.

Damian's eyes met hers. "Welcome."

A soft chime echoed above.

One by one, the committee members stood, then turned and left in silence, like shadows dispersing.

Only Damian and Evie remained in the circle of light. She looked down at the ring, and the silence stretched.

As the final echo of the chime faded, members of the inner council came one by one to offer Evie quiet congratulations. The gestures were restrained but genuine, a rare currency in this room. She answered with calm grace, though her heart was still pounding.

The Chamberlain stepped forward with a bow and led them through wide oak doors into a private dining room steeped in history and power. The long table gleamed under the weight of crystal and silver, lit by the soft glow of a towering chandelier. Conversation resumed in low tones, faces relaxed now that the formalities were behind them.

Evie took her seat between Damian and a quiet, sharp-eyed woman she had not met. Courses arrived without fanfare, an elegant sequence of classic European fare, expertly executed and precisely portioned. Champagne, Burgundy, and Bordeaux flowed freely but never to excess. The meal was ceremonial as much as celebratory, punctuated by occasional toasts but never names. In Umbra, anonymity was a principle, even among allies.

Damian remained composed, his attention split between the table and Evie. He said little but raised his glass when it mattered.

When the final course was cleared and coffee and Armagnac made their rounds, Damian stood and crossed to her. The hum of conversation continued, but the moment between them felt cordoned off, private.

He took her hand, then reached into his coat pocket. "I nearly forgot," he said softly, placing a set of keys in her palm.

Evie turned them over, recognizing the shape and the small enamel tag. Her breath caught.

The Knightsbridge house.

The place where she had spent holidays, where he had first begun to test her potential. Silent breakfasts. Shadowed debriefings. A warmth that had almost become something more.

She looked up, uncertain. "Damian…"

His expression was unreadable, but kind. "It is yours now. You will need a base in London."

She searched his face for an echo and found only a faint nod before he stepped back.

It was not a love letter.

It was trust.

And it was enough.

She closed her hand around the keys and whispered, "Thank you."

Across the room, council members were rising again. The evening was drawing to a close. Tomorrow, the real work would begin.

Evie stood a little taller.

She was one of them.

There would be no going back.

Al, seated nearby with a glass of Armagnac, leaned in and grinned. "Grab the keys before he changes his mind." He winked, then added, gentler, "I cannot give you a second house, but I am having it redecorated for you. My interior specialist's card. Set a time. Make it yours."

Evie was briefly speechless. Overwhelmed, she hugged him hard. "Thank you," she whispered, voice thick.

When she stepped back, her gaze drifted to Damian, and tears welled. Weeks ago, her name had been engraved on a bullet. Now, a ring on her finger, keys to a life she had never dared imagine. House, belonging, trust. No one prepares you for this.

"I do not know what to say," she told him, trembling.

Damian's smile touched the corners of his eyes. "You do not have to say anything. You are home now. You are one of us. You will be looked after."

As the room emptied and the grandeur faded back to formality, Evie rode with Damian toward the Ritz, turning the ring on her hand, watching the metal catch the low light. He said nothing. The glances he gave her were enough.

"I should confess something," she said at last, voice low. "When I saw the keys, I hoped you would take me there again."

He did not answer at once. Only the hum of the engine and the soft rhythm of the tires. Her words settled between them, light and heavy at the same time.

Then he spoke, calm and measured. "Evie, the house is not about where we have been. It is about where you are going."

She looked down, the keys pressing into her palm. His answer was not cruel, but it cut. "It was ours once," she said softly. "It is where you taught me everything. It is where I," She stopped, the last thought too dangerous to name.

He exhaled, a small, almost regretful smile tugging at his mouth. "It was a place. Nothing more. What matters is what you make of it now."

She turned to the window. Her reflection blurred in the glass. Frustration tightened in her chest, and with it, resolve.

"So, you are saying it is up to me."

He did not look at her. "It always has been."

She nodded slowly and let the silence settle.

The car moved through the quiet London streets. The past lingered in the space between them. The future waited ahead, vast, unclaimed, and hers.

Chapter 26

The grand façade of the London Ritz loomed against the night like a monument to restraint. Its glowing windows promised comfort, but to Damian, they felt more like distant stars, unreachable and sterile in their perfection.

The doorman's white gloves and polished brass fittings caught the glow of the streetlamps. A faint perfume of roses lingered in the lobby, cut by the dry scent of waxed marble. Guests moved with practiced elegance, their laughter pitched low, their eyes lingering too long on Damian and Evie as they crossed the floor.

He stepped out of the car first, movements crisp and efficient, every detail controlled. Logistics were armor. Details, distractions. Behind him, Evie followed, the soft click of her heels a delicate, rhythmic counterpoint to the silence between them.

The elevator hummed its quiet ascent, a low mechanical whisper between two people who had said everything and nothing. Damian kept his gaze ahead, but he could feel her watching him. Not with judgment. Something worse. Hope.

When the doors opened, he gestured for her to go first. Always the gentleman. Especially when it cost him.

Outside her suite, she turned to face him. "Goodnight, Damian," she said. Softly. A thread of excitement. Vulnerability. Maybe even an invitation.

"Goodnight, Evie. And congratulations." Polite. Measured. Final.

She waited a beat, long enough for a different answer, then nodded. Damian walked away without looking back. He felt her gaze following him, hot and silent, all the way to his door.

Inside, the click of the lock sounded too loud. He stood still; palms pressed against the wood as if anchoring himself. Then he exhaled sharply, as though purging what he had not said.

Another five minutes. That was all it would have taken. Another five minutes in her orbit, and the walls he had spent years building would have come down like wet paper. She did not know how close she came.

He shook his head, stripped off his bow tie, and moved through the room with purpose. Jacket off. Shoes aligned. Everything in its place. He imposed order on the chaos inside him, each ritual a safeguard.

He picked up the phone.

"Good evening, Lukas." His tone was smooth, composed. "We will fly to Salzburg at eleven. Please have the plane and ground transport ready." Salzburg was not a business. It was a pause, a sliver of reprieve after Rome and the investiture, nothing more.

Next, he dialed again.

"James, thank you for handling the Leonardo file," Damian said, his voice shifting warmer. "The execution was exemplary."

He noted a figure on the hotel notepad for James's bonus, then crossed to the closet.

A suede caramel blazer, a grey cashmere turtleneck, and grey slacks. Quiet power. Armor for tomorrow.

Under the hot water, the tightness in his shoulders began to loosen, but not enough. As he dressed for bed, the thought of Evie lingered, persistent beneath the surface. She had stood there, radiant and unsure, waiting for him to reach out. And he had done what he always did: closed the door.

He lay down and stared at the ceiling. Sleep did not come.

Morning broke cool and pale over London, the air carrying the damp edge of November. Damian was already awake when the call came for their car. Lukas moved with quiet care, making sure luggage was ready, documents in order, and timing exact.

The drive to the private hangar was quick at that hour. Security recognized them at once, the gates swinging open without a word. The Gulfstream waited on the apron, crew in place, engines starting a low, steady hum. They boarded without delay; the cabin already set for the short flight to Austria.

The Alps rose from the clouds as they crossed into Austrian airspace, peaks dusted with the season's first snow. Salzburg appeared in the valley below, its spires and rooftops bright in the thin, slanting light. The car was waiting on the tarmac.

Just beyond the aircraft, Lukas shook Damian's hand, then Evie's. "I will head to Vienna first," he said. "The flat needs a sweep, and there are matters to settle. I will join you tomorrow."

He stepped into a second car and was gone.

The drive into the Old Town was quiet, streets edged with bare branches and late autumn leaves drifting in the breeze. The Goldener Hirsch greeted them with its centuries-old calm, polished wood, warm textiles, and the faint scent of beeswax and stone. The staff bowed discreetly; their recognition never spoken but understood.

They spent the afternoon as tourists, something neither had done in too long. From the Archbishop's palace, they looked over the city, the

Salzach cutting a silver path through the rooftops. They walked the Getreidegasse, past wrought-iron shop signs and windows glowing with warm light. Damian paused once to buy her a silk scarf in deep green, its sheen catching the afternoon sun. He did not explain the choice, and she did not ask, but she wound it once around her neck as though it had always been hers.

At a café tucked in a narrow alley, the brass tables glowed under soft lamplight. Evie ordered a slice of Sachertorte, its glossy chocolate glaze catching the light, while Damian chose a plate of apple strudel with vanilla sauce.

She closed her eyes as she tasted the cake, savoring the richness. Damian, indifferent to her dessert, broke a piece of pastry with precise ease, the steam fragrant with cinnamon and baked apples.

"You've been here before," she said, watching the way his gaze lingered not on the plate but on the square beyond the window, where students drifted past with books under their arms and bicycles rattling over cobblestones.

"Many times," he replied. "Salzburg rewards repetition. Each visit shows you something different. The light on the mountains, the rhythm of the markets, the silence when the students leave for winter."

She tilted her head, intrigued. "And what do you notice now?"

"That it is orderly without being rigid. Civilized, but not soft. A city that remembers its past and refuses to apologize for it."

Her lips curved faintly. "Spoken like a man who feels at home here."

Damian regarded her for a moment, the ghost of a smile tugging at the corner of his mouth. "I feel at home where order still holds. It never lasts as long as it should."

For a while, they sat in silence, the clink of cutlery and the low murmur of German voices filling the space around them. Outside, the bells of the Franciscan church rang the half-hour, solemn and resonant. Evie traced the rim of her coffee cup, considering his words. She wondered how much of him was shaped by cities like this, how many walls he had built not only for defense, but to preserve something fragile beneath.

Damian broke the quiet with a single question. "Do you like it?"

She nodded slowly. "It feels…honest. Like the city isn't trying to be more than it is. I like that."

He raised his cup in a small salute. "Then you understand why I return."

As the evening settled, they made their way to St. Peter's. In the forecourt, braziers glowed, and the air was rich with mulled wine. They drank from heavy mugs, the spice and warmth a welcome counter to the cooling night. Inside, the vaulted stone refectory held a steady heat. Candlelight flickered on ancient walls, and each course arrived with unhurried grace, the music of a harpsichord drifting in the background.

Damian raised his glass once, studying her across the flicker of flame. "You should remember this," he said quietly. "Moments like these. They do not last."

She met his eyes, unflinching. "That's why they matter."

His gaze held hers, something unreadable behind it. "You're learning faster than most."

"Or maybe I just listen," she countered.

For a moment, the corners of his mouth threatened a smile, but it never fully formed.

After dinner, they walked through moonlit streets. The air was crisp, carrying a faint scent of woodsmoke from chimneys. Damian glanced at her profile in the silver light and felt the stillness that came when the noise of the world fell away.

"Do you miss it?" she asked quietly.

"Miss what?"

"Before Umbra."

He paused, steps slowing over the worn cobblestones. "I do not remember enough of it to miss."

She nodded, accepting the truth of it, but the quiet that followed carried weight.

They crossed the Domplatz, their footsteps muted by centuries of stone. The cathedral tower rose above them, throwing long shadows.

By the time they reached the Goldener Hirsch, the church bells struck midnight. The sound followed them inside, fading only when they reached the corridor to their rooms.

They parted without ceremony.

In her room, Evie removed her coat and let her gaze rest on the Umbra ring on her hand. For a moment, she studied it, feeling again the weight of its meaning. She turned it slowly, the silver catching candlelight, a reminder that beauty and burden could share the same form.

When she lay down, sleep came almost at once, deep and without dreams.

Chapter 27

Evie woke to the low murmur of rain brushing the windows. Distant thunder rolled like a warning. She lay still a moment, cocooned in warmth, then rose and drew back the curtains.

Her phone glowed in the dim room. An inbound message from Damian: I don't want to wake you, but when you are up, we need to go.

She was out of bed in an instant, the residue of sleep gone before her feet hit the floor. A quick shower chased the chill from the old stone walls. Clothes on, bag packed, she reached the lobby within minutes.

Damian was already there at a small table near the window, a silver pot of coffee steaming in the November light. He looked up and smiled, but the current under it was wrong. This was not routine.

The contrast with last night was sharp. Celebration and warmth had given way to something quieter. He spoke without preface.

"Egon was killed last night. In his home."

The words landed like a dropped stone. Quiet. Final.

Evie's breath hitched. Disbelief, anger, dread flickered across her face. Egon's steady presence, his pointed advice. More than a senior figure, a stabilizing force.

Outside, mist tapped the roof in a steady rhythm, as if keeping time with the weight settling in her chest.

"The details are still coming in," Damian said, voice even with steel under it. "Egon returned to his house on the Gold Coast last night. His assistant arrived this morning, got no answer, let himself in." A beat. "They found him in bed. Two shots. Clean."

Evie closed her eyes. The sleek lines of Egon's lakeside home. The assistant moves through silent rooms. Two shots, close range. Not a killing. A message.

She swallowed hard.

No one said it, but it was clear: if someone could reach him in Zurich, no one in the Collective was untouchable.

They left the Goldener Hirsch after breakfast, Salzburg holding the quiet of a late autumn morning. The air was cool and clean, touched with woodsmoke from the hills. Damian's pace was steady, collar turned up; Evie matched his stride without a word.

The driver waited just beyond the pedestrian zone. Cobblestones gave way to an open road and then the airport perimeter.

Lukas had left the day before by train to Vienna, then on to Zurich. He would meet them upon arrival.

At the FBO, their jet stood ready. Damian exchanged a quiet word with the captain and boarded, Evie close behind. The flight to Zurich was smooth, the sky a pale wash of November. Damian read secured updates without comment, his expression fixed. Evie sat back, thoughts caught between last night's warmth and the morning's edge.

They landed just past midday. Umbra muscle waited at the steps, silent in dark coats and gloves. Damian and Evie took the lead SUV. The convoy moved off with unhurried discipline.

Their route looped past the main terminal as Lukas's flight from Vienna reached the gate. He appeared through a controlled exit with a single bag, eyes already searching. A clasp of hands with Damian, a nod to Evie, and he slid into the seat.

The drive south to Cham was uneventful. Bare fields under a soft gray sky. The lake, then the gates of Villa Villette. Inside, stillness broke. Vehicles lined the drive, polished flanks catching the muted light. Council members arrived and clustered in low conversation. Urgency lived in the air, a shared understanding that the ground had shifted.

Damian took the veranda steps in measured strides. The SUV eased toward the garage and vanished.

Evie followed, stretching stiffness from travel. Across the courtyard, Lukas moved in calm orbit, greeting arrivals, directing staff, readying the house. Engines ticked as they cooled. Passengers emerged in dark coats and purposeful silence. The inner council was gathering.

Damian paused beneath the awning, scanning faces with a look equal parts welcome and assessment. Evie started toward him, gravel crunching underfoot, the lake wind carrying faint woodsmoke.

He stood flanked by members of the inner council. Coats damp. Expressions set. Around them, two dozen operatives formed a silent perimeter. Heavily armed. Sunglasses on despite the gray.

This was not protocol. This was a response.

Damian caught her eye and raised a hand. Hold back. She obeyed, taking the edge of the space.

She watched. Not fear. Something colder. Dread.

Minutes passed. Damian stepped away from the circle and crossed to her. His shoulders were wet, his movement unchanged.

Lukas appeared and set a shawl across her shoulders. She nodded thanks.

"You are not to go anywhere alone," Damian said. "Even on the grounds. Full protection."

She nodded. No protest.

"I want to go to the range," she said quietly.

Damian considered, then gave one nod.

"Ten minutes," Lukas said. "I will accompany her."

"Take a full team," Damian replied.

Mist thickened as they walked to the gun house, Lukas a step ahead, a four-man detail spread around them.

In the range, the familiar weight of the gun brought a narrow comfort. Focus. Control. Something she could hold.

She took her stance and adjusted her grip. The shot cracked through damp air.

Another.

Again.

Each steadier than the last.

She could not fix what had happened. She could sharpen herself.

Mist drummed the roof like a metronome. Lukas, watchful and exacting, guided her through each drill with quiet care. Minimal touch. Murmured correction. Praise only when earned.

Each shot dulled the echo of the morning. Egon, in his house, receded to the edge. The clean mechanics of a weapon moved to the front.

Under Lukas's direction, her groupings tightened. She moved faster between targets. Held steadier. He demanded more; she delivered.

For a while, the gun house was a haven.

When the mist lightened, they walked back. The earlier buzz had shifted to a thinner, tenser quiet.

Staff moved with sober efficiency. Lunch was underway. The air held a kind of anticipation that needed no name.

In the dining room, the full council had assembled. Damian sat at the head, still as marble. Faces along the table were carved by restraint. The timing, hours after Evie's investiture, made the message unmistakable.

Evie did not linger. She went upstairs, changed into a clean sweater, and curled into the window seat with a book she did not read, eyes on the mist outside.

Downstairs, Lukas resumed his post outside the dining room. Silent. Steady.

Lunch came and went. Plates cleared with ghostlike grace. Little conversation. The scrape of silver on porcelain. Paper lifted. Orders taken.

The council stayed cloistered most of the afternoon, dissecting every angle. Strategy. Risk. Loyalty. Betrayal. Egon's murder was an incursion. Their answer would be swift.

By dusk, the doors opened. Members emerged tired, sharp, and resolved. Hands clasped. Orders confirmed. Faces unreadable.

Bags were packed. Vehicles queued. Commands flowed in a practiced cadence. The villa stood as a fulcrum.

Evie came downstairs, her steps soft in the hush. Outside, the mist had cleared, leaving a clean scent in the air.

Damian waited on the veranda, steady amid departures. She joined him.

Together, they saw off each council member, handshakes and kisses on the cheek. Formal, and not only formal.

With the last car gone, the villa exhaled.

Chapter 28

Damian went straight to the kitchen. Cooking was how he processed. For some, meditation. For him, mise en place.

He set a fresh duck on the butcher block. The faint, gamey aroma hinted at what would come. A heavy pan. Olive oil from Dario's groves in Umbria. The gas clicked and flared. The oil shimmered.

He began with a sofritto: onion, celery, carrot, garlic. Then the duck, joints separated with care. The kitchen filled with the beginnings of comfort.

He crossed to the stereo and chose von Suppé's Charge of the Light Brigade. Brass and gallop filled the space, drama echoing the mix of chaos and resolve inside him.

The duck hit the pan and sizzled. Passata, a splash of stock, a cinnamon stick, a pour of white wine. Steam rose. He eased the flame low and steady and let the sauce reduce. Let his mind do the same.

Evie stepped in and watched a moment.

"I thought I would cook tonight," he said, still at the stove.

"I see that," she said, gentle, curious.

He washed his hands, reached for an Amarone, uncorked it with a soft pop, and poured three glasses.

"Evie, I will tell you everything," he said, meeting her gaze. "But not tonight. Tonight, I want to make dinner. And sit. And not think about the rest."

"Understood," she said, and took the glass.

They clinked. The wine slid down warm and deep. Steam and music filled the kitchen. Not peace, but close enough to pretend.

Lukas appeared in the doorway, drawn by scent and sound. "I smelled ragù halfway up the stairs," he said. "If you are playing cavalry music, it must be duck night."

"Just in time for the oranges," Damian answered.

"Good," Lukas said, rolling up his sleeves. "I like this part."

They moved in a practiced rhythm, zesting and juicing blood oranges. Citrus brightened the room, cutting through meat and wine. The pan hissed and sighed.

"The staff had a bet," Lukas said. "They prepared pappardelle expecting Bolognese."

"Have I become predictable?" Damian asked.

"Not predictable. Familiar. I have been in your service more than half my life."

"At least I surprised you with the duck," Damian said, dry.

From her perch at the counter, Evie laughed. "Two handsome men in the kitchen, and both can cook. What more could a girl ask for?"

They exchanged a look and broke into smiles.

Lukas dropped the fresh pappardelle into boiling water. Damian finished the sauce, then tossed the pasta through, adding a splash of water for silk. He turned off the gas.

"Dinner is served," he said, satisfied.

They set the table. The air held ragù and fresh pasta, warm and inviting. Conversation loosened.

"Damian, this is incredible," Evie said after a bite. "You are going to ruin me for every other meal."

"I would hope so," he said. "It took three hours before it agreed to taste like anything."

"So," Evie said, eyes bright, "funniest kitchen story?"

Damian took a sip. Lukas was faster.

"West Africa," he said. "Government minister. Lovely setting. Damian insists on dessert. Cherries jubilee. He is at the stove, all going to plan, then gunfire."

Evie's smile faltered. "Wait, what?"

"Bullets flying," Lukas said, enjoying himself. "Security shouting. The minister under the table. Damian keeps stirring as if he is auditioning for a cooking show."

"Cherries jubilee is about timing," Damian said. "You cannot rush it."

"A boy, maybe sixteen, storms in, hands shaking with an old 1911," Lukas went on. "He hits, in order: Damian's wineglass, the bowl of cherries."

"Twice," Damian added.

"Twice," Lukas agreed. "Then the ladle. The one he was using to pour the kirsch."

Evie stared. "Oh my God."

"This angered him," Lukas said, solemnly.

"The ladle had been in my family since that afternoon," Damian said with mock gravity. "Practically an heirloom."

"The boy freezes under that look," Lukas said, laughing. "Then Damian raises the ladle and runs at him. Remember, there is kirsch in it, it is on fire, liquid pouring out. So, the boy who came to shoot his first minister is now chased down the street by an angry descendant of Escoffier with a flaming ladle."

"Distant relation on my mother's side," Damian said with a wink. "Hardly worth mentioning."

"You chased him?" Evie gasped, laughing.

"Five hundred meters," Lukas said, proud. "Mid service. When he came back, security almost did not let him into his own house."

"I may have resembled a lunatic," Damian said.

"And the best part?" Lukas finished. "He completed the cherries jubilee and served it to applause."

Damian slipped into his study and returned with a mounted plaque: a bent, scorched ladle with two neat holes. The brass tag read: Wounded in the Line of Duty.

Evie stared. "This is absurd."

"Respect," Damian said, perfectly solemn. "He was wounded in the line of duty."

Laughter rolled, deep and helpless. Tears pricked at the eyes. The image of a flaming ladle and a fleeing gunman cut the day's heaviness cleanly in two.

"I always thought your stories were half exaggeration," Evie said, breathless. "Never again."

They cleaned the kitchen together. The staff stood ready, but Damian insisted: those who made the mess cleaned it.

Hands busy, voices light, laughter echoing in the beams.

Lukas mentioned emails and excused himself. Damian and Evie drifted to the small library, a room tucked away from the world. Something orchestral played low. Shelves of weathered volumes breathed paper and polish and time.

They settled into armchairs. A low fire flickered. Conversation ran out, and they let the silence stretch. Not awkward. Companionable. Under it, something stirred.

Evie watched him. She remembered other nights like this, before Cham, before Rome, before London's weight. When what they shared felt effortless and fragile. She missed that. Missed him. The quiet curve of his smile when his guard slipped.

Tonight, he was hard to read. Polite. Warm. Distant.

Was it caution? Final?

She weighed her next move. One word might bridge the gap. Or widen it.

She let the moment be. The music was balm. The fire was soft. The world, for once, was still.

Fatigue found her at last. She curled on the couch, breathing slowly. Damian glanced over and saw the tension leave her face. She looked younger like this. Vulnerable, at peace.

He watched a while. Something unspoken crossed his features, fondness shaded by a quiet sorrow. He rose, left, and returned with a blanket. He folded it around her. She shifted, nestling deeper.

He brushed a strand of hair from her forehead and set the lightest kiss there.

"Dream the dreams of angels," he murmured.

He straightened, gave her one last look, and slipped out. The music continued, low and steady, as he climbed the stairs alone.

Chapter 29

The morning mist still clung to the trees when Damian found Evie in the drawing room, barefoot, curled into a velvet chair with a mug of tea and a half-finished book in her lap. Her hair was slightly tousled, her eyes distant. She looked up as he entered, reading his mood in an instant.

"You are pacing inside your head," she said softly.

He gave a tight smile. "I need air. Movement. Quiet that is not loaded."

Evie studied him for a beat. "You are going to go crazy here."

"I already am," he admitted, glancing toward the window where the rain had begun to let up. "Mark has everything in hand. He will link with London and keep me informed."

She nodded, sensing something else behind his words.

Damian leaned on the mantel, casual but deliberate. "Let us go to Colmar."

Evie's brow lifted. "Colmar?"

"It is not far. Quiet, beautiful. We will take Seraphina." His eyes flicked to hers, gauging her reaction. "She has not been out in a while."

Evie smiled, the weight of the past few days easing a fraction. "You are really letting me drive Seraphina?"

"I am going to let you learn how to drive her."

They showered, packed for an overnight, and walked to the garage. The Bugatti Tourbillon gleamed, deep metallic paint catching the light like a blade being unsheathed.

Evie approached reverently. "God, she is beautiful."

"You should get used to that feeling."

Evie opened the door and slid into the passenger seat, the leather creaking softly. Damian took the wheel, buckling in with the same calm he brought to boarding a jet.

The engine purred to life, smooth and deep. A sound of restrained power.

Evie grinned. "She does not just whisper, she growls."

"She will roar if you ask nicely."

They drove. The peaks fell away as the lowlands opened. Seraphina settled under his touch, responsive and fluid. Evie watched the way he tilted the wheel through a sweeping curve, the neat heel and toe on a tight descent, the gear change so clean it felt like breath.

"You make it look easy," she said.

"It is when you listen to her."

"You two speak the same language."

"So do you. You will."

Silence returned. Only the rush of the road, clean air, and the steady hum of a machine built for speed and quiet. Not escape. Recovery in motion. A reminder they were still breathing, still choosing direction.

Evie leaned her head against the cool glass, watching mountains mirrored on the lake. "I never get tired of this view," she said. "Unreal."

"It is one of the few things that still feels untouched," Damian said.

"It makes everything else feel manageable," she murmured. "Like the rest of the world can wait."

He let the hum of Seraphina fill the space. Then, "We do not stop enough. We say we will, but something always comes up."

"You chase the next crisis," she said, smiling.

"And you dive into it."

"Touché."

They rolled through Zurich as the city blinked awake. Storefronts opening. Cyclists threading the curves. Life beginning.

"Ever think about leaving it all behind?" Evie asked, watching the lake. "Disappearing somewhere quiet. Living like normal people."

"There is no such thing as normal," he said after a moment. "And there is no leaving this behind. Not for me."

She nodded, and something in her eyes dimmed.

They followed the A1 west, then north toward Basel. Fields flickered by; trees bright with autumn fire. Bern slid past in a blur of arcades and cobbles, then the dark spires of Fribourg. Near the border, the land softened into Alsace, vineyards rippling over hills, stone farmhouses under old oaks.

At the Swiss–French crossing, they were waved through.

"I remember waiting hours for a bored officer to stamp a passport," Damian said.

"You miss it?"

"Not the bureaucracy. I miss knowing the world had edges."

She watched vineyards slide by, green and gold in the late autumn light.

Colmar drew close, a quiet promise. The last kilometers passed in companionable silence. Damian's hand shifted on the wheel. With a flick, Seraphina surged, the engine's growl low and satisfied. The scenery blurred.

"The French are more relaxed about speed limits than the Swiss," he said, grinning.

Evie laughed, exhilarated. "This is the antidote to everything. Speed, sun, no questions."

Mulhouse flashed by like a postcard. The A35 curved toward Colmar, wide and empty. Sunlight glinted along Seraphina's hood. Motion, purpose, possibility.

At Anneau du Rhin, the Bugatti settled into a low purr as Damian cut the ignition. Evie stepped out, crisp air carrying the scent of fuel and anticipation.

A tall man in a tailored jacket approached. "Madame," he said, shaking her hand. "Welcome to Anneau du Rhin. We have been expecting you."

Beside him stood the test driver, compact and steady. "We start with control drills," he said. "Master control. Speed later."

Damian gave Evie a small nod and stepped back to check the perimeter and the security team.

She drew a breath as revving engines rose in a chorus. A different kind of battlefield.

"Let us begin," the representative said. "She is waiting for you."

Evie brushed her fingers along the carbon fiber and smiled. "So am I."

A few paces away, Damian finished with the detail and looked at her not as an operative, but as the woman he had chosen to invest in.

"All set?"

Her eyes caught the light. "Let us do this."

She spent the morning in Seraphina's cockpit, the cabin wrapping her like a fitted glove. The instructor's voice crackled in her headset, precise and unyielding. "Again," as she peeled around hairpins, tires singing.

It was more than speed. It was discipline. Brake before the apex, hold the line, trust the downforce. Suede gloves tightened. Eyes scanned ahead, absorbing data, anticipating every shift.

By midmorning, she stopped thinking about the car. They were no longer separate. The engine's growl matched her pulse, the chassis moved with her breath. Mechanical symbiosis.

Between sessions, she reviewed telemetry on a tablet. Acceleration curves, reaction times, corrections. Analyze. Improve.

Damian watched from a distance, arms crossed, a small, private smile. He did not interrupt. He knew better.

Later came performance drills. Emergency maneuvers. Wet surface handling. A false deer is bolting across the track. She did not flinch. The car shifted beneath her as if waiting for that moment.

By the final session, she was at speeds she would not have dared in the morning. The edge of the track blurred, whispering danger and daring her to blink. She did not.

Helmet off, hair damp against her brow, pulse still thrumming, she walked toward Damian with a grin that had not been there in days.

"I was right to name her Seraphina," she said, wiping her brow. "She is not a car. She is a weapon."

Damian handed her a towel; his eyes unreadable. "She is," he said. "And so are you."

Chapter 30

The sun had slid low, and the paddock smelled of hot rubber and spent fuel. Mechanics moved like practiced shadows around open hoods, torches bobbing across polished metal. It was the small, private chaos of motorsport, the precise kind of disorder that suited people who liked things controlled but raw. Mark approached with a grave line in his face, his gait measured as if he were carrying the weight of the message in his shoulders.

"Damian," he said without preamble. He kept his voice low. "We intercepted a communication. Your name came up. So did the track."

Damian's expression changed in a single, audible shift. He drew himself straighter, the careful mask of veneer filling in. "Thank you, Mark," he said. The words were polite but sharpened at the edges. "It is time to go."

Evie slid into the Bugatti's driver's seat without hesitation. The cockpit smelled of leather and hot metal. Her fingers settled on the wheel as if they belonged there. "Let us get out of here," she said. No question. No tremor.

The engine answered like a living thing. When she released the parking brake, the car lunged into motion, low and sure. Damian settled beside her, scanning the paddock with a practiced calm. The main gate sat ahead, a narrow aperture in the fence, and beyond it the access road that threaded out toward Alsace. At the gate, a nondescript sedan waited, engine idling like a patient animal.

"That car should not be there," Damian said, eyes narrowing. He flicked his head as if scanning the horizon. "Stay calm. Drive past."

Evie did as she was told. The Bugatti glided by, the world slurring at the edges as they picked up speed. In the rearview, the sedan pulled out and fell in behind them, distance closing to a cautionary measure. It assumed itself invisible in the wrong way, the sort of tail that watches without making the mistake of drawing attention.

The pursuit began with the quiet patience of predators. Through winding Alsace lanes, the shadow kept pace, never closing fast, never dropping back entirely. It was a presence in the mirror, a pair of headlights that tracked them like a measured heartbeat. Damian stayed in contact with Mark, weighing options, calibrating reaction to risk. No confrontation in the open. Not with civilians on narrow roads.

They passed vineyards, neat rows feathering the valley sides, small houses set back from the road like careful ornaments. The Bugatti ate distance in smooth strokes; Evie drove with an economy of motion, hands steady, breath even. Her calmness steadied Damian more than anything he had access to.

Near the M35, his patience thinned. He glanced at the mirror and then forward, mapping a plan in a single breath. "We cannot let them follow to the border. Time to end this," he said.

"Tell me," Evie replied.

He outlined it quickly to Mark. "Form a rolling roadblock. Side by side, just under the limit. Close their sightlines. Box them in. On my mark, we accelerate and open a gap."

Mark's voice came back clipped. "Copy. We will move now."

Damian turned to Evie. "Now. Go."

She dropped a gear and pushed the throttle. The car lunged, the engine singing in a high, clean note. Trees smeared into streaks. Speed rose, and the world narrowed to lines and mirrors and the scent of warmed brakes. He called Lukas on a secondary channel. "We are inbound. A tail is on us. Prep the perimeter."

"Security is active," Lukas replied. "Perimeter teams in motion. Expect the convoy."

Damian patched to Umbra's London desk. "Threat at Colmar. Pursuit underway and contained. I want eyes on every node between here and Cham."

"Activating coverage," the woman said. "You will have a secure corridor."

On the road, the plan took shape. Two of Mark's vehicles slipped across both lanes and moved abreast with the Bugatti. They cut the tail's line of sight, sliding into position like phantoms. Drivers trained in these movements, muscle memory replacing hesitation. The sedan found its options narrowed, exposure growing with every mile.

Evie drove them toward two forty. The Bugatti held; it was built for this hunger, powerful and balanced. The tail's reaction was hesitant. With Mark's car boxing them, the sedan attempted a slip and then pulled back, indecision showing as a suggestion rather than a threat.

They did not speak for several kilometers. Between them was only the sound of the engine and the crackle of the radio. Then Damian allowed himself a small, wry comment. "Well driven."

"We were not giving them the last word," she answered without changing her line. Her voice was dry, precise.

When they neared the Swiss border, he shifted their plan. "Speed limit now. We are changing routes." He thumbed the nav and entered the alternate. "We will leave the A1, take the A2 to Egerkingen, through Aarau, then south through Muri to Cham. Indirect. No one will expect it. The Bugatti handles those roads better than anything following."

They threaded through the countryside dotted with chalets and bare vines. Mist curled in the shallow hollows. Evie carved the curves with the confidence of someone used to trusting throttle and line, every movement economical and exact. The rhythm of the road became a kind of meditation, focusing on reducing fear to something manageable.

Status updates arrived in bursts. "Mystery vehicle pulled off near Basel," Mark said at last. "No longer in pursuit. We will regroup at the villa."

"Good," Damian said. The relief was small and sharp. "See you in an hour."

Past Muri, the knife-edge of tension eased. The stone towers of Muri receded in the rear window, small and composed against a flat, ordinary sky. Evie kept her hands light on the wheel. The car ate the first narrow lanes without hurry. Evie kept her speed under the limit. Fields ran by in long green ribbons. Cows lifted their heads and watched them pass, bells chiming in the open air like an old clock. Farmhouses had shutters painted brightly and stacks of wood that said the place had weathered winters and would weather more. They drove on. The road rose and fell with low hills. The sky threw its light across the hedgerows. A distant line of the Alps sat on the horizon, patient and pale. The car smelled faintly of leather and coffee. Evie left the window cracked a fraction so the cold could touch the back of her neck. It kept her awake.

Cham arrived without drama. The road straightened and the first flash of blue opened at the end of the line of trees. Masts pricked the air at the marina like a forest turned to wood. Boats rocked gently against their moorings. The town had a measured air, tasteful in a way the harbor clubs were not. People walked dogs. An old man fed the pigeons. That level of ordinariness was why they had chosen this place.

The villa rose where the trees thinned, a cut of stone in the dimming light, stoic and guarded. The gates opened, and they entered as if returning from a normal day. Lukas and the estate team were already moving, faces set, systems activating.

Mark arrived with the convoy not long after, cars folding into the drive with practiced choreography. Damian allowed a rigid, weary grin to break the tension. "What took you so long?" he asked, deadpan, and in the exchange was a release, a reminder that somewhere beneath the business there were still men who could joke to keep from falling apart.

The reprieve lasted less than an hour. A message slid across one of the secure channels, and the room snapped alert. Mark read it and his face drained. "Another council member is dead," he said. He named the victim. "Count von Klimt. Bavaria. He was out hunting. Long range. Professional."

Damian moved to the hearth and stood; his hands dropped to his sides. The fire warmed the stone but not him. "Where?" he asked.

"Egon in Zurich," Mark said after a beat. "Klimt in Bavaria. This is not scattered. It is coordinated."

Silence pooled at the edges of the room. Two assassinations, days apart, in secure places, by methods that carried the signature of care and distance. It could not be random.

Damian paced once, control never faltering, but tension barely contained. He let the anger shape itself into orders. "This will not do."

His voice sharpened into iron. "Emergency session. London. Tomorrow morning."

The room reacted like a living engine. Mark took his headset. "I will push our German channels. Scrub every movement. Recon the terrain. We find the shooter."

Lukas coldly enumerated measures. "Tighten all travel and house security. Assume nothing is secure. Sweep every manifest. Change every route immediately."

Damian fixed Evie with a look that weighed and contained more than instruction. "Sort our movement to London. Quiet, fast, redundant comms. We are not going in blind."

She straightened and accepted the task with the same calm that had seen them through the chase. The villa shifted shape. Where there had been respite, now there was a machine: phones, screens, maps unfurling, staff moving like a practiced militia. Safe rooms locked, doors sealed, channels encrypted.

Outside, the night lay cool and indifferent. Inside, the world they had built rearranged itself around a single truth. The sanctuary had become headquarters.

Chapter 31

The next morning, Damian, Evie, Lukas, and Mark gathered downstairs just before five. The villa was still, its long corridors lit only by sconces burning against the dark. Outside, the lawns were silver with dew, and mist clung low to the hedgerows. Their expressions were somber and contained, the unspoken truth of the night's news hanging between them.

Two black SUVs rolled to the entrance, engines humming with quiet readiness. The drivers wore plain clothes, but with the posture of men who did not miss details.

At the lead vehicle, Lukas moved first. He took the passenger seat and was already in his comms net, confirming perimeter status, routes, and fallback positions. Mark climbed in behind him, broad shoulders filling the bench seat as he scrolled through overnight briefs. Damian and Evie entered last, settling into the rear. The second SUV closed in behind them, carrying the rest of the security element.

The convoy slipped down the gravel drive, headlights cutting through the mist, and merged onto the A4. The world outside was hushed, towns shuttered and lifeless at this hour, farmhouse lights the only evidence of wakefulness. The air was damp, carrying the smell of wet earth and pine.

Evie rested her gaze on the passing landscape. Lakes lay flat and dark as slate, the surface disturbed only by a ripple of waterfowl lifting at their approach. Roadside trees blurred in bands of shadow, their branches dripping under the weight of fog. The hum of the engine and the hiss of tires on wet asphalt became the only soundtrack, steady and mechanical, almost comforting.

Beside her, Damian sat composed, his posture effortless but unyielding. The only hint of strain lay in his jaw, clenched a fraction too tightly, and in the hand resting against his knee, fingers flexing once before stilling. He had not spoken since the villa, but his silence was not absence; it was weight.

At Zurich Airport, the convoy swung past the commercial terminal toward general aviation. The Gulfstream waited on the apron, its tail light glowing red in the half-dark, engines whispering at idle. The curfew had only just lifted, and they had the first slot. Timing was precision, not convenience.

Mark disembarked first; his economy of movement was almost ritual. He checked bags, gear, and the manifest with quiet exactitude. No word was wasted; none needed to be. Each of them stepped into their roles as if into uniforms, discipline disguising fatigue.

At the foot of the stairs, Damian paused. He scanned the misted apron once, eyes moving from fence line to terminal windows, then up to the faint silhouette of the control tower. Nothing lingered, nothing shifted, yet the ritual of assessment mattered. Only then did he incline his head for Evie to precede him.

The pilot offered a brisk greeting at the door. Damian returned it with the brief nod of a man who valued professionalism above warmth. Before he could step inside, two figures approached across the tarmac from the small terminal. Ernst Müller, tall, his overcoat cutting a severe line in the fog, and Sophia Keller, elegant even at this hour, her hair pinned precisely, her heels crisp against the tarmac.

Ernst extended his hand. "Damian, thank you for the lift to London. I wish it were under better circumstances."

"Likewise," Damian said, gripping firmly. "We need steady minds at the table. Thank you for coming."

Sophia turned her attention to Evie. Her gaze flicked to the Umbra ring on Evie's finger, the smallest shift of her brows betraying thought before her expression smoothed again. "Have you had any time to breathe since the investiture?"

Evie returned the nod politely. "Yes, thankfully. My current role is mostly keeping Damian from invoking the V-word."

Sophia's lips curved. "Vendetta?"

Evie's smile was faint but real. "He is circling it. Do not give him a reason to jump."

"I will tread lightly," Sophia replied, and for a moment the severity in her face softened into something almost amused.

Inside, Damian conferred with Mark over the manifest, each detail verified twice. Lukas monitored the secure channels, voice low as he cycled through coded check-ins with teams across Zurich, Geneva, and Vienna. The cabin itself felt different this morning, not the sanctuary it often was, but a stage set for calculation. Two council members had been killed in the days. There would be no routine flights for some time.

The door sealed with a muted hiss. The engines rose, spooling into a steady climb of sound. Damian closed his eyes for a fraction of a second, then opened them as the Gulfstream rolled to the runway.

The aircraft surged forward, wheels pounding the asphalt until lift carried them into the pale light. The mist fell away beneath the wings, and Switzerland shrank into cloud. Ahead lay London, and a council that would demand answers.

The Gulfstream leveled into its climb, engines softening into a steady hum. Cabin lights warmed against pale leather and polished walnut, a cocoon against the dark sky outside. Yet there was no ease in it. The air felt weighted, the silence dense enough to press against the chest.

Damian sat in the forward seat on the left, Evie beside him. Across the aisle, Sophia Keller adjusted her coat with the precision of someone who never allowed fatigue to show. Ernst Müller took the seat behind her, shoulders set, his frame almost too large for the space. Lukas remained at the rear, headset on, murmuring in clipped tones to the Zurich security net. Mark sprawled opposite him, reviewing dossiers on a tablet, his eyes moving with the sharpness of a soldier marking targets.

A tray of coffee and water was set out by the attendant, but few reached for it. Evie accepted a cup, the steam rising like a small ritual, something normal against the unreality of assassination and pursuit. She sipped, listening more than speaking, letting the currents of power shape themselves in the pauses.

Sophia broke the silence first. Her voice was low, precise. "Two in less than a week. Egon in Zurich. Von Klimt in Bavaria. Both killed in places we thought untouchable."

Ernst's response was blunt, the Bavarian in him showing. "Not untouchable. Only comfortable. Comfort breeds mistakes."

Damian opened his eyes, gaze steady on the table between them. "These were not mistakes. They were executions. Coordinated, deliberate, meant to prove reach. We must treat them as the opening act, not the end."

Sophia's eyes narrowed. "And you believe the tail in Alsace was connected?"

"Of course, it was," Damian replied. His tone was iron, clipped of any doubt. "Pressure from one direction, surveillance from another. Someone is probing our defenses, mapping our responses. If we treat each as isolated, we hand them the initiative."

Mark set his tablet down, voice dry. "The shot that took Klimt was long range, clean. Russian equipment. But the tail in France was Western. Mixed methods, mixed signatures. Someone wants to blur the trail."

Lukas looked up from his comms, his accent heavier when tired. "Or to tell us that alliances we dismissed as impossible are already formed."

For a moment, no one spoke. The hum of the jet filled the silence.

Evie broke it softly. "Then the question is not only who, but why now."

Sophia studied her over the rim of her glass. "You are new to this table, but you are not wrong. The timing is precise. Your investiture, Damian's return to London, the Leonardo closure, it is all too tightly aligned."

Damian leaned back, eyes narrowing. "Which means they are watching more closely than we thought. And closer still, if they knew Klimt's habits in the Bavarian Forest."

He glanced at Evie, then back at the council members. "That is why we are going to London. We cannot answer this piecemeal. We must decide if this is a hunt or a war."

The words settled over them like the weight of the jet itself pressing through the thin air.

Evie finished her coffee in silence, setting the cup down carefully. She knew her place was to listen, but she also knew Damian had placed her here for a reason. Tonight, she was not an apprentice or an operative. She was a witness at the threshold of power.

The Gulfstream crossed into French airspace, stars dimmed by cloud, the city lights of Europe glowing faintly below. The men and women inside did not look down. Their eyes stayed forward, on London, on the emergency session that waited like judgment.

Chapter 32

The tires kissed the runway and held. London rose through mist like a city remembering itself. The Gulfstream rolled long and straight, reversers murmuring, the first light of morning catching on wet tarmac and beadlets of fuel rainbowing in the puddles. No one spoke. Inside the cabin, the seatbelt signs chimed, soft as a spoon on porcelain.

The stairs dropped. Cold air reached up into the fuselage with a clean smell of jet exhaust and rain. Damian stood, paused a heartbeat at the threshold, then stepped down. He scanned the apron the way a soldier reads a map. Fence line. Hangar doors. Tower glass. Two blacked-out SUVs idled beyond the marshaller, engines low and steady. Lukas was already on comms. Mark came down behind them, unreadable as stone. Sophia and Ernst followed with the precise economy of people who knew they were being watched even when they were not.

They moved as a file across the wet concrete. Doors opened. The first SUV took Damian forward and left. The second carried the rest of the security element. No one wasted a word. The city's early pulse reached them as a distant thrum, sirens faint in the rain-smoothed air.

Inside the lead vehicle, the driver kept his eyes on the mirrors. Mark took the far bench, shoulder to the window, phone flat in his palm. In the third row, Lukas sat beside Evie. The glass was dark. Streetlights ran along it like pale fish in a river.

Damian was half-turned in the middle row, watching nothing and everything. The set of his jaw was the only tell. Thumb against the lion on his signet once, then still. When the convoy cleared the perimeter road and slid onto the main artery, Lukas leaned closer to Evie as if the truth, like a secret, could only be told at this distance.

"There is a story," he said. "When Damian was seventeen. Montreal. City championship. His team was down forty-nine to nothing at the half. In the locker room, he wrote on the wall with a marker: 'This is our house.' Then he played music. Loud. Angry. For fifteen minutes, he led as they chanted and jumped and screamed. It would have scared anyone who was not involved. The noise was unbearable. They came out to start the second half, not jogging but stampeding. They broke down doors, ran through fences, not to destroy but because it was in the way, and nothing would stand in their way. Opening kick, return for a score. One play later, the other team drops the ball. Another score. In ninety-six seconds, forty-nine to twenty-one. They won, seventy-two to forty-nine. When he is not playing, he is on the side, jumping, screaming, and motivating. He tore his vocal cord and could not speak for months. He did his valedictory in sign language."

Evie stared at him. "That cannot be real."

"It is real," Lukas said. "He is not only a restraint and strategy. When he chooses to fight, he is a hurricane."

She looked toward Damian. He sat very still, eyes half-closed, thumb tracing the lion again, a single pass like a ritual. The road hissed under wet tires. The river flashed through breaks in the buildings, quicksilver and grey.

"Is that what he hums before the fire starts?" she whispered.

"That music is not nostalgia," Lukas said. "It is a signal. He is lacing his boots."

Up front, the driver eased them through a sweep of traffic. Wipers beat a time that matched no human heart. The city drew closer, glass and stone rising into the weather.

Damian opened his eyes. He did not look back, only forward, as if the road itself were a question he had decided to answer. "We go straight to One Hundred," he said to Sophia and Ernst. No one argued. The radio hissed and clicked as the second vehicle adjusted position.

They took the river road and then cut toward St James. Streets were slick and glowing. Newspapers lay in doorways like abandoned birds. A cyclist ghosted past and vanished at a light. The convoy turned under a canopy of plane trees, stopped at an unmarked entrance, and rolled in.

From the outside, One Hundred was angles and restraint. Inside, it was a fortress. The private ramp breathed them into a bright, dry silence. The air held the faint smell of lacquer and cold metal. Operatives moved without wasted effort, the choreography of a place that had practiced this approach under brighter days and darker ones.

At the biometric gate to the war rooms, each of them presented a token. The pane read heat and print, and pulse and then released with a muted click. No ceremony. No words. Security did its job, and in doing it became invisible again.

They crossed a corridor where art had been chosen to communicate nothing. The elevator rose, quiet and inevitable, floor numbers glowing in a sober column. The hum of ascent settled beneath the heavier pressure in the car, the kind that comes not from speed but from intent.

Damian did not move. He did not need to. Something in him had already changed somewhere between cloud and city, between runway and road. In the reflection on the elevator's stainless steel, he looked like himself and not like himself. Familiar lines, unfamiliar temperature.

By the time the doors opened on the council floor, the decision had been made for him. He stepped out first. The others followed.

He did not look for clarity anymore.

He was preparing for war.

Chapter 33

The corridors of One Hundred emptied with the hush of stone swallowing sound. Council members broke into knots of conversation, aides trailing with files and clipped whispers. Damian walked through it without slowing, Mark shadowing his left shoulder, Sophia and Ernst just behind. Evie and Lukas followed, silent observers, the press of tension still clinging to them.

Dinner was suggested in passing, but there was no debate. After days of funerals, flights, and hard decisions, the night demanded ritual. Food, laughter, and the semblance of normalcy could be as strategic as any communiqué.

Evie offered The Ledbury at nine. Damian agreed with a brief nod, then lifted his phone, voice abrupt. "Oi. The Duck at seven, then The Ledbury at nine." He ended the call without flourish.

Evie blinked, remembering the eloquence with which he had commanded the council chamber. Now he spoke like a man ordering taxis. It startled her, then steadied her. He could switch masks with ease, but they were all him.

By dusk, Soho was alive. Lanterns glowed behind steamed glass, neon washed across wet pavement, and the sharp scent of ginger and soy drifted through the night. Outside The Duck and Rice, Al waited beneath the awning, cigarette dangling, smile crooked and familiar.

The embrace he and Damian shared was brief but unguarded, an old rhythm replayed without hesitation. They stepped back, measuring one another with the quick once-over of men who needed no words.

"Huntsman," Al said, tugging Damian's lapel. "Very you. Shame you will spill soy sauce on it in twenty minutes."

Damian grinned. "Then I will send the bill to your tab."

Al turned to Evie, his tone softening. "Miss Fastest-Woman-in-France." He kissed her cheeks, his cologne sharp with tobacco and bergamot. "You gave the boys in Colmar something to talk about for months."

"Good," Evie laughed. "Maybe they will stop talking about Nice."

"I doubt it," Al said with a wink. "But one can dream."

Lukas's handshake was precise as ever. "You are late."

"Fashionably, darling. Always."

Inside, warmth hit them like a wave. The pub was a wall of chatter and clinking glasses, kitchen heat rolling out with bursts of garlic and chili. A string of lanterns glowed low, painting the room in copper and gold. Their table in the back was half-hidden, discreetly guarded, but the noise and bustle made it feel like a sanctuary.

They ordered without ceremony: baskets of steaming dumplings, crisp pork belly, foaming pints. When the beer arrived, Al raised his glass. "To old friends, new missions, and not getting shot at dinner."

"Cheers to that," Damian said, the grin tugging wider than Evie had seen in weeks.

The first toast gave way to stories. Al teased Damian about Marrakesh, a misjudged poker game that ended with Damian driving across the

Atlas in a borrowed Mercedes. Damian countered with a dry recollection of Al losing half a million in Zurich, saved only because Damian bought the bank that held the note. Even Lukas allowed himself the faintest chuckle.

Evie sat back, listening. The weight she had carried from Colmar and Cham eased under the warmth of banter. She had never seen Damian so unarmored. When he laughed, it was low and rough, the kind of sound pulled from a deeper place. She realized with a start that Al was the only man alive who could make him laugh that way.

She leaned toward Lukas; voice low. "They are like two old souls."

"Yes," Lukas said. "Flame and fuse. Either would give you the shirt off his back. Both would die for the other without hesitation."

The moment stayed with her, even as the night moved forward.

By eight thirty, they slipped back into the city, leaving behind the warmth of the pub for the polished hush of Notting Hill. The Ledbury greeted them with restraint: white linen, hushed service, stemware catching the light like crystal bells. The contrast was sharp but deliberate. Raucous laughter first, then refinement.

Course after course arrived like choreography. Smoked eel with apple. Venison, seared to perfection. A wine flight that revealed more with each pour. The four of them shifted between easy laughter and low murmurs of strategy. Al leaned in now and again, speaking names and places Damian filed away without comment. Evie watched, noting the seamless weave of friendship and power.

By dessert, an intricate tower of citrus and vanilla, conversation softened. Al recounted a half-remembered escapade in Marrakesh. Damian answered with a dry aside about bail money. Evie laughed until her sides ached. Even Lukas's eyes gleamed with something like amusement.

When they stepped into the London night, the air was damp with the promise of rain. A car waited at the curb, black and discreet. Damian paused, eyes lifting to the restless skyline. He thought of Egon. Of Klimt. Of the storm still gathering. But for now, trust held. Loyalty held. Laughter held.

He slid into the car beside Evie. Lukas followed; Al behind. The door shut with the soft thud of inevitability, sealing them back into motion.

Tomorrow would demand answers. Tonight, had given them strength.

Chapter 34

Morning light in London was pale and sharp, cutting across the city like glass. Shadows stretched long and thin, carving edges into stone façades and wet pavement. Damian woke before his alarm, his body already aligned to discipline. The shower was brisk, cold enough to bite, heat following only as he needed it. He dressed in charcoal and white, authority without effort. His hair lay neat, his expression guarded. Something had shifted.

Downstairs, the Ritz was hushed. The breakfast room held its usual elegance, polished silver, pressed linen, the faint aroma of tea and toast, but today it felt sterile, almost too still. The clink of cutlery and low murmur of voices could not disguise the undercurrent, the awareness that something beyond control was moving in their world.

Evie arrived a few minutes later. She moved with grace, though it was edged with tension. Black trousers, a soft blouse, a fitted cardigan. Her ponytail was sleek, her boots quiet against the carpet. Her eyes swept the room automatically, as though she had learned to see threat before she saw comfort.

Lukas was already seated with a half-finished coffee, posture immaculate, gaze sharp. He rose to greet them, his tone formal yet warm. "Guten Morgen. You both slept?"

"Well, enough," Damian replied, though it was a lie neither bothered to challenge.

Menus were opened and closed without thought. Orders placed with no memory of what they had chosen.

Security was present in ways subtle and blunt. Mark stood near the entrance, arms folded, jaw set, scanning every entry and exit. Two plainclothes operatives occupied other tables, feigning indifference, their eyes too alert. It was not paranoia. Not this week.

"Tense," Evie murmured as her tea was poured.

"Because we do not yet know how deep it goes," Damian said.

The phone rang. The sound was not loud, yet it cracked across the table like a gunshot. Damian turned slightly, answering with a voice taut and controlled. "Yes?"

"Are you alone?" Al's tone was flat, stripped of all his usual irreverence.

"Not exactly."

"Listen. I found something you will want to see. Not over the phone."

"How bad?"

"Bad enough I am calling before breakfast. Meet me in an hour. The usual place."

"I will be there."

Damian ended the call and slid the phone away, his expression unreadable.

Evie watched him. "That did not sound social."

"Al found something," Damian said. "Quiet meeting."

"Can I come?"

"No." His reply was sharper than he intended, then softened. "I need you at the office. Eyes open. Lukas will stay close."

"Are we expecting trouble?"

"I am expecting answers. Not all of them will be clean."

He rose. Lukas stood immediately.

"I will brief Mark," Lukas said.

"No need," came the voice from behind them. Mark had drifted closer, silent as a shadow. "You are not leaving alone."

"They will stay out of sight," Damian answered.

"They had better. If something happens to you,"

"It will not."

Mark's stare was flinty, but he said nothing further. He signaled to two nearby operatives: a tall man with a buzz cut and a wiry woman with a scar curling behind her ear. They moved without hesitation.

Outside, a dark green Bentley idled at the curb, understated and elegant, the kind of car London barely noticed. Al sat behind the wheel, a cigarette low between his fingers, expression stripped of humor.

"Get in," he said.

They drove in silence. London passed outside, the city murmuring with buses, shop shutters rising, delivery vans double-parked. Inside, the quiet was heavier than the noise.

"Why the Courtauld?" Damian asked at last.

"Because no one listens there," Al said. "Students are too tired. Faculty are too obsessed with pigment decay to notice two suits in a side gallery."

"So, it is serious."

"It does not belong in any of our usual places," Al replied. "And I prefer not to be overheard."

Somerset House loomed ahead, the Courtauld folded inside its stone embrace. The museum's hush enveloped them as they entered: marble floors dulled the city's clamor, air cool with centuries of varnish and dust. They walked without speaking until they stopped before Manet's A Bar at the Folies-Bergère.

"One of my favorites," Damian said.

"Mine too," Al murmured. "Look at her. Like she knows exactly what you have done."

They stood in silence. The painted barmaid's gaze was flat, her hands resting on bottles and fruit, a mirror behind her alive with masks.

Al's voice was low. "Yesterday, someone said something that would not leave me. Twins. The Leonardos. Identical sons. Everyone knew Silvestro. The other stayed in the shadows. Then he vanished."

"You think he is still out there?" Damian asked.

"I think he is the one pulling the strings."

Damian studied the canvas again. The reflection seemed darker now, the faces behind the glass more sinister. He nodded once. "We go back to One Hundred. Now."

They turned, their steps echoing off marble, the gallery's solemn beauty receding behind them.

Outside, the city struck hard. Grey skies, brisk wind, the smell of wet stone. Damian stepped down onto the pavement, his foot slipping on the damp stone. He caught the railing.

A sharp scuff behind him.

He spun. Al staggered back, a bloom of red spreading across his shoulder.

"Al." Damian caught him as he faltered.

"It is a scratch," Al gritted, breath short.

A hooded figure vanished into the crowd, swallowed by London in an instant.

"We are getting you to a hospital," Damian said, voice like iron.

"No." Al's grip was tight, eyes steady despite the blood. "Go to One Hundred. Fix this."

Damian held his gaze for a long second, then nodded once. "Take care of him," he told the team.

He flagged a cab, sliding inside with a single command. "One Hundred St James. Fast."

The driver hit the accelerator, and the city blurred. Damian's mind raced: assassinations, false trails, a hidden twin. The pieces were aligning, but into what he did not yet know.

They screeched to a stop. Damian threw notes at the driver and ran inside.

"Emergency assembly," he told security. "All London personnel in person. Remote link for the rest. Thirty minutes."

He was already moving, corridors, stairwells, down into the data center's cold glow. Screens bathed the room in sterile light, keyboards clattering as staff snapped to attention.

"Leonardos," Damian barked. "Everything. The twin. Records, aliases, locations. Confirmation, history, movement. Now."

The supervisor's fingers flew. Windows bloomed across the monitors: bank records, family histories, travel logs, blurred photos pulled from years-old files.

Minutes later, Damian stepped into his office and called the agent assigned to Al.

"We are at A and E," the agent reported. "Stable. He is being a handful."

Damian heard Al's voice behind the line, loud and defiant. "There's a bloke with a broken femur two beds down. Go fix him. I've got a scratch and a bruised ego."

A rare smile tugged at Damian's mouth. If Al was yelling, he was alive.

"Keep me posted," Damian said. "Any change, I want it immediately."

"Yes, sir. Relief is en route. I will file a full report on handoff."

"Good. And do not let him get thrown out."

"I would give the odds even," the agent muttered, half-amused.

Damian ended the call. For now, Al was safe.

"Sir," the technician called. "The Leonardo file is ready."

Damian crossed into the briefing room adjoining his office. Monitors glowed, filling the space with fractured light. Faces of the Leonardos spread across the screens: Silvestro, known and gone, and another, blurred photographs, passport copies under false names, border crossings half-erased from record. A ghost of a man moving through Europe's veins.

"Giampaolo Leonardo," the technician said. "Born minutes after Silvestro. Disappeared from public records at nineteen. We have fragments, Zurich, Milan, Madrid, and Istanbul. He used at least seven aliases, all low-level but consistent. He never stayed visible long. His trail went cold five years ago."

Damian leaned closer, eyes narrowing. "Not cold. Buried."

The technician hesitated. "We are cross-referencing financial flows. Shell companies. Small but precise movements through Luxembourg, Liechtenstein, and Monaco. Quiet money. Patient money."

Damian stood silent, thumb running over the lion on his ring. The storm was no longer just on the horizon; it was here, pressing against their walls.

In another wing of One Hundred, Evie sat with Lukas, reviewing the night's intercepts. Her eyes moved across coded transcripts, lines of chatter, none of it yet clear. She felt the shift in the building, the tempo quickening, the air heavy with preparation. Somewhere beneath the floor, Damian was putting the pieces together.

Upstairs, he straightened, voice cutting through the hum of the data center. "This is not just survival," he said. "It is a campaign. And it begins here."

Chapter 35

The main monitor glowed with a decrypted dossier. Legal documents, faded clippings, stray signatures. Then the line that mattered:

Giampaolo Leonardo.

Brilliant. Withdrawn. Five languages. A mind tuned for precision but no taste for the social whirl Silvestro had mastered. Their father had favored the flash, and Giampaolo had withered in that shadow until he vanished.

No death certificate. No change-of-name record. No forwarding address. Tax filings ended in 2009. No passport renewals. Banking blackout after a final transfer: one million euros into a Liechtenstein shell. The company name was redacted.

Nothing after.

Not disappearance. Ghosting. Deliberate. Professional. Planned.

Damian leaned back, eyes narrowing at the glow. Why? Revenge against the father. Jealousy of the brother. Or something deeper, something hidden in the family's books that no one outside Umbra had ever seen. He clicked into known associations. A short list of tutors, academics, and two shell directors. One contact had been flagged three years earlier. A thread to pull later.

Giampaolo was not merely gone. He was building something. Watching. Waiting. And now he had begun to move.

There was an elegance to it, a discipline Damian could respect. But after Egon and von Klimt, there was no return to shadows. Someone was backing him. Someone with reach, maybe even state support.

Damian compiled a preliminary report and pushed it to the council. Then he called Lukas.

Lukas arrived minutes later, absorbed the dossier in silence, then gave a single nod. "I will find him."

"Where is Evie?" Damian asked.

"She is chasing something down," Lukas said. There was the faintest hesitation.

"Alone?"

"No. One of Mark's men is with her. She is covered."

Damian let it stand, though unease coiled in his gut.

Hours passed. Damian and Mark worked side by side, analysts sweeping feeds across Europe. At last, a Zurich tower ping surfaced: Giampaolo's device near Egon's house days before the murder. Meeting or surveillance, it didn't matter. Damian's instincts said personal.

Mark deployed his contacts without ceremony. If there was an extraction to be made, Mark would deliver.

Even so, Damian's thoughts circled back to Evie. She was brilliant, capable, lethal in ways few operatives could match. But she moved first and counted the cost later. Lukas had reassured him. Still, the knot stayed tight.

A new call cut through. "Possible visual in Mayfair," an analyst said. "Near the Grosvenor."

An hour later, a black Audi idled outside the Grosvenor. Damian stepped onto the pavement with Mark and a younger officer, Alex. The hotel's façade gleamed with old money restraint; elegance designed to vanish its guests.

Mark peeled off to reception, blending in with the steady rhythm of travelers. Damian and Alex took the lift. The mirrored walls hummed, reflecting faces that looked too composed for what waited. A text pinged on Damian's phone: Room 602.

The lock yielded with a soft click. They entered.

The room smelled faintly of expensive cologne. Wardrobes pressed sharp creases into empty suits. Toiletries lined the counter with mathematical precision. No clutter. No fingerprint of life.

Mark joined them minutes later. "No booking under his real name. The alias traces to a ghost we've seen before."

Alex knelt, sweeping the desk. His hand paused, then lifted an envelope taped beneath the wood.

Damian slit it open. Passports. Papers. The face was younger, the hair different, but the eyes were Giampaolo's. He had been here.

They resealed the envelope, replaced it exactly, and left the room as untouched as they had found it.

On the pavement, cold air cut sharply. Damian dispatched Ryan to relieve Alex and hold surveillance. Then he stepped outside, collar up against the wind, phone already in hand.

He called Evie. No answer.

He swore under his breath.

"Back to One Hundred," he told Mark.

The war room glowed under recessed lights, screens alive with feeds and chatter. Damian debriefed in clipped precision: timeline, alias, likely stay patterns.

Ryan called with an update. "Al's out of surgery. Clean hit, muscle only. The doctor says forty-eight hours. Knowing him, he'll be up in twenty-four."

Relief flickered, hidden quickly. "Good. Keep security in his room. Quiet but visible. Around the clock."

Mark nodded. "Already set."

The meeting wound down. Damian checked his watch. Seven oh four. Still nothing from Evie. He called again. Voicemail. She did not go dark without warning. The knot pulled tighter.

A message pinged from the analysts: Room 602 reservation canceled.

Damian called Alex. "Any movement?"

"Nothing," Alex said. "No one matching the profile. Dead all day."

Dead all day. Yet the room had been scrubbed too clean. The documents are still taped under the desk. Clothes pressed and waiting. A ghost had walked through and erased himself.

If Giampaolo canceled without lifting a thing, someone had tipped him. They were burned.

Damian stood in the chill outside One Hundred, a cigarette steady between his fingers. Smoke rose into the blurred city lights. Somewhere out there, Giampaolo Leonardo was moving again.

Next time, they would not miss.

He dialed Evie one last time. Silence.

The hollow ache that followed was not professional. It was something heavier, threaded with fear.

When he finally looked up, Lukas was crossing the street toward him, composed as ever, unreadable in the night.

Chapter 36

Evie's heart pounded as she slipped into the press of Piccadilly. Midday light pooled on wet stone, and the city moved like a living organism, all elbows and umbrellas and the rasp of bus brakes. She had left One Hundred late in the morning to meet a contact, then circle back to Damian with whatever she could pry loose. Plans dissolved the instant she saw him.

Silvestro.

He should have been dead. She had left him in Venice, in the pale mist along the Grand Canal. She remembered the way the water lapped at the stones, how the smell of brine clung to the night, the exact angle of her wrist as the blade slid between ribs and found the dark. The last light in his eyes had gone to ash. It had been clean. It had been final.

Yet there he was, breathing London air as if the grave had never noticed him.

She did not make a scene. Her gaze was anchored to the small details that never lied. A faint hitch in his step from an old training injury. The way his shoulders bunched when he read a crowd. The slight tilt of his head when he used a glass as a mirror. There was no doubt. Not a lookalike, not a brother conjured by rumor. The man ahead of her wore his history like a well-fitted suit.

Instinct spoke first. Follow.

Evie slipped into the current of bodies. Tourists raised their phones toward glittering signs. Office workers cut diagonals with heads low and shoulders set against the drizzle. The air smelled of rain and roasted chestnuts and engine heat. Silvestro moved with purpose, never hurrying, never lingering, always near the shelter of awnings and glass. He was cautious, but not cautious enough for her.

She reached for her phone and thought of Damian. One call and a perimeter would knit itself around this street. One call and angles would close. She lowered her hand. One glance down and she might lose him in a stairwell or a service entrance and watch the city eat him whole. Not now. Not when the impossible walked twenty paces ahead.

They slid across the mouth of Piccadilly Circus. Neon hummed. Screens threw color on slick cobbles. A bus sighed to a halt. A street performer struck flint, and fire leapt from a steel pan, bright against the grey. Evie took the near side of a group of tourists and used their cluster as cover. Silvestro's head turned, scanning reflections in a café window. She angled her face to a passing umbrella. His eyes passed over her and kept going.

He cut toward Leicester Square, past the theater posters and the smell of popcorn drifting from an open foyer. The crowd thickened, then thinned as a shower shook loose from the low sky. Evie's coat darkened with rain. She kept her breathing steady and let her stride match the city's rhythm. If he accelerated, she accelerated. If he drifted across a lane of foot traffic, she drifted with a different pack and let their bodies blur her outline.

For a moment, she saw the Ritz across the road. Green awnings, polished brass, a promise of warmth. She pictured Lukas leaning on a thought he had already solved, Damian reading a room like a ledger and balancing columns no one else could see. She kept moving.

Covent Garden opened like a stage set, all ironwork and echo. Street musicians tested new songs against the space. The Royal Opera House rose in pale stone and glass, serene and indifferent. Silvestro cut away from the arcades into a narrow run that led toward Seven Dials. Evie shortened the distance by three steps and then gave it back. He glanced over his shoulder. She turned to a shop window and studied the reflection that mattered. He looked past her again.

Seven Dials radiated in streets like spokes. The geometry here punished mistakes. He could take any of seven exits, and one wrong guess would end the pursuit. Evie took the left edge of the circle and drifted toward a storefront with darkened glass. The pane showed his shape stretched into a sheen. He chose a street that favored the river. Good. The flow of the city would carry them toward open ground where a watcher could be watched.

He entered a lane barely wide enough for a van. The brick was wet and cold, the rain now a fine mist that clung to hair and lashes. He stopped at a junction and pretended to check a message. His head turned in a measured sweep. Evie slid into a recessed doorway and flattened her profile. The bricks pressed their pattern into her shoulder. Water slipped from a broken gutter and tapped the stone with a maddening regularity.

She counted under her breath. Ten. Twenty. Thirty.

His gaze touched the doorway and moved off. His hand brushed the inside of his coat, a gesture casual enough for a civilian and coded enough for anyone who knew the weight of weapons. He pocketed the phone and walked on.

Evie let him have five meters and then took the corner. Her pulse was loud, a deep rhythmic knock. This was not fear. This was attention at its highest setting.

The city sloped toward the Thames like a thought returning to its source. St. Paul's drifted into view, stone shouldering the sky, steady as judgment. The London Eye blurred in the mist; a pale crown set above the water. On the South Bank, umbrellas unfurled and closed, unfurled and closed, a garden of careful flowers. Silvestro was a constant thread through it, always one pace quicker than comfortable, never fast enough to draw eyes.

She tested the impossibility again. She had watched him die. She had felt the last resistance fade. In Venice, the water had carried the memory away, but not far enough. She tasted brine in a London rain and made herself breathe.

How did he live? Did he live at all? Was she seeing a marvel of surgery and money? Was she hunting a double built from old footage and fresh arrogance? Or had she failed in the one act that defined her? The questions skimmed, then sank. She had no luxury for ghosts.

The river widened and took the light into itself. Tower Bridge rose ahead, its towers softened by weather until they seemed carved from cloud. Beneath the eastern arch, the stone wore a sheen where rain had found the same path for a hundred years. Silvestro paused. His eyes searched the edge of the crowd. He stepped into a shadowed cut that would be invisible to anyone who did not already know it was there.

Evie's nerves sang. She crossed two beats late to keep the angle. The doorway held only a strip of darkness and a smell of old mortar. She listened. Shoes on a wet stone. A muffled footfall. He turned again, quick and precise. She slipped down a side passage and hugged a wall, one hand open and close to the knife she had not yet allowed herself to draw.

The corridors narrowed into a lattice of service routes and forgotten alleys. Water dripped from unseen pipes. A strip of torn flyer clung to a brick, its ink bleeding into something unreadable. Evie took the bend fast and light.

Nothing.

The passage ended in a black wooden door chained from the inside. To the left, a stairwell dropped to a basement delivery bay. To the right, a deeper dark with no echo of breath. She stilled herself until her ears ached from trying to hear.

Gone.

Her chest lifted against a vise. She scanned high for a fire escape, low for shoe scuffs, along the walls for the telltale smear of a hand. The rain made everything look like movement. The quiet made every drip a signal. She waited and let the first wave of fury crest and break.

"Not now." The words were smoke in cold air. "Not after all this."

She pressed her palm against the brick and felt the stone take the heat from her skin. Failure announced itself with no mercy. She let it soak into her bones for the length of a slow breath, then pushed away. Anger cooled into resolve. If he could vanish here, he could appear anywhere. That meant he would. That meant she would be ready.

The Thames sounded like a long exhale. She took the path back, past the hush of the National Theatre and the turned faces of statues made permanent by weather. The city smeared into grey and gold, lamps casting small coins of light onto wet paving. The Tower sat in its own gravity on the opposite bank, old enough to have seen every kind of disappearance.

She crossed toward Westminster and its clean lines against the sky. The clock face glowed behind a gauze of rain. She walked faster. Damian would listen first and judge after. That was the order she needed. She would give him the impossible and watch him turn it into a plan.

St James's Square gathered her back into its composed geometry. The doorman at One Hundred opened the door without surprise. Warm light pooled on marble. The receptionist looked up, polished and kind, the precise antidote to London's wet edges.

"Good afternoon, Ms. Blackstone. How may I help you?"

"Is Mr. Cesarini in?"

"Mr. Cesarini left about thirty minutes ago," she said. "He mentioned going to the Ritz. He was trying to reach you. He seemed concerned."

Evie drew her phone from her coat. The black screen stared back. She slid it across the desk in a silent request.

"Of course," the woman said. A cable appeared from a drawer. The screen sparked to life and notifications stacked like accusations. Twelve missed calls from Damian. Six from Lukas. Three system pings from the security net asking for acknowledgments. Guilt flickered, hot and brief. She pushed it down. There was no time for shame. Only movement.

She dialed. Damian answered on the first ring.

"Evie. Where have you been?" His voice was tight, the edges honed by worry that refused to admit itself.

"I am on my way to you," she said. "The Ritz. The bar at nine."

"Before, if you can."

"I need a shower and dry clothes," she said, steady. "Then I will come to you."

She ended the call, thanked the receptionist, and stepped back into the rain.

The walk to the Ritz was short and heavy. Traffic hissed by in sheets. Headlights smeared themselves across puddles. She pulled her coat in close and felt the ache in her legs now that the chase was a memory. Silvestro's outline hung in the air in front of her, a negative she could not unsee.

In her suite, she left a trail of damp cloth to the bathroom and turned the water hot. Steam rose and fogged the mirror to a blank coin. The spray thudded across the knots in her shoulders and along the spine that had held her upright through the city. Heat lifted the scent of London from her skin. The sound filled the room and offered a kind of mercy. It could not reach the place where doubt had planted itself.

If he was alive, someone had built a miracle from money and medicine. If he was a double, someone had studied the original with a lover's obsession. Either way, someone wanted her to chase ghosts through her own city.

She closed her eyes and let the water run until the room felt like a secure box. Then she made herself move.

A cream silk blouse that held its line. A charcoal skirt that skimmed and obeyed. La Perla beneath, private and deliberate. Black suede Louboutins, tall and quiet. Her reflection settled into clarity. Not a woman who had lost a quarry. A woman who intended to finish a job.

She reached the door and stopped. The knives. The pause lasted only an instant. She opened the drawer, took the slender sheath, and strapped it to her thigh. The weight was small, familiar, and correct. The skirt fell back into place. The weapons were part of the silhouette now. Not a declaration, only truth.

She crossed the corridor to the elevator, pressed the call button, and watched the floor numbers fall. The mirrored doors offered her a last look. Calm face. Clear eyes. No sign of the storm she carried. The lift opened. She stepped inside.

By the time it reached the lobby, she had already placed the city's map in her head. Streets and angles and entrances. The bar would be light and brass, and conversation. Damian would be in a corner that let him see the room and the door, and the reflection in the glass behind the barman. She pictured his profile, the way he weighed every second, the thumb that found the lion on his ring when thought sharpened into decision.

She walked toward him through the marble and the hum. He was the fixed point she could allow herself.

The chase was over for today.

The hunt was not.

Chapter 37

She had been so sure. Silvestro is alive. Now gone again, slipping through her fingers like water. She pressed her coat tighter, city lights bleeding through the mist in streaks of color. Her muscles ached with cold and frustration. Her mind was sharper than ever, honed by disbelief.

She could not ignore what she had seen. Either he had survived the impossible, or someone had rebuilt him in image and manner. Either way, she needed answers.

In her suite, she stripped off her damp clothes, letting them fall in a heap, and stepped under the rainfall shower. Heat poured over her spine, washing away the grit of the day but not the doubt lodged beneath her ribs. She closed her eyes. The spray could not touch the place where fear and certainty had braided together.

Tomorrow she would find him again. And finish it.

Steam clung to her skin as she wrapped herself in a thick towel, then moved with deliberate calm through the room. She dressed with care, layer by layer, as if each piece were armor. A cream silk blouse that caught the lamplight. A charcoal Valentino skirt that skimmed and fell with exacting grace. La Perla beneath, a private assertion of choice. Black suede Louboutins, four inches of silent authority.

Her reflection in the mirror was everything she required. Sharp. Composed. Ready.

At the door, she paused, her hand brushing the elevator button, then stilled. The knives.

She turned back, crossed to the dresser, and drew the slender sheath. With practiced ease, she strapped the blade high against her thigh. The familiar weight steadied her. The Valentino dropped over it in a clean line, concealing everything. Invisible, never forgotten.

Fully dressed, fully armed, she stepped into the elevator. The brass doors closed with a hush, soft light glancing off her heels as she descended. The bar waited below. Damian waited below.

Meanwhile, Damian sat alone at the Ritz bar, a Dark and Stormy in hand, its ginger heat a poor excuse for calm. The brass rail and marble counters threw light and shadow across his face, cutting his features into angles.

He had changed after leaving 100. Black turtleneck, tailored blazer, dark slacks, Italian shoes. Simple, precise, the uniform of control. He checked his watch, then checked again, until the count blurred past five.

Evie's silence had unsettled him more than he liked to admit. She was never unreachable without cause. Hours had passed with her line dead, Lukas's calls unanswered. Search teams were minutes from launch when she finally rang. A dead phone. A tactical mind and legendary instincts, tripped by something so banal. He had laughed, but the sound tasted bitter. She was fine. The fine was not enough tonight.

He took a measured sip and forced his thoughts still. She would come. She would have answers.

Lukas appeared, moving with that deliberate economy of his, and slipped onto the next stool.

"Just stopping by," Lukas said, a faint smile touching his mouth. "Did not want to vanish without a good evening."

"You vanished earlier," Damian replied. "All well."

"A quiet day," Lukas said. "Productive. I have dinner plans."

There was no elaboration. Damian did not press. If something mattered, Lukas would share it. They exchanged a few more words, grounded in their banality, before Lukas adjusted his cuffs and slid back into the hotel's softened light.

Left alone, Damian let the amber swirl in his glass and scanned the bar. Crystal clinked. Conversations rolled low. Shoes brushed polished floors. The Ritz was a safe stage for waiting.

He thought of Evie. She would arrive dressed to kill, and yet there was more to it lately. Something in her had shifted. Elegance sharpened into a statement. Fabrics whispered; silhouettes declared. She was not dressing to impress. She was dressing to declare.

He admired the psychology. He admired her.

Anticipation stretched taut beneath his calm.

And then she entered.

He felt it before he saw it, the room's air shifting, heads turning, conversations dipping by instinct. Her heels struck marble, measured and sure. Evie paused at the entrance, radiant and controlled, eyes sweeping until they caught his. He raised his glass, a rare smile surfacing.

She began to cross the room, gaze fixed.

Then she slowed.

Behind Damian, a couple rose from their booth. The man slipped his partner into her coat with practiced ease, a gesture so intimate and familiar that Evie stopped dead.

Her breath caught.

The tilt of his head, the offering of an arm. Memory seared through recognition.

Her eyes widened.

Him.

The world collapsed to a single point. Sound dissolved into a hum.

It was him.

Evie tore off her heels and ran.

Damian turned to greet her just as she saw it, the man's hand disappearing inside the woman's coat. Not tenderness. A draw.

Gun.

No time to shout. Only instinct.

Her hand shot beneath her skirt. Steel met her fingers. One motion. Draw and release.

The knife flew, a whisper through the air before the scream.

Silvestro Leonardo.

The blade struck his shoulder as the gun cleared his grip. He cried out, the shot cracking wide, shattering a bottle behind the bar. Glass rained. Patrons screamed.

Evie was already moving. Her second knife left her hand before the first had landed.

Damian dropped for cover, his pistol drawn, his mind still struggling to register the impossible: Evie, barefoot, skirts torn, lethal and absolute.

The second knife found its mark.

It tore his throat open. His eyes widened, shock flooding them as he clawed at the blade, blood spilling bright across his collar. He gurgled, staggered, knees buckling, and collapsed.

For half a heartbeat, there was silence. Then chaos erupted. Screams. Chairs scraping. Bourbon and cologne soured with the metallic weight of blood.

Damian rose slowly, glass crunching underfoot, heart hammering.

Evie reached him, breath ragged, rain still glistening in her hair, hem torn, eyes steady.

"Are you all right?"

He nodded once, too slow, still catching up to what had happened.

"You just,"

"Silvestro Leonardo," she said, voice level. "He was going to shoot you."

Umbra security burst in first, plainclothes and sharp-eyed, scanning, ready to strike.

Damian raised his hand. "Hold perimeter. No interference."

They froze, alert, waiting.

Hotel security followed, hesitant. One look at Damian, the knives, the blood, and they stopped.

"Stand down," Damian said, calm and low. "It is contained."

The first scream had already carried into the lobby. Guests were pouring out, some sobbing, some stiff with shock, clutching coats and handbags as if they were lifelines. Chairs lay overturned, broken glass glittered across the floor like ice. Staff moved in nervous circles until Umbra agents redirected them, steady hands disguising lethal precision.

Two operatives closed the main entrance, another secured the fire exit, while a fourth moved to the body. Gloves snapped, the knife in Silvestro's throat eased free, and sealed in a sterile pouch. His pistol was bagged next, and the pool of blood spread wider with each second.

"Clear the scene," Damian ordered. His voice cut clean through the noise.

Orders rippled outward. Agents blotted blood, swept shards, and replaced bottles from the cellar. The wreckage became controlled disorder, staged to pass for an accident. Guests who remained were quietly ushered out; their protests muffled by reassurances.

Evie stood at the center, barefoot, skirt hem frayed, blood speckled on her sleeve. Yet she looked unshaken. Composed in the storm.

Damian's eyes stayed on her. He had no words for what he had just seen, only the truth that had landed with the knives. She was no longer a step behind him. She was the line itself, drawn hard between him and the darkness that hunted them.

"You just saved my life," he said, his voice quiet.

Her gaze did not waver. "It will not be the last time."

Chapter 38

The bar was chaos

Glass shards glittered on the floor like fallen stars, and the metallic scent of blood hung heavy in the air. Patrons huddled near the exits, hushed and wide-eyed, as uniformed hotel security ushered them away from the scene.

Damian and Evie stood together near the body. Giampaolo's body. Lifeless, a dark stain spreading beneath him. Evie's breathing was steady, but he could feel the tension radiating off her.

"And this time you will stay dead," she said.

Damian touched her elbow lightly. "Evie. Wait."

Her eyes flicked to his, wary but alert.

"I have been trying to call you all day," Damian said. "There is something you need to know."

Her gaze did not soften, but curiosity stirred. "What is it?"

"That is…was Giampaolo Leonardo. He was Silvestro's twin."

The words landed like a dropped stone.

Evie froze, her brows knitting as her mind raced. "Twins," she repeated.

"Yes. Twins. Al and Mark both confirmed it."

Her eyes dropped to the body at her feet. Shock bent toward comprehension, then sharpened into something harder. "I killed Silvestro in Venice."

Damian nodded. "And this was the other one."

Mark pulled the wallet from the corpse, rifled quickly, and handed it over. "They are good. Very good."

"Russian," Damian asked. "It would make sense if he had backing."

Mark grunted in assent but stopped when hurried footsteps thundered down the corridor.

Hotel security burst into the bar and began asserting control, guiding guests toward the exits and pulling tape across the room.

Mark moved at once, his voice clipped as he spoke into a secured line. He cut across the room with the ease of a man long practiced in battlefield triage.

Uniformed officers entered, but before they could speak, another presence filled the doorway. Tall, commanding, plainclothes, authority carried in his step.

"Commissioner Wright," Mark said, recognition sharpening his tone. "I did not expect to see you tonight."

Wright gave a brisk nod. "I could say the same, Mr. Lawrence. I was dining in the Palm Court when I heard shots."

"We have it contained," Mark replied. "One fatality."

Wright's expression hardened. "The headlines write themselves."

Damian remained silent, his face an unreadable mask.

Mark lowered his voice as Wright drew closer. "The man on the floor is Giampaolo Leonardo. He was involved in the murders of two colleagues in Europe, possibly more. He was armed with a Russian Grach pistol. We will make the files available through secure channels. There was also a woman with him, but she disappeared in the confusion."

Wright listened without interruption, his gaze flicking to Evie where she stood composed and still amid the wreckage. His jaw set.

"Get them out of the country. Tonight. I will clean this up."

Mark nodded. "Understood."

Damian stepped forward, his voice level. "I am not leaving yet. I need to see Al."

Wright's eyes narrowed. "Mr. Cesarini, I do not think that is a good idea."

"I owe him that much," Damian said.

The commissioner's tone sharpened. "Then send him a card. You have two hours. I will assume you have a jet waiting at London or Farnborough. File your plans, fuel it, and leave. If you return to the UK, I want notice. No surprises."

The message was clear. They were liabilities now. Valuable, but too hot to hold.

They left the bar together, passed through the lobby, and stepped into the elevator. On the sixth floor, Lukas stood waiting, Damian's suitcases lined neatly beside him.

Evie scanned the hall, her own luggage conspicuously absent.

Damian caught the look and leaned close, a trace of humor at his mouth. "He thought it improper to pack your unmentionables."

A quiet laugh slipped from her, low and edged with fatigue. "Of course, he did."

Lukas stared forward with dignified silence.

"I will take care of it," Evie said. She disappeared into her suite and returned minutes later with her bags; her composure restored.

Together they descended, moving as one through the controlled storm of the Ritz. Police tape glared beneath the chandeliers. Flashbulbs sparked as the press gathered outside, the scent of scandal clinging to the night air.

The doorman stood his post without flinching, top hat immaculate, and opened the great glass doors with practiced grace.

Outside, a black limousine idled at the curb. Their bags were loaded quickly, and the door closed with quiet finality.

Inside, silence settled.

London's streets slid past; their beauty dulled by what had been left behind. Mark spoke in low tones on his phone, coordinating with Umbra's operations. Damian leaned forward, touched his shoulder, and said one word.

"Venice."

Mark met his eyes, nodded, and altered the manifest. Marco Polo Airport.

Evie sat beside Damian, her expression unreadable, adrenaline burned to ash, leaving calculation in its place. Across from them, Lukas studied the road behind, eyes restless in the mirrors.

The limousine reached the private tarmac. The driver opened the door. Cold night air carried the tang of fuel and the hum of engines.

The Gulfstream waited under pale floodlights, sleek and silver, poised to outrun the fallout.

Mark oversaw the final checks, then turned back. "I will handle Wright. You get her out. Venice is quiet for now."

"Check on Al," Damian said.

"Already did. He is awake. He swore at a nurse. He will live."

Relief flickered in Damian's eyes. They clasped hands once, firmly, then parted.

Damian, Evie, and Lukas boarded the jet. Lukas seated himself in the rear, tablet glowing. Damian and Evie faced one another, chairs angled, silence stretched between them.

The pilot's voice came over the intercom. "Ladies and gentlemen, welcome aboard. We will be departing for Venice shortly. Please buckle up. Skies are clear tonight."

The engines roared, the jet gathered speed, and with a surge, they rose from the runway, London shrinking behind them.

Evie watched the window, then turned back. "When I saw your messages, I dressed quickly. I was on my way down when I realized I had forgotten my knives."

Damian's lips twitched. "Women's intuition."

"Or paranoia."

"Either way, it saved me." His eyes fell briefly to her skirt.

She lifted the hem a fraction, revealing the third knife still strapped against her thigh.

Damian raised a brow, impressed. "Three lives," he murmured. "Mine included."

The Gulfstream descended hours later into the silence of Venice.

Rain slicked the tarmac at Marco Polo, runway lights stretching long across the puddles. A salt wind carried in from the lagoon.

They moved without delay. The Donzi waited at the private dock, engines low, crew discreet. Their luggage was loaded swiftly.

Evie sat beside Damian beneath the narrow canopy as the launch tore across the dark water. Her coat wrapped tight, her hair damp with mist. Neither spoke. Behind them, the mainland lights faded.

Ahead, Venice rose from the fog, towers and domes materializing like ghosts sharpened by steel. The canals shimmered under muted lamplight. The city was awake, but hushed, as if holding its breath.

The Palazzo Cesarini appeared, a silhouette of stone and shadow.

At the dock, Umbra sentries stepped forward, hands clasped, eyes sharp. Lukas keyed them inside.

The palazzo's marble hall spread open, heavy with polish and history. Damian paused at the base of the grand staircase and turned to Evie.

"You should rest. We will debrief in the morning. Mark has intel on Giampaolo's movements. We will need clear heads."

Evie nodded, though her gaze lingered. "And you?"

"I will be in the Linen Room."

She studied him, then placed her hand lightly on his chest. "Do not stay up all night."

"No promises."

She turned, climbing into the shadows above, leaving Damian alone in the silence of his house.

Chapter 39

The days turned into weeks. Palazzo Cesarini, now affectionately dubbed "101" in a nod to their London base, shifted from quiet stronghold to command post. With Damian unable to return to the UK, committee members drifted toward Venice, some for strategy, others for refuge. All came for clarity.

The palazzo, ivy-clad and heavy with centuries, proved an ideal sanctuary. Vaulted ceilings, marble corridors, and tranquil gardens offered both privacy and peace. Damian, the composed host, made sure no one felt like a guest. Lukas, meticulous and unflappable, managed everything from morning espresso to the precise placement of briefing folders on polished tables.

Arrivals were met not with protocol but with warmth. Soon, the house hummed. Strategy sessions filled the library. Maps and dossiers spread across antique desks. Conversations ran late over grappa, the room lit by steady fire and low lamplight.

The work was serious, the mood not grim. Damian's calm and Lukas's attentiveness fostered something rare: camaraderie. Even Al, newly arrived from London to convalesce, found ease in the city. He walked narrow streets, folded himself into the lagoon's rhythm, and let quiet architecture do what doctors could not. Color returned to his face. So did his dry humor.

By evening, long oak tables hosted dinners that felt ritual rather than celebration. Arguments, laughter, and the disciplined restraint of people who knew the cost of indulgence. The wine flowed. The focus held.

The gardens, stripped of bloom but not of beauty, became confidences made visible. Bare trellises cast delicate shadows. Stone fountains whispered under winter air. Paths turned into places for private reflection, quiet negotiation, and the occasional stolen moment between shifting alliances.

In the background, Giampaolo's estate unraveled. Leonardo Industries, purged of rot, was absorbed and divided. Useful assets were folded into the organization's holdings. Shell companies were neutralized or converted. Within weeks, the name itself was gone. The affair wound down, and with it the turbulence.

As the dust settled, Evie received what few ever earned within Umbra: a command of her own.

There was no ceremony. Only a sealed envelope delivered by Mark, unmarked but unmistakable. Inside: authorization.

Her own team.

And not just any team. The Ghosts.

They were whispered about even inside the Collective. Operatives deployed only when silence was paramount and outcomes were not in doubt.

That evening, Mark met her in the library and handed over a slim dossier. "They are yours," he said. "Selectively. Use them like a scalpel, not a hammer."

Evie sat alone at the long table after he left. Firelight flickered across polished wood and the stack of files. One by one, she opened them.

Sparrow. Rayne. A legend even among legends. Rayne had shadowed Evie through Madrid without ever being seen, a ghost through checkpoints. Network destabilization was her art. There was the story about the White House, a towel that had changed hands and histories. Another about a minor state holiday that bore her name in Turkmenistan. The anecdotes contradicted each other. The pattern did not. Close work. Contact killing. Efficiency.

Wraith. Xander. Vaults and embassies. Panic rooms and departures that looked like disappearances. His photo was a grainy still from a Kabul extraction. The notes were spare. Does not speak unless necessary. Never late. Leaves nothing.

Nyx. Selene. Last seen in Osaka. Sparse file. Bloody results. A trail of silenced names. On assignment. Evie flagged the page. No one remained on the periphery forever.

The last sheet listed three empty slots.

"Select carefully," Mark had said. "The committee approved six. You have three. Fill the rest."

Evie leaned back, fingertips steepled, letting the weight of it settle. This was not a promotion. This was positioning. They were not giving her the Ghosts. They were testing whether she could command them.

She felt no pride, only the hard, clean satisfaction of inevitability. She reached for a pen, considered, and added her first name at the top.

Chapter 40

With the immediate threat extinguished, the committee began to prepare for departure. Homes, families, and quiet nodes of power drew them outward. The Russian connection would require inquiry and, soon enough, reckoning. The timetable belonged to them again.

The last dinner ended gently. After-dinner drinks were finished. The fire burned low. Members retired one by one, soft footfalls fading along the marble.

Outside, fog returned and lay a pale veil across the canals. The city hushed. Water lapped against stone in an unhurried, tidal heartbeat.

Damian stood by the tall window with a glass of black rum, the city lights distant and blurred. When Lukas entered, it was without announcement, only the soft catch of the latch and the rhythm of familiar steps.

"Herr Damian," Lukas said quietly. "May I have a moment?"

Damian set the glass on the sill and turned. He knew Lukas well enough to hear the weight beneath the request. This was not routine.

"Of course," Damian said. "Sit."

Lukas remained standing, hands clasped in the old soldier's pose. "I have been in your service for over twenty years. Not once have I considered leaving."

Damian tilted his head. "But now you do."

"Yes," Lukas said. "Not from disloyalty. Because I believe Fräulein Evie needs someone beside her. Someone who understands what she is stepping into, what the Houses will expect, and what the weight will demand. She must not repeat the mistakes of those before her."

Silence held. Damian had leaned on Lukas through storms that had never reached a ledger. To lose him would be to feel a shift in every quiet operation. Yet the truth stood clear in Lukas's voice. This was not abandonment. It was a legacy.

"You would leave me, for her," Damian said. There was no bitterness. Only truth.

"If you say no, I will stay," Lukas answered. "I would never betray you."

"And if I say yes."

Lukas's eyes steadied. "Then I will serve her as I have served you. Loyalty. Discipline. A clear line between impulse and action. I will make sure she survives what is coming."

Damian studied him in the firelight. Shadow, shield, compass.

"Do you believe she will accept you?"

"She will, if you tell her it is right."

A breath. A glance at the dying fire. "I could refuse."

Lukas stood unmoving.

"You would stay," Damian said.

"Yes."

"Even if it meant ignoring what you believe must be done."

"Yes."

Damian lifted his glass and watched the steam of the rum rise. "You have been my most trusted man, Lukas. Not a servant. Not only an advisor. A constant."

"It has been my honor, Herr Damian."

Another quiet beat. Then Damian lifted his gaze. "I will not refuse you."

Lukas's exhale was small, controlled, and seen.

"You will go to her," Damian said. "Keep her grounded. Teach what I cannot. Do it knowing my trust does not change?"

"Thank you," Lukas said.

Thirty minutes later, Evie entered. The room's energy shifted. She was composed, and Damian saw the purpose that had brought her.

"I need to talk to you," she said.

Damian did not answer at once. He took a measured sip. "I said yes."

She blinked. "You do not even know what I,"

"I said yes," he repeated, calm and steady.

She drew a breath. "Lukas came to me with an idea."

"I said yes."

Evie frowned. "He wants to work for me. I cannot accept that unless I know you are truly all right with it."

"I meant it the first time," Damian said. "If he believes his place is now with you, I trust that. I trust him. I trust you."

Her breath caught. She nodded once. "Okay."

She stepped forward and folded herself into his arms. It was simple and warm. She held on a fraction longer than habit allowed, long enough for him to feel the shift.

When she pulled back, her eyes were brighter. "Thank you."

He reclaimed his glass and found a smile. "Besides, it is time I learned to tie my own shoes."

Evie laughed, tension breaking loose, and dropped into the chair across from him, one leg tucked under, finally at rest. Somewhere along the way, the line between becoming like him and becoming herself had blurred. She had already crossed it.

After a shared drink, she excused herself. The door closed, and the room settled. Restlessness pressed against Damian's ribs, a slow weight that would not shift. He needed air.

He knocked on Al's door. Despite the hour, Al was ready.

"Walk," Damian said.

"What took you so long?" Al replied.

The palazzo's oak door shut behind them. The December night bit clean and sharp, laced with salt and stone. Their breath drifted in pale ribbons and vanished into fog. Venice in winter offered a quiet stripped to essentials.

At the Accademia Bridge, the canal stretched black and wide, broken by small fires of light. The dome of Santa Maria della Salute loomed spectral through vapor.

They crossed in silence. On the far side, Dorsoduro gave them shuttered cafés and alleys of stone. At the water's edge, the lagoon lay still and dark, fog clinging to its skin like held breath.

Al spoke first. "You know what you are going to do. So do it."

Damian drew a slow breath, pulled a pistol from his coat, and tipped a single round into his palm.

The casing gleamed faintly. One word was etched into the brass.

Evangeline.

He stared at it, then flicked it into the lagoon. The splash was small but final, louder in meaning than in sound.

Al slipped an arm around his shoulders. "Come on. Let us find a beer."

They turned back into the fog. The city took its footsteps and made them part of its own.

The lagoon, eternal and indifferent, erased the ripple.

Afterword

A Note on the Text

While some locations referenced in this novel, such as The Ritz London, Rules, The Duck and Rice, Maio in Milan, Da Romano and Al Covo in Venice, and Villa Villette, are real, others, like 100 St. James's Square, are fictional. 100 was inspired by 6 St. James's Square, the former headquarters of Rio Tinto, where I once worked.

Villa Villette, now a restaurant, remains a beautiful place to spend an afternoon in the garden or on the verandah watching the Zugersee. Al Covo, owned and run by Diane and Cesare Benelli, continues to be one of Venice's true treasures, and I make a point of visiting every time I am in the city.

The palazzo depicted as the Cesarini residence is inspired by the Palazzo Barbaro, though it has been reimagined for the purposes of this story.

As for Al, my brother from another mother, well, Al is real. You cannot make up someone like Al; you have to experience him and, if you are lucky, survive him.

All characters, organizations, and events portrayed are fictional, and any resemblance to real persons, living or dead, is purely coincidental, except, of course, Al.

Acknowledgements

I am deeply grateful to those who stood by me through the long shadows and the bright mornings alike.

To my wife, Nicole, and my children, Levi and Hayden: Thank you for the patience, encouragement, and the endless conversations that shaped these pages.

To my mentor and friend, Andrea, for your steady hand and sharper insight than I deserved.

To my book club: Karen R, Sheina K, Jackie G, Dave Y, Big Mike, Marion D, and Nadine BP, thank you for being my Guinea Pigs and for the feedback

To the readers who find their way into this house of shadows, this book is, in part, yours.

And finally, to the Umbra Collective itself, for proving that some ideas demand to be written.

* Every story owes its life to those who believe in it first. *

About The Author

Jules D'Isep is a writer fascinated by the intersection of power, secrecy, and loyalty. Drawing on a background in Russian Studies and International Business, he crafts stories where the unseen forces that shape our world take center stage.

When not writing, Jules can be found in an airport lounge, either dreaming of a new city to explore or finding his way back to Venice for dinner, always in search of the next shadow to chase.

The House of Umbra is his latest exploration into the murky depths of ambition and power.